CHRISTOPHER BUSH
THE CASE OF THE BONFIRE BODY

CHRISTOPHER BUSH was born Charlie Christmas Bush in Norfolk in 1885. His father was a farm labourer and his mother a milliner. In the early years of his childhood he lived with his aunt and uncle in London before returning to Norfolk aged seven, later winning a scholarship to Thetford Grammar School.

As an adult, Bush worked as a schoolmaster for 27 years, pausing only to fight in World War One, until retiring aged 46 in 1931 to be a full-time novelist. His first novel featuring the eccentric Ludovic Travers was published in 1926, and was followed by 62 additional Travers mysteries. These are all to be republished by Dean Street Press.

Christopher Bush fought again in World War Two, and was elected a member of the prestigious Detection Club. He died in 1973.

By Christopher Bush

The Plumley Inheritance
The Perfect Murder Case
Dead Man Twice
Murder at Fenwold
Dancing Death
Dead Man's Music
Cut Throat
The Case of the Unfortunate Village
The Case of the April Fools
The Case of the Three Strange Faces
The Case of the 100% Alibis
The Case of the Dead Shepherd
The Case of the Chinese Gong
The Case of the Monday Murders
The Case of the Bonfire Body
The Case of the Missing Minutes
The Case of the Hanging Rope
The Case of the Tudor Queen
The Case of the Leaning Man
The Case of the Green Felt Hat

CHRISTOPHER BUSH

THE CASE OF THE BONFIRE BODY

With an introduction
by Curtis Evans

DEAN STREET PRESS

Published by Dean Street Press 2018

Copyright © 1936 Christopher Bush

Introduction copyright © 2018 Curtis Evans

All Rights Reserved

The right of Christopher Bush to be identified as the Author of the Work has been asserted by his estate in accordance with the Copyright, Designs and Patents Act 1988.

First published in 1936 by Cassell & Co.

Cover by DSP

ISBN 978 1 911579 95 3

www.deanstreetpress.co.uk

INTRODUCTION

THAT ONCE vast and mighty legion of bright young (and youngish) British crime writers who began publishing their ingenious tales of mystery and imagination during what is known as the Golden Age of detective fiction (traditionally dated from 1920 to 1939) had greatly diminished by the iconoclastic decade of the Sixties, many of these writers having become casualties of time. Of the 38 authors who during the Golden Age had belonged to the Detection Club, a London-based group which included within its ranks many of the finest writers of detective fiction then plying the craft in the United Kingdom, just over a third remained among the living by the second half of the 1960s, while merely seven—Agatha Christie, Anthony Gilbert, Gladys Mitchell, Margery Allingham, John Dickson Carr, Nicholas Blake and Christopher Bush—were still penning crime fiction.

In 1966--a year that saw the sad demise, at the too young age of 62, of Margery Allingham--an executive with the English book publishing firm Macdonald reflected on the continued popularity of the author who today is the least well known among this tiny but accomplished crime writing cohort: Christopher Bush (1885-1973), whose first of his three score and three series detective novels, *The Plumley Inheritance*, had appeared fully four decades earlier, in 1926. "He has a considerable public, a 'steady Bush public,' a public that has endured through many years," the executive boasted of Bush. "He never presents any problem to his publisher, who knows exactly how many copies of a title may be safely printed for the loyal Bush fans; the number is a healthy one too." Yet in 1968, just a couple of years after the Macdonald editor's affirmation of Bush's notable popular duration as a crime writer, the author, now in his 83rd year, bade farewell to mystery fiction with a final detective novel, *The Case of the Prodigal Daughter*, in which, like in Agatha Christie's *Third Girl* (1966), copious references are made, none too favorably, to youthful sex, drugs and rock and roll. Afterwards, outside of the reprinting in the UK in the early 1970s of a scattering of classic Bush titles from the Golden Age, Bush's books, in contrast with those of Christie, Carr, Allingham and Blake, disappeared from mass circulation in both the UK and the US, becoming fervently sought (and ever more unobtainable) treasures by collectors and connoisseurs of classic crime fiction. Now, in one of the signal developments in vintage mystery publishing, Dean Street Press is reprinting all 63 of the Christopher Bush detective novels. These will be published over a period of months, beginning with the release of books 1 to 10 in the series.

Few Golden Age British mystery writers had backgrounds as humble yet simultaneously mysterious, dotted with omissions and evasions, as Christopher Bush, who was born Charlie Christmas Bush on the day of the Nativity in 1885 in the Norfolk village of Great Hockham, to Charles Walter Bush and his second wife, Eva Margaret Long. While the father of Christopher Bush's Detection Club colleague and near exact contemporary Henry Wade (the pseudonym of Henry Lancelot Aubrey-Fletcher) was a baronet who lived in an elegant Georgian mansion and claimed extensive ownership of fertile English fields, Christopher's father resided in a cramped cottage and toiled in fields as a farm laborer, a term that in the late Victorian and Edwardian era, his son lamented many years afterward, "had in it something of contempt....There was something almost of serfdom about it."

Charles Walter Bush was a canny though mercurial individual, his only learning, his son recalled, having been "acquired at the Sunday school." A man of parts, Charles was a tenant farmer of three acres, a thatcher, bricklayer and carpenter (fittingly for the father of a detective novelist, coffins were his specialty), a village radical and a most adept poacher. After a flight from Great Hockham, possibly on account of his poaching activities, Charles, a widower with a baby son whom he had left in the care of his mother, resided in London, where he worked for a firm of spice importers. At a dance in the city, Charles met Christopher's mother, Eva Long, a lovely and sweet-natured young milliner and bonnet maker, sweeping her off her feet with a combination of "good looks and a certain plausibility." After their marriage the couple left London to live in a tiny rented cottage in Great Hockham, where Eva over the next eighteen years gave birth to three sons and five daughters and perforce learned the challenging ways of rural domestic economy.

Decades later an octogenarian Christopher Bush, in his memoir *Winter Harvest: A Norfolk Boyhood* (1967), characterized Great Hockham as a rustic rural redoubt where many of the words that fell from the tongues of the native inhabitants "were those of Shakespeare, Milton and the Authorised Version....Still in general use were words that were standard in Chaucer's time, but had since lost a certain respectability." Christopher amusingly recalled as a young boy telling his mother that a respectable neighbor woman had used profanity, explaining that in his hearing she had told her husband, "George, wipe you that shit off that pig's arse, do you'll datty your trousers," to which his mother had responded that although that particular usage of a four-letter word had not really been *swearing*, he was not to give vent to such language himself.

Great Hockham, which in Christopher Bush's youth had a population of about four hundred souls, was composed of a score or so of cottages, three public houses, a post-office, five shops, a couple of forges and a pair of churches, All Saint's and the Primitive Methodist Chapel, where the Bush family rather vocally worshipped. "The village lived by farming, and most of its men were labourers," Christopher recollected. "Most of the children left school as soon as the law permitted: boys to be absorbed somehow into the land and the girls to go into domestic service." There were three large farms and four smaller ones, and, in something of an anomaly, not one but two squires--the original squire, dubbed "Finch" by Christopher, having let the shooting rights at Little Hockham Hall to one "Green," a wealthy international banker, making the latter man a squire by courtesy. Finch owned most of the local houses and farms, in traditional form receiving rents for them personally on Michaelmas; and when Christopher's father fell out with Green, "a red-faced, pompous, blustering man," over a political election, he lost all of the banker's business, much to his mother's distress. Yet against all odds and adversities, Christopher's life greatly diverged from settled norms in Great Hockham, incidentally producing one of the most distinguished detective novelists from the Golden Age of detective fiction.

Although Christopher Bush was born in Great Hockham, he spent his earliest years in London living with his mother's much older sister, Elizabeth, and her husband, a fur dealer by the name of James Streeter, the couple having no children of their own. Almost certainly of illegitimate birth, Eva had been raised by the Long family from her infancy. She once told her youngest daughter how she recalled the Longs being visited, when she was a child, by a "fine lady in a carriage," whom she believed was her birth mother. Or is it possible that the "fine lady in a carriage" was simply an imaginary figment, like the aristocratic fantasies of Philippa Palfrey in P.D. James's *Innocent Blood* (1980), and that Eva's "sister" Elizabeth was in fact her mother?

The Streeters were a comfortably circumstanced couple at the time they took custody of Christopher. Their household included two maids and a governess for the young boy, whose doting but dutiful "Aunt Lizzie" devoted much of her time to the performance of "good works among the East End poor." When Christopher was seven years old, however, drastically straightened financial circumstances compelled the Streeters to leave London for Norfolk, by the way returning the boy to his birth parents in Great Hockham.

Fortunately the cause of the education of Christopher, who was not only a capable village cricketer but a precocious reader and scholar, was taken up both by his determined and devoted mother and an idealistic local elementary school headmaster. In his teens Christopher secured a scholarship to Norfolk's Thetford Grammar School, one of England's oldest educational institutions, where Thomas Paine had studied a century-and-a-half earlier. He left Thetford in 1904 to take a position as a junior schoolmaster, missing a chance to go to Cambridge University on yet another scholarship. (Later he proclaimed himself thankful for this turn of events, sardonically speculating that had he received a Cambridge degree he "might have become an exceedingly minor don or something as staid and static and respectable as a publisher.") Christopher would teach in English schools for the next twenty-seven years, retiring at the age of 46 in 1931, after he had established a successful career as a detective novelist.

Christopher's romantic relationships proved far rockier than his career path, not to mention every bit as murky as his mother's familial antecedents. In 1911, when Christopher was teaching in Wood Green School, a co-educational institution in Oxfordshire, he wed county council schoolteacher Ella Maria Pinner, a daughter of a baker neighbor of the Bushes in Great Hockham. The two appear never actually to have lived together, however, and in 1914, when Christopher at the age of 29 headed to war in the 16th (Public Schools) Battalion of the Middlesex Regiment, he falsely claimed in his attestation papers, under penalty of two years' imprisonment with hard labor, to be unmarried.

After four years of service in the Great War, including a year-long stint in Egypt, Christopher returned in 1919 to his position at Wood Green School, where he became involved in another romantic relationship, from which he soon desired to extricate himself. (A photo of the future author, taken at this time in Egypt, shows a rather dashing, thin-mustached man in uniform and is signed "Chris," suggesting that he had dispensed with "Charlie" and taken in its place a diminutive drawn from his middle name.) The next year Winifred Chart, a mathematics teacher at Wood Green, gave birth to a son, whom she named Geoffrey Bush. Christopher was the father of Geoffrey, who later in life became a noted English composer, though for reasons best known to himself Christopher never acknowledged his son. (A letter Geoffrey once sent him was returned unopened.) Winifred claimed that she and Christopher had married but separated, but she refused to speak of her purported spouse forever after and she destroyed all of his letters and other mementos, with the exception of a book of poetry that he had written for her during what she termed their engagement.

Christopher's true mate in life, though with her he had no children, was Florence Marjorie Barclay, the daughter of a draper from Ballymena, Northern Ireland, and, like Ella Pinner and Winifred Chart, a schoolteacher. Christopher and Marjorie likely had become romantically involved by 1929, when Christopher dedicated to her his second detective novel, *The Perfect Murder Case*; and they lived together as man and wife from the 1930s until her death in 1968 (after which, probably not coincidentally, Christopher stopped publishing novels). Christopher returned with Marjorie to the vicinity of Great Hockham when his writing career took flight, purchasing two adjoining cottages and commissioning his father and a stepbrother to build an extension consisting of a kitchen, two bedrooms and a new staircase. (The now sprawling structure, which Christopher called "Home Cottage," is now a bed and breakfast grandiloquently dubbed "Home Hall.") After a falling-out with his father, presumably over the conduct of Christopher's personal life, he and Marjorie in 1932 moved to Beckley, Sussex, where they purchased Horsepen, a lovely Tudor plaster and timber-framed house. In 1953 the couple settled at their final home, The Great House, a centuries-old structure (now a boutique hotel) in Lavenham, Suffolk.

From these three houses Christopher maintained a lucrative and critically esteemed career as a novelist, publishing both detective novels as Christopher Bush and, commencing in 1933 with the acclaimed book *Return* (in the UK, *God and the Rabbit*, 1934), regional novels purposefully drawing on his own life experience, under the pen name Michael Home. (During the 1940s he also published espionage novels under the Michael Home pseudonym.) Although his first detective novel, *The Plumley Inheritance*, made a limited impact, with his second, *The Perfect Murder Case*, Christopher struck gold. The latter novel, a big seller in both the UK and the US, was published in the former country by the prestigious Heinemann, soon to become the publisher of the detective novels of Margery Allingham and Carter Dickson (John Dickson Carr), and in the latter country by the Crime Club imprint of Doubleday, Doran, one of the most important publishers of mystery fiction in the United States.

Over the decade of the 1930s Christopher Bush published, in both the UK and the US as well as other countries around the world, some of the finest detective fiction of the Golden Age, prompting the brilliant Thirties crime fiction reviewer, author and Oxford University Press editor Charles Williams to avow: "Mr. Bush writes of as thoroughly enjoyable murders as any I know." (More recently, mystery genre authority B.A. Pike dubbed these novels by Bush, whom he praised as "one of the most reliable and resourceful of true detective writers"; "Golden Age baroque, rendered remarkable by some extraordinary flights of fancy.") In 1937 Christopher Bush became, along with Nicholas Blake, E.C.R. Lorac and Newton Gayle (the writing team of Muna Lee and Maurice West Guinness), one of the final authors initiated into the Detection Club before the outbreak of the Second World War and with it the demise of the Golden Age. Afterward he continued publishing a detective novel or more a year, with his final book in 1968 reaching a total of 63, all of them detailing the investigative adventures of lanky and bespectacled gentleman amateur detective Ludovic Travers. Concurring as I do with the encomia of Charles Williams and B.A. Pike, I will end this introduction by thanking Avril MacArthur for providing invaluable biographical information on her great uncle, and simply wishing fans of classic crime fiction good times as they discover (or rediscover), with this latest splendid series of Dean Street Press classic crime fiction reissues, Christopher Bush's Ludovic Travers detective novels. May a new "Bush public" yet arise!

Curtis Evans

The Case of the Bonfire Body (1936)

"Then he died from a crack on the head," Wharton said. "And I'd give a fi'pun note to have a good look at that head."

"It's the hands that intrigue me," Travers said.

"Why?" fired Wharton.

"Personal predilection," prevaricated Travers, "and infinitely less horrible."

The Case of the Bonfire Body

If *Murder is Easy*, as the title of a Thirties detective novel by Agatha Christie assures us, what is rather harder, surely, is getting rid of what archaically might be termed the "evidences of murder," beginning, naturally enough, with the body. In real life, which purportedly is stranger than fiction, murderers have infamously resorted to such expedients as cellar burial (Hawley Harvey Crippen), acid baths (John George Haigh) and blazing cars (Alfred Rouse), while in fiction crime writers--their criminal creativity fostered by commercial, if not personal, need--have employed all these real murderers' methods and more, including a tar boiler (see John Rhode's *Proceed with Caution*), dismemberment (Gladys Mitchell's *The Mystery of a Butcher's Shop*) and others so morbidly ingenious (not to mention horrific) that out of deference to readers they must not be named here. In Christopher Bush's fifteenth Ludovic Travers detective novel, *The Case of the Bonfire Body* (*The Body in the Bonfire* in the US), Bush contributed to the field of crime fiction his own bravura take on the vexing problem of corpse disposal, one that stands high in this particularly grisly pantheon.

In the event that the body is discovered, a clever murderer aims to erect a second line of defense, namely preventing identification of the body by duly appointed investigating authorities (or, as is so very often the case, those dangerously clever and deplorably nosy amateur freelancers who with alarming frequency stumble upon crime scenes in vintage mysteries). Hence all sorts of ingenious efforts to obfuscate identity have been made by murderers in the annals of classic detective fiction, from Dorothy L. Sayers' debut Lord Peter mystery, *Whose Body?* (1923), where a corpse clad only in a pair of pince nez is discovered deposited in a bathtub, to the late Sayers admirer P.D. James's *Unnatural Causes* (1967), in which a headless and handless corpse is found floating in a dinghy. In *The Case of the Bonfire Body*, Christopher Bush offers for our ghoulish delectation not only a burned body, but one, like that of murdered mystery writer Maurice Seton in James's *Unnatural Causes*, with its head and hands removed. Never has Bush's lamppost-lean, bespectacled and well-bred sleuth, Ludovic "Ludo" Travers, had a more gruesomely challenging case dropped indecorously into his lap.

The case commences when Ludo, driving in his Rolls Royce with his loyal manservant, Palmer, down Oxford Road in London on a heavily befogged Guy Fawkes Night, encounters a panting pedestrian at his car window, who is prating something about a body in a bonfire. The panic-stricken pedestrian, it transpires, is a minister, Reverend Giles Ropeling. While leading a troop of scouts on Guy Fawkes Night, the clergyman to his mortification discovered that the "Guy" in a local bonfire was no straw dummy but rather a human corpse! This initial setting recalls Agatha Christie's "Murder in the Mews," the title tale in a 1937 novella collection by the Queen of Crime (though it originally appeared in an American magazine in December 1936) wherein a killing similarly is staged on Guy Fawkes Night.

In his book *Snobbery with Violence: English Crime Stories and Their Audience* (1971), Colin Watson contended that mystery writers during the Golden Age of detective fiction kept violence "conformist, limited, unreal" with "fastidious expressions that convey nothing of the terrible glistening mess that is made of human butchery". Yet Christopher Bush, in his description of the dreadfully disjointed body that Ludo Travers surveys on Guy Fawkes Night, artfully manages to retain sensitivity while not stinting on unpleasantness:

> At last his eyes fell slowly to the thing that lay by the brushwood edge—the naked body of a man, chest upwards and a newspaper over its middle. It was a smallish body, not much larger than that of a well-grown lad, but plump enough and with matted hairs of badger grey. One quick glance at where the head had been, and Travers was turning his eyes away, for there was nothing but a hacked-off bloody stump against the folded sacking that had been placed for a pillow. Much cleaner were the hacked wrists from which the hands had gone, for there one saw the bluey-white of the joints.
>
> But about the whole of that trunk, and its mere contact with the cold slime of the trodden earth, was something so bestial that a new horror came over him. . . .

Here Christopher Bush, like the fictional Ludo Travers a veteran of the First World War, vividly recalls words—"a nightmare of earth and mud"—written about the conflict by French author Henri Barbusse, another Great War veteran. The salacious American publisher's blurb, on the other hand, simply hyped the horror of it all for sensation-hungry mystery fans: "For those who like their murders with none of the punches pulled, Christopher Bush has concocted one of the most sanguinary ever conceived. It is not for the squeamish reader—let that warning be sufficient!" Ludo's Scotland Yard superintendent ally, George "The General" Wharton, on the other hand, remains characteristically phlegmatic throughout the ghastly affair. "I'll find that head if I dig up half the country," the General vows.

Soon it appears that the unidentified and incomplete corpse may be connected to the stabbing murder of a respected Hampstead doctor. But, in that case, was the corpse the doctor's slayer or the doctor's victim? And what of the hand, cut off from the wrist, which is fished from a sewer? Did the hand, which may have held the knife which killed the doctor, come from the unidentified corpse, or from some other corpse, yet undiscovered? With a multiplicity of corpses, body parts and identities floating around, *The Case of the Bonfire Body* offers one of the most challenging conundrums that the crafty Christopher Bush ever contrived, both for his determined crew of crime investigators--Travers, Wharton, Chief Inspector Norris, Dr. Menzies and Sgt. Lewis are all present and active--and his devoted legion of mystery readers.

CHAPTER I
THE CURATE WHO RAN

THE FOG LAY heavy along the Oxford Road. Even the inside of the windscreen of the Rolls was filmed with its mist, and it blurred the horn-rimmed spectacles of Ludovic Travers, so that driving was a tedious and harassing affair. Then as the car drew warily into the outskirts of Garrod's Heath, the yellow curtain lifted somewhat and became swirly and more patchy, and Ludovic Travers hoped, and with a hope never more fervent, that he soon would see the last of it. So he slowed the car down by the grass verge for what he trusted would be the last wipe of his horn-rims.

"Not very promising for Guy Fawkes' Night, sir—if I may say so," remarked Palmer, his man. Though Palmer had valeted Travers's father and had probably known the infant Ludovic in his first pram, he still broached a conversation with primness and much diffidence.

"I don't know." The lightening of the fog had brought Travers a cheerfulness, and in any case he was always prepared to argue and theorise. "Mayn't the fog make it Guy Fawkes' Night with a difference? Glamour and mystery, and all that sort of thing? Not merely crude flames from obvious bonfires, but super-glow-worms in the enshrouding mist. Just imagine it, Palmer. All England encircled with them."

The thought amused him and he was smiling to himself as he gave those monstrous spectacles a last polish and moved the car on. Palmer cast a damper on that facetious outpouring of poetical claptrap.

"All the same, sir—if I may say so—the children won't like it, sir. It isn't much use having bonfires and letting off fireworks if you can't see them, sir." "Maybe you're right," admitted Travers, eyes on a patch of fog ahead. "But it may all be gone by to-morrow. Guy Fawkes' Night is to-morrow, isn't it?"

"To-day is the fourth, sir," said Palmer, with that quaint, incipient bow of his.

Soon the fog grew even more patchy, so that at times the road was clear for a hundred yards. The grass verges disappeared and there were paved paths and the first houses of what even a stranger would have known as a high-class suburb.

"One of the most select of the London dormitories—Garrod's Heath," Travers remarked reflectively. "Tremendously wealthy population, one always gathers."

"I suppose this *was* the heath, sir," said Palmer, with a wave at the Common.

"Undoubtedly," Travers told him. "All that's left of it, and still pretty huge. Rather like a home-grown park, don't you think? Gorse always in bloom, and the whole spot charmingly desolate."

It was then that Palmer made a sudden movement as he caught sight through a swirl of fog of a man who ran ahead in the open road by the gorse at the Common edge. Then Travers saw him and slowed down the car at the strangeness of it, for the runner was not dressed for sport, and he ran like the wicked, with none that pursued. As the car drew nearer, Travers could hear his pantings which were those of a man at the end of his tether but still urged to an effort by desperate haste. His clothes were those of a clergyman—a youthful vicar or a curate, it might be—and with some queer intuition that was not even yet a thought, Travers sounded the horn and shot the car abreast. Then the curate heard the sound of it, staggered to a halt, and turned.

"Pardon me," began Travers, "but is anything the matter? Is there anything I can do?"

"Yes," said the other, and panted hard. Phrases like *muscular Christianity* and *the Church militant* were trite in Travers's mind, and in the brief seconds before the man spoke again he watched the quick breaths that curled to fog in the raw air of that early afternoon.

"It's terrible!" He panted again. "Terrible. It's a body . . . the head cut off . . . and the hands. In the bonfire there."

Travers swivelled his long legs and his six-foot three was out of the car in a flash.

3 | THE CASE OF THE BONFIRE BODY

"You mean—a murder?"

"I don't know." The curate shook his head bewilderedly, but his breath was coming back. "It's a naked body. A man's."

Travers frowned in thought.

"You were running for the police?"

"Yes," the other told him and his face lighted with an idea. "Perhaps I might—I mean, you'd be so good as to give me a lift?"

Travers frowned again and for a moment made no move. Then he nodded.

"My man will take you if you show him the way. But where exactly is the bonfire?"

A minute later he was threading his way through the gorse, and the sound of the Rolls was lost. The heathy paths were dry and the whole place was like a maze with the tall, obscuring gorse, and the clumps of silver birches and the thickets of thorn, but sometimes there would be a grassy clearing that gave a view ahead. Then there was the sound of young voices and Travers steered that way till he saw faggots and brushwood scattered in the open, and two Boy Scouts whom the curate had mentioned.

But for the moment Travers kept his eyes from the thing that lay like a huge white slug among the scattered pieces of wood. His eyes took in the ruts that had been made by a cart or lorry, where no real track was, then he drew up to the awed pair who still warily watched.

"I've just met your scoutmaster," he said, "and he told me I should find you here. My car's taken him to the police-station."

He smiled friendlily as he ran his eyes over them. One lad looked a good two years older than the other.

"You tell me all about it," he said. "Why's the bonfire all scattered about, for instance?"

In less than no time both scouts were talking. Travers gathered that the local troop had an annual bonfire and, by permission of the local council, the Common was always the site. Faggots and brushwood had been brought on his lorries by the father of one of the scouts, and they had been piled higgledy-piggledy to make a rough pyre. That much had been begun on the Saturday and completed by the Monday night.

Then that same night the B.B.C. had broadcast a talk by an expert in bonfires, saying how they should be built for better burning and longer lasting, so the scoutmaster—the Rev. Giles Ropeling of Travers's recent acquaintance—had decided to pull down the crude mountain and re-erect it scientifically. Just about an hour ago had been the time agreed on, and it was when about half of the material had been thrown aside that the body had been discovered. A hole seemed to have been made well into the side of the heap and the trunk pushed in and the hole concealed.

Then the older lad offered to show just where the body had been found. Travers, whom the mere thought of blood made wince, was horrified.

"You'd better stay here, as Mr. Ropeling told you. You see, whoever put the body here must have left footprints."

A nod and a smile and he moved off to the ruined bonfire. At last his eyes fell slowly to the thing that lay by the brushwood edge—the naked body of a man, chest upwards and a newspaper over its middle. It was a smallish body, not much larger than that of a well-grown lad, but plump enough and with matted hairs of badger grey. One quick glance at where the head had been, and Travers was turning his eyes away, for there was nothing but a hacked-off bloody stump against the folded sacking that had been placed for a pillow. Much cleaner were the hacked wrists from which the hands had gone, for there one saw the bluey-white of the joints.

But about the whole of that trunk, and its mere contact with the cold slime of the trodden earth, was something so bestial that a new horror came over him, and as he backed slowly away there was the sound of voices, and he turned and waited. Four men came round the path by the tall gorse: policemen, two of them, and Ropeling, and a fourth man who advanced with hand outstretched.

"Inspector Mott, sir. I don't know if you remember me."

He named a certain case, and mentioned Travers's association with Superintendent Wharton of the Yard. Travers remembered.

"Mr. Ludovic Travers, isn't it, sir?"

Travers admitted it, and the curate all at once cut in.

"Not the Mr. Travers who wrote *The Economics of a Spendthrift*?"

Travers admitted the fact. The inspector coughed.

"If you're ready, gentlemen, we'll see what there is to see."

Travers protested, if none too ardently, that he was merely a spectator. And Garrod's Heath was in any case well beyond the area of the Yard.

"I'd like you to have a look, sir," Mott said. "My Chief Constable can't get here for a bit. The doctor's due now though." He halted. "You might send those lads of yours home, Mr. Ropeling, sir. Enough to give 'em the horrors."

"I've been thinking," Ropeling said. "Mightn't we search the gorse for the—er—missing parts?"

"Rather a bit gruesome, don't you think?" said Travers gently. "Besides, the police will be doing that scientifically almost at once."

He stood looking down at that body. Once more the thought of its icy coldness made him shudder, and then suddenly, headless as it was, it seemed a strange impersonal thing; and when the inspector stooped all at once and canted it to its side, his own eyes could survey it in detail with never a wince.

Mott moved the sacking pillow away. "This is what it was wrapped in?"

"Yes," said Ropeling, and gulped. "It was half in and half out and it came right out when I pulled the sacking."

"You never ought to have moved it," Mott told him reprovingly. "Still, now it's where it is it might as well go to the station when the doctor comes. That sounds like him now."

The doctor it was. He heard the story of the finding and made his quick examination. But after it he knew as little as before. The body had no trace of a shot or stab, and even the post-mortem might never establish the cause of death, unless such causes were within the organs of the trunk itself.

"Such as poison?" suggested Travers.

Mott drew Ropeling aside for a word and came back alone.

"We always know where to find Mr. Ropeling when we want him," he said. "But about what you were saying, doctor. I've got an idea. If you ask me, he died from a smashed skull. Somebody bashed him dead and then cut off the head so that the cause of death shouldn't be known."

"You mean, a charge of murder could never be brought?"

"That's it, sir. Not unless we find the head. Not only that. If the head ain't found, we'll never know who he is. That's one reason why it was cut off. To conceal identity."

"And the hands?" asked Travers suavely.

Mott had his reply pat. "Why shouldn't the hands have given away who he was—same as his head? What if he had some deformity, or tattooing, or fingers missing?"

"Maybe," said Travers. "But what about that mark on the left ankle, doctor? Looks to me like some sort of a cut."

"An incision it is," the doctor said, "or the beginning of one." He rubbed his chin and frowned perplexedly. "Surely it couldn't be?"

"Why not?" said Travers. "Something disturbed the murderer or else he'd have cut off both feet as well. He'd actually begun on one ankle and then he stopped."

But although there was scarcely a break before Travers resumed the thread of his argument, an idea had suddenly come, and he hooked off his glasses and began a quick nervous polishing—a trick of his when at a loss or on the edge of discovery. And then some strange intuition made him keep the thought back, though in the words that came was matter enough for reflection.

"He had made up his mind to cut off the feet. Let's imagine therefore that he did it. But the feet show no distinguishing marks—save a certain amount of grime which announces his class and his distaste for baths. Why then cut off the feet?"

"But he *didn't* cut off the feet!" said Mott triumphantly. "He realised there wasn't any need to cut them off, because they hadn't any distinguishing marks—like the hands."

"Maybe you're right," said Travers, still wholly unconvinced. "But what about that sacking?"

The sacking carried no marks whatever, and might have come from anywhere. One of the policemen volunteered the statement that he had seen some lying about on the fringes of the Common itself.

"Might be some of that!" said Mott, eyes opening wide. "That'd make it a local murder."

"Old sacking's as common as paper," the doctor said. "Wherever you get an open space you get surreptitious dumping of refuse and rubbish and discarded sacking like this."

But the sacking was stout enough and on it the doctor and a constable bore off the body to where the ambulance waited on an invisible side road. Travers remarked that there was nothing he himself could do, and as the fog looked like thickening at any moment, it might be as well if he made town at once. Mott pocketed the card, then gave a shrewd look.

"You're an old hand at this sort of game, sir. Got any ideas at all? Anything that makes you think—so to speak?"

George Wharton once said of Ludovic Travers that the fact that there are two sides to every question was for him merely an incentive to hunt for a third. So Travers at once forgot the fog. He smiled dryly.

"Have you?"

"Well"—the wind went only momentarily from the inspector's sails—"I have, sir, and I haven't. All I do know is that whoever did that mutilating wasn't any too good a hand at the game. In fact, sir, I wouldn't call the parts cut off. I'd call them hacked off, sort of anyhow."

The air was suddenly more raw and Travers hitched round his ears the collar of his heavy overcoat.

"You mean that no medical man did it?"

"That's it, sir."

"Then I don't agree with you, I'm afraid," said Travers casually, and at the prospect of theorising his hands once more went to his glasses. Mott looked surprised. Travers smiled charmingly.

"For instance, let's assume we've arrived at the definite fact that a medical man did not do the mutilating. How does it help? Out of what the Press would call the teeming millions of this isle we eliminate about one twentieth of one per cent. Rather slow that, even for the exhaustive method, don't you think?"

"You've got to start somewhere, sir."

"True enough," said Travers whole-heartedly. "But when you make a start by insisting that no man with medical knowledge did it, even there I'm not inclined to agree with you. If a medical man did it, would he have been such a fool as to do the job scientifically and so narrow the search down to men like himself? No, he'd have hacked the parts off, so as to throw off the scent people like you and me."

The eyes of the inspector had opened wide and Travers knew himself in the presence of a good listener. But he moved to more solid ground after such shifting sophistries.

"Still, all that leads us nowhere. How did the body get here? That's the essential point?"

"There you've got me beat," Mott said. "But whoever he was, he must have had local knowledge or he'd never have come to the bonfire."

Once more Travers was polishing his glasses, and blinking away into the raw, misty air.

"I wonder," he said, and hooked the glasses on again. "Why were the head and hands removed, for instance?"

"Why, so as it shouldn't be known who he was —and what killed him."

"Let's keep to the first point," Travers said. "Say the disfigurement was done to conceal effectively the identity of the victim. Now, but for that talk on the radio, this bonfire would never have been disturbed. The trunk would never have been discovered until it had been burnt to a charred mass. That, I think you will agree, would have been sufficient concealment of identity. A man with local knowledge would simply therefore have hidden the body in this bonfire and not have done his work of disfigurement twice—by cutting off in addition the head and hands."

Mott frowned. "I see what you're getting at, sir. Mind you though, there isn't any reason why he shouldn't have made assurance doubly sure."

"True enough," said Travers amiably. "But let's go further. The doctor thought from a first observation that the man was killed yesterday evening. Stomach content at the post-mortem might determine the fact more closely. You and I know, however, that the body couldn't have been put here in broad daylight. What was the weather like last night?"

"Thick, sir, but moonlight—if you know what I mean. A peculiar sort of light, and yet you couldn't see twenty yards ahead."

Travers nodded. "A diffused light, in fact. You could see well enough for a small circle round yourself." His hand went out to the far main road by which he had come. "Hundreds of cars use that road. It's one of the arteries of traffic. A car, if it liked, could draw clean in off it through one of the rides and into the gorse. There'd be no courting couples about on account of the fog and damp. Now where was the man killed?"

"Heaven knows, sir."

"Exactly. He might have been killed anywhere and transported here by car. Everybody knows this Common and its peculiarities. Half motoring England must have passed it one time or another. Very well then. The murderer knew this Common and intended to hide the body among the gorse. As he was carrying it in the sacking to the loneliest depths, he blundered by chance on the bonfire. Then the idea came to him to make assurance doubly sure."

Mott clicked his tongue. "That's it, sir—for a fiver!"

Travers smiled. "I wouldn't go so far as that. All the same, if I were you I'd go over the grass round this Common for the marks of tires. And I'd search the Common paths for the footmarks of someone who was carrying the tidy weight of the best part of a dead man."

Mott nodded, then his eyes rose again.

"Any other ideas, sir?"

"No," said Travers, and frowned. Then the question came off-handedly. "I suppose the curate —Mr. Ropeling—rather lost his head when he saw that body? Been here long, has he?"

"I don't know that he has, sir." Mott cast a crafty look. "Be about twelve months probably. Decent sort, too. The inoffensive kind, if you get me, sir. But what was that about losing his head?"

"Just an idea," said Travers airily, "and if I mention it, it's in the strictest confidence. Put yourself in his place when the body was found. What would you have done? Left those two lads here alone?"

Mott frowned prodigiously. "Can't say I would, sir."

"Of course you wouldn't," said Travers heartily. "You'd have stayed here with that horrible thing yourself, and you'd have sent off both boys—one for a doctor and one for the police."

"Yes," said Mott and nodded slowly. "Yes, I reckon that's what I'd have done. But surely you don't think—?"

"Of course I don't," Travers told him. "If you remember, you asked if I had ideas. The curate was one of the answers. Besides, he wouldn't be the first man who lost his head."

He hitched the collar of his coat once more round his ears and the inspector must have thought his departure imminent, for the question came hurriedly.

"Before you go, sir, just what would you do if you were in charge of this case yourself?"

"Faint, probably," said Travers. "But if I were you, and my Chief Constable agreed, I'd do this: I'd have a regiment of men methodically search this Common, with a special eye for newly dug ground and the buried head and hands and clothes. I'd have the district combed for missing men—just in case. Above all I'd get that body into the hands of a Scotland Yard expert at the earliest moment. He'll find out more about the dead man in a day than theorising would in a year." His hand went out. "Good-bye. I shall keep an eye on the papers to see what's happening. I don't expect you'll want me for anything, but if you do—"

A farewell smile and a nod and he was making his way to where he judged the car to be. But as he drove those last miles to town he was singularly quiet, and not wholly for the treacherous fog that kept his eyes to the road. The eyes might watch and the hands move by instinct, but the thoughts were as swirling as the fog itself. Yet behind all the theories one immovable thought lay as a background. He had crammed advice down Inspector Mott's throat—to call in the Yard. That might mean George Wharton, and where Wharton went, there would he himself contrive to be also.

CHAPTER II
DEATH OF A DOCTOR

IT WAS CHANCE and a friendship with George Wharton that had first turned Ludovic Travers into an unofficial aid of the law; and the paradox of the matter lay in the man himself and—on the showy surface—his utter remoteness from the official and conventional. Never was man less sleuth-like. About Travers was nothing of the ramrod back, the brisk authority and the uncertain cockneyisms of the stage detective. If in fact he looked anything at all, it was what he was—the authority on economic history and the perpetrator of certain volumes of delicious irony with which even the half-informed connected his name.

But when Travers fell in with George Wharton and experienced the thrills of his first murder case, the gentle satirising of the social system and the quaint play of mere words were all at once futile and savourless. And as books for him were no question of bread-and-butter, the real flavour of life lay thereafter in a discipleship of Wharton, and writing was a thing to be returned to only in the stagnant intervals between murders.

Wharton found that unofficial partnership profitable and to his liking, for he had for Travers an admiration and even an affection which the camouflage of gruntings and gruffness could never quite conceal. Travers, as he had come to know, was a square peg that miraculously fitted a round hole. Neither his wealth nor his sureness of breeding made a pandering appeal to the Old General, as the Yard knew him. What Wharton could appreciate, for all his leg-pulling and obvious ironies, was that Travers had a charm of manner and an atmosphere of sympathy that could elicit truths where the clamour of the law could only fail. The alert brain that had once amused itself with epigrams and such written trifles could now flash with startling intuitions. At times, it is true, they might savour of the fantastic, but there were other times when they led to short cuts. And above all Travers had the knack of discerning in the unobserved and commonplace the one thing vital and most needed.

It was after five o'clock when the car came at last to the broader road by the Park, and Travers turned southwards to the Embankment. The fog, still awkwardly patchy, would soon be dense if all the signs held true, so Palmer was sent home with the car while Travers called at the Yard.

Wharton happened to be in. He had finished a belated tea and was wiping with a voluminous handkerchief that vast overhanging moustache which made him the living spit of Chester Conklin or of an elderly Samuel Small. At the sight of Travers's six-foot three of lamp-post leanness, he gave a benevolent glance over the tops of his antiquated spectacles, then rose beamingly.

"Well, well, well; if it isn't Mr. Travers!"

Never had he looked more the amiable paterfamilias. Travers took the proffered hand and glanced down reprovingly.

"No bedroom slippers, George? Why deny yourself that supreme touch?"

Wharton guffawed. "You will have your little joke. Get that coat of yours off and sit down for a bit. Have some tea. You won't? Then try some of this in your pipe."

He fussed round till Travers was seated, then drew his own chair alongside and gave an arch glance over the spectacle tops.

"And what brings you out a night like this?"

"I've just come back from an auction on the far side of Buckinghamshire," began Travers. "There was a Ralph Wood figure I wanted for myself, and a coin my brother-in-law asked me to pick up if it went reasonably."

"A coin?" frowned Wharton, and then nodded. "Of course, though. He's a collector. What was the coin? Anything special?"

Travers brought it out of his waistcoat pocket. It was a silver coin of the size of a florin, and seemed in a state of superb preservation. Wharton twisted it about in his fingers and made faces at it.

"And what would that be worth?"

"About sixty pounds," Travers said. "It actually cost me forty guineas."

"Forty guineas!" His eyes bulged. "You're not taking a rise out of me?"

"God forbid," said Travers. "But there are only seven of these that are actually known. Its popular name is the Limerick Crown. One of a set of trial pieces cast for Cromwell for a minting he intended at Limerick, but which never materialised."

"And you brought it along specially to show me?" said Wharton, aping an anticipatory gratitude.

Travers shook his head. "Afraid I didn't. The fact is I came home through Garrod's Heath—"

"Garrod's Heath?" Wharton registered surprise. "Funny thing you should mention Garrod's Heath. We've been having inquiries from them recently." He waved at some papers on the desk behind. "What I've been working at this afternoon, as a matter of fact. They've had a regular plague of burglaries down there the last year or two. Keep on breaking out like the plague. I expect you've read about them."

"I believe I have," said Travers. "But what I ran across on the Common there was what was left of a murdered man."

Wharton raised his eyebrows. Travers told him the whole story from the episode of the running curate to a short synopsis of the talk with Mott, and ended with the remark that Garrod's Heath was beyond the jurisdiction of the Yard—unhappily.

"Unhappily?" said Wharton.

"Only in the sense that you people mayn't get called in," explained Travers. "But there's a certain amount of hope. I may say I did some useful propaganda work. Without actually being importunate, I practically insisted to Mott that the Yard was his only chance."

Wharton grunted. "What do you think we are? New grocery stores or something, touting for custom?" Then he settled himself more comfortably in his chair and prepared to take a ghoulish interest. He might have been some kindly member unavoidably absent from a Lord's Test and preparing now to hear in detail how the day had gone. "Head hacked off, was it? And the hands." He grunted. "Don't know what you think, but it seems to me Mott was right. There was something about those hands that might have revealed identity."

"It was a bestial performance," said Travers, almost savagely. "Either a madman's work, or something caused by sheer desperate necessity." He gave a slow reminiscent shake of the head. "Reminds me of something I once quoted to you on a certain case and which had the amazing fortune to fit in with an unknown context. Remember it, George?"

When beggars die there are no comets seen;
The heavens themselves blaze forth the deaths of princes.

Wharton grunted once more. "All of which means what?"

"Merely this. If the murdered man was a nonentity, why trouble to disfigure the corpse? Once be sure, in fact, that head and hands were removed for the purposes of concealing identity, and then you should be equally sure that the murdered man was a public or notorious personage."

"Splendid!" said Wharton, and chuckled. "All that remains to do is wait till such a personage becomes posted as missing—"

The rest of the heavy irony was lost to posterity. The phone shrilled and Wharton swivelled round instinctively. From his own end there came little more than "Quite so" and "Very good" but no sooner did he replace the receiver than he was getting to his feet.

"Sorry, but there's a matter I've got to attend to. You wouldn't like to pop in again later?"

"Don't like the fog," Travers told him. "And I'm rather frightened about that murder getting on my mind. It was the most horrible thing I've ever run across."

Wharton held out a good-night hand at the top of the stairs where their ways parted.

"I shouldn't be surprised if you don't have to do a lot more thinking about it yet."

"I expect I shall," said Travers ruefully, oblivious to Wharton's sparring for a climax.

"And so do I," said Wharton, already moving off. "What I'm now due to discuss, if I'm not mistaken, is an application for us to go down to Garrod's Heath."

Travers stared but Wharton was lost to sight round the corridor bend.

It was the homeward hour and the pavements were thick with pedestrians as Travers steered a careful way along Whitehall. The fog was still patchy, though with a visibility of never more than twenty yards. But towards Trafalgar Square it was suddenly scarcely more than a yard or two and he funked the intricate crossings to the Strand and kept left towards Piccadilly. One main crossing only, and he made his way up the Haymarket and turned for home. It was as he passed the shell where the Tube station used to be, that he heard the chimes of St. Martin's strike six. At the same moment his eyes fell on something for which they had grown accustomed to look whenever he passed that way— a seller of matches who always stood in a slight recess by the station door.

Travers, it may be repeated, was a student of human nature. The discovery of an original type had for him something of the thrill of the acquisition of a new Ralph Wood figure. And that seller of matches was certainly an original type—with a definite difference. There was about him nothing amusing or quaint or even pathetic. It was rather that Travers sensed in him some deeps of personality which the man himself guarded and which it would be a rudeness to appraise or familiarise. So Travers, in the nine months since he had become aware of the man's existence, had attempted neither talk nor inquiries, but had contented himself with the bestowal of coins and a friendly smile. "Thank you, sir," the man would say, and therein lay something of that originality of type, for there seemed a brusque dignity in the gratitude, and the voice— gruff and almost inaudible—had in it nothing of apology or shame.

Moreover that arch-theoriser Travers had in this particular instance no need of theorising, for the man spoke tacitly his own story. A neatly printed notice hung round his neck; a notice in itself original—

> CAST OFF BY THE SEA
> NO WORK
> NO DOLE

A greying torpedo beard gave him the look of a ship's captain and there was something of the patience of the sea in the way he would tirelessly stand, with no movement but to shift at times his tray of matches from one hand to the other. Maybe his eyesight had lost him his job—depression or no depression—for he wore dark glasses and had the stillness of a man whose eyes have ceased to rove. Then there was a curious kind of fisherman's hat that he wore, and a reddish muffler knotted round his neck, and in cold weather tied over mouth and throat as if he suffered from some weakness of the chest.

There was a bitter rawness that cut to bone and marrow, and Travers was surprised to see him at his post. The muffler was over nose and mouth but he had no overcoat, and there was an obvious thinness about the blue reefer that was buttoned beneath the muffler round to his ears. An old-fashioned red mitten was on the hand that held the tray but the fingers through it were blue with cold.

For the first time in his life Travers almost spoke. "Take this and get off home," it might have been, or, "Go and get yourself a good hot drink." But something held him back and it was about himself that there seemed a momentary shame as he dropped a hasty half-crown in the tray. Somehow he would have liked to meet those eyes and give a cheery nod, but the eyes were invisible behind their glasses, though he saw the movement of the head and heard the muffled thanks.

It was no more than five minutes from there to St. Martin's Chambers. Palmer took his master's coat and hat and asked about tea.

"A bit too late I think," Travers said, and then thought of something. "Any thermos flasks we can spare, by the way?"

Palmer thought there was at least one.

"There's a man who sells matches outside the old Piccadilly station," Travers said. "A man of about fifty or so, and an old sea-captain by the look of him. You've seen him there perhaps."

Palmer remembered the man and ventured to describe him as a gentleman fallen on evil days. But when he came back with the flask of hot tea, Travers had thought of something else.

"Anything I can reasonably spare in the way of overcoats? Something quiet if possible. It wouldn't do for him to be wearing anything showy or palatial. What about that blue?"

Palmer laid it out for inspection. Travers nodded approval and Palmer, wrapped up to the ears, departed like a second Wenceslas. Travers, having done his good deed for the evening, poured himself out a sherry and drew up a chair to the dining-room fire.

His thoughts at first hovered round the social system, depressions and unemployment; then focused themselves on the case of the match-seller, wondering what wires might be pulled to find the man a job. Then the thoughts shifted still farther back to the horror of the earlier afternoon; hurried quickly forward again, and cheered themselves with the prospect of new work with George Wharton. Then the sound of Palmer's door was heard and Travers called him in.

"He took the things?"

"And very grateful he was, sir," Palmer reported. "I was only just in time, sir. He was that moment going."

Before Travers could speak, the phone rang. He nodded to Palmer that he would take the call himself.

"Hallo! That you, Mr. Travers?"

Travers smiled as he knew the voice for Wharton's.

"Travers speaking. What's in the wind, George?"

"That operation of your sister's for appendicitis. Who was it did it?"

A cloud flashed across Travers's sun.

"Bendall, of Wimbeck Street. At his Hampstead nursing home. Why're you asking? Mrs. Wharton isn't ill, is she?"

"No," said Wharton. "But I thought I remembered your telling me he did the operation. That's why I'm letting you know about Bendall in case you'd like to come round. His operating days are over."

"You mean he's dead?"

"Stabbed in his own surgery," said Wharton curtly. "The knife's still in his ribs."

CHAPTER III
WHARTON GAPES

THE FOG was thicker than ever as Travers cut through Soho to his rendezvous with Wharton at Oxford Circus. Wharton said that Chief-Inspector Norris was already at Wimbeck Street and the usual crowd with him.

"He'll have the preliminaries done by the time we get there," he said. "Now tell me about the man. I suppose you saw a good bit of him. What'd you gather about him while Mrs. Transom was in his hands?"

"Precious little," Travers said. "He was recommended to us by a friend and we had an interview at my place as being most convenient and then my sister went into the nursing home. He struck me as alert and highly competent. But since I'm talking to you, I may add that he was the sort with whom I shouldn't have liked to have dealings in other than a professional way. I can't say more because I've nothing to go on but instinct."

"You wouldn't have trusted him, you mean?"

"That's what it amounts to. I did gather that he had few interests outside the nursing home, or private hospital or whatever you care to call it. He was a practising surgeon, I take it, with no panel practice and a strictly limited clientèle. He was a wealthy man and could afford to pick and choose."

"Elderly?"

They halted for a minute to get their bearings in the fog. Wharton found some landmark or other and steered Travers across the road.

"You were asking about his age," Travers said. "I'd put him at over sixty. A fine figure of a man in his younger days but he'd developed something of a stoop. It gave him a kind of predatory air. I shouldn't be surprised if it contributed to my prejudices."

Wharton crossed the road again and announced that they were in Wimbeck Street. Another minute and they were at a door where a constable was stationed. Norris met them in the narrow entrance-hall.

"We're getting on, sir," he said. "A fine set of prints on the knife. And we've timed it down to five-past six."

Travers liked Norris. He was the patient, relentless sort who takes no step but on firm ground. He was of the military, ramrod type, and in one splenetic moment Wharton summarised him in the remark that if he had had a moustache he would have waxed the ends. Now as they moved on, Norris indicated a door to the left.

"The waiting-room, sir. There's a patient in there—a Mrs. Dormant—you might like to see."

Wharton grunted a something and swayed his way on to an open door. That surgery was the spit of a hundred others, with its smell of dope, its desk and paraphernalia, and its handsome cabinet of drugs and medical oddments. The print men were at work and Menzies, the police-surgeon, was peering through his glass at the slit of a wound through the back ribs of the corpse. Wharton nudged Travers.

"That him all right?"

Travers took a quick look at the dead face, and nodded.

"Where's the knife, Menzies?" Wharton said.

Menzies waved back and went on with his peering.

It was a triangular-bladed knife with a point like a needle. Wharton had a squint at it through his glass. Travers saw plainly the white powder-marks of the prints.

"Sharpened up for the job," said Wharton, and grunted. "The prints gone yet?"

"Ten minutes ago," Norris told him. "We might have a ring through at any time."

"How was the body found? On the floor?"

Norris indicated the chalk marks. It looked, he said, as if the doctor had spoken to the patient—

"Patient?" Wharton said, and glared.

"You'll hear about that, sir," Norris told him imperturbably. "It was a patient who did him in. This patient was probably spoken to by the doctor in the usual way and then the doctor turned towards the desk here to make the usual entry in his book. That was when the patient slipped the knife between his ribs, as soon as his back was turned."

Wharton nodded. "Been through his pockets yet?"

"Not a thing worth mentioning," Norris said.

Wharton pursed his lips. "And how'd the patient get in?"

"A maid admitted him in the ordinary way. There's usually a nurse here to do the job but it was her evening off duty."

"Let me have a word with the maid," Wharton said. "Outside there will do. Where's that book you mentioned?"

"I've taken it over myself, sir," Norris said. "I reckoned it might come to getting in touch with every patient whose name's mentioned in it."

Wharton nodded approval and moved off to the hall, Travers at his heels.

The parlour-maid was a good witness. When the nurse was off duty it was for her to admit patients and show them into the waiting-room, and after some brief calculation she said the nurse had often remarked that they rarely came to more than thirty a week.

"And who did you admit to-night?"

"A man first," she said. "It was just six o'clock and I know that because I thought to myself they was pretty sharp on time."

"And how much later was it when you admitted a lady?"

"At about five past, sir, or just before."

The vital facts that emerged were these. At six o'clock to within a few seconds a patient was admitted to the waiting-room. He had a definite stoop, was black-bearded, and said in a high-pitched, almost squeaky voice that he had an appointment. His age would be somewhere in the fifties, and at first the maid thought he was coming about his leg, for he walked with a slight limp. Then she guessed it was his teeth, for one jaw was swollen and he kept a hand held to it. The nearest Wharton could come at his height was that he was a little shorter than himself. The rest of her account seemed likely to be overlapped by that of the second patient—the Mrs. Dormant.

Norris came bustling out with news. Wharton got in a question first.

"Any memo pad on the doctor's desk?"

"There's a pad with one entry," Norris said. "I meant to have shown it to you. It just says *J. Scott —6:00*"

"J. Scott," said Wharton, and paused. "And he came at six o'clock all right. Probably made an appointment by phone. Still, you might hunt for a letter in case he wrote. Anything else?"

"A fine set of prints on the inside chair," Norris said. "You can almost trace out what happened to the very word."

"And how?" asked Wharton with a raising of eyebrows.

"No prints in the waiting-room round where he sat," Norris said. "None on this door-knob, so he kept his gloves on all the time. The doctor sat in this chair and he sat in that. The doctor asked him about himself and told him to take off his overcoat and things, which he did, and when he sat down again he gripped the arms of the chair the same as anyone would if they were nervous-like. When he'd done the job he simply shot on his things again— there's this mark where he touched the chair where he'd laid them—and had his gloves on too and was out and gone. Mrs. Dormant will bear that out."

Wharton nodded noncommittally and moved off to the waiting-room. Detective-Sergeant Lewis was taking a statement and he stood by when Wharton took over.

The new witness was housekeeper at a place farther along the street. It was just before five-past six when she was admitted by the maid, to whom she put the whispered question if she were the first. The maid smiled, whispered back that there was one other, and showed her into the waiting-room. By the time she had sat down, the indicator went, which was the usual buzzer controlled from the surgery displaying a sign—NEXT PATIENT, PLEASE—in the waiting-room. Thereupon a man in a dark overcoat, hand to jaw, rose from the chair just inside the door and made his way out. Although Mrs. Dormant had been regular in her visits for a fortnight—Wharton gathered that the doctor was seeing her regularly as a special favour and to oblige his own housekeeper— she, like the maid, had never clapped eyes on the man before, and she saw little of him save a quick glimpse of his back. But on the buzz the doctor had come to the surgery *door* as his custom was, and she heard him giving the patient a good evening.

After that there was just the faintest sound of voices from the other room and in a very short while she lost track of things because she picked up a periodical with some pages of recipes and was busy reading. Then it seemed to her that she had heard the outer door and—less clearly—she seemed to remember a "Thank you, doctor. Good night." So with an eye on the sign and an ear for the buzzer, she sat on. Then, as she confessed, she put her ear to the wall and could hear no sound of voices, and it was at a quarter-past six that she peeped out into the hall. The doctor's housekeeper—Mrs. Keepage—was at the stairs and about to go up. The two were acquaintances and conferred and the upshot was that Mrs. Keepage listened at the surgery door, then tapped and entered.

"Never mind a general statement. Concentrate on a description of the man himself and get it rushed out," Wharton told Lewis. "Use the name J. Scott. It was probably a fake but you never know."

He moved out to the hall again where an operator was running a phone extension to the surgery.

"Any ideas yet?" he asked Travers.

"None that you haven't found for yourself," Travers said. "Affected limp. Fake beard."

"Why fake?"

Travers gave a shrug of the shoulders. "Guesswork, of course, but he'd padded out one cheek to help his disguise and give an impression of toothache, and he kept his hand to his jaw so as to make sure the fake beard didn't come loose."

Wharton shot a look at him, then nodded. "I reckon that was it. If so, Lewis is wasting his time."

So back to the surgery again. Menzies said the ambulance was waiting and he might as well get the body away.

"Got any close-ups of him?" Wharton asked Norris. "If not, prop him up and take a couple."

Travers winced. Menzies and the body had gone when he turned away from surveying the half-dozen prints on the red-distempered walls. Then the phone went but it was only the operator testing the extension. A second or two and it went in earnest. Wharton took the receiver, and inside fifteen seconds was hanging up.

"Prints unknown," he said to Norris. "Which is what we ought to have anticipated from the start. A pro would have had more sense than to broadcast his prints. All he left, he'd have wiped off."

"Surely there's no man sufficiently uninformed nowadays as to be unaware of prints and what they imply?" Travers said. "An amateur murderer would have wiped them off."

"Always assuming he had time and hadn't got the wind up," added Norris.

"Precisely," smiled Travers. "Then you'll have to assume that he didn't give a damn. It's possible that prints or no prints he was dead sure he couldn't be connected with the murder."

"There'll be plenty of time for theorising," Wharton cut in impatiently. "Now the waiting-room's clear I'll see the housekeeper there. Lewis, you take his keys and go through every drawer in the place."

Now if there was a thing wherein Wharton flattered himself it was in his handling of women. He had a repertoire of innumerable angles of approach, but with the housekeeper his was the role of sympathiser.

"A sad business, this, Mrs. Keepage," he said. "A terrible business, in fact, for you and all of us."

"It is indeed, sir," she said, and Travers noted how her eyes were dry.

"Pray sit down," Wharton said. "Let me draw that chair to the fire."

Travers stood in the background; watched, listened and admired. That housekeeper was a colourless, adequate sort of soul, but Wharton got his answers pat, and the right ones.

"You've been with him a good time, I expect?"

"Five years, sir," she said. "Ever since he came here."

"You must have got quite used to all his ways then," said Wharton, and did a bit of quick thinking. "But you were saying he came here only five years ago. Where exactly did he come from?"

"I don't know. I never heard him say."

"All the household staff was new?"

"Yes," she said. "He engaged me first and I engaged the new staff. There's only the two and the chauffeur."

"A chauffeur, is there?" Wharton said. "And where's he live?"

"He's single," she said. "He's at the Old Mews, leading out of the Square. That's where the car's kept."

Wharton caught Travers's eye and Travers unobtrusively departed. In a minute he was back again and picking up the lost threads. Mrs. Keepage was in fact in the act of telling Wharton about a queer thing that had happened the previous evening.

Dr. Bendall, it appeared, had announced at lunch-time, just after he returned from his usual morning visit to his nursing home, that he would be going out that evening and might be late for dinner, the usual hour for which was seven-thirty. Where he was going was somewhere in the country, for Mrs. Keepage had later seen the chauffeur who had told her that the master had inquired about the practicability of going to the far suburbs in the fog. The chauffeur's reply had been that to drive the car would be slow and dangerous work, and if an Underground station lay anywhere handy to wherever it was that the doctor was going, then he advised taking it. The doctor thereupon nodded and apparently accepted the advice.

Now there was nothing unusual about that for it was sometimes the case that he was called to consultations and professional business that took him out of town. The curious thing was that he came home just in time for dinner after all, and in a furious temper. First he growled out that he had been made a fool of, and then he began blaming the phone, and after the meal he did some telephoning and Mrs. Keepage heard him asking someone if he knew anyone of a certain name.

That was all very vague. Mrs. Keepage, for instance, had listened to the doctor's outburst during the brief time she was in the dining-room, but had not quite understood what it was all about, and the sooner she got out of the room, as she said, the more comfortable she would be feeling. So Wharton went patiently over the story again, having a hunch there was something in it, and then a tap came at the door and Norris announced that the chauffeur was there.

"Bring him in here," Wharton said.

He was a man of about thirty-five and of no particular individuality, though it was plain that the news of the tragedy had come as a shock. But all the news he could give was a confirmation of the housekeeper's story, and he had not the faintest idea where his master had gone the previous evening. Wharton accompanied him out, shook hands effusively and said he knew where to find him.

"His alibi's plumb all right," whispered Norris, as soon as the door had closed. "Several cars kept round there and he was helping a man on a job." Wharton came back to the housekeeper and began on a new line.

"Now who were his relatives, Mrs. Keepage?"

"I don't think the poor gentleman had any," she told him.

"None at all?" said Wharton, with a raising of eyebrows.

"Well, he had a daughter, sir, but she's dead. He always kept her photograph upstairs in his bedroom."

"I wonder if you'd mind fetching it," Wharton said.

The sending was probably no more than a ruse for a quick conference with Travers.

"Not getting anywhere for the moment," he said, "unless there's anything in that yarn about him being made a fool of last night. What's your own idea?"

Travers gave a helpless shrug of the shoulders. Even theories seemed at the moment far too substantial.

"So this is the daughter," Wharton said, when he had adjusted his antiquated specs. "Charming-looking lady. Married, was she?"

"I don't think so, sir. I never heard the doctor say so."

Wharton gave a look of indescribable archness. "Then if he hadn't a relative in the world, where was he going to leave all his money? He had plenty, hadn't he?"

"He certainly had, sir," the housekeeper told him with a prideful nod. "I know for a fact, sir, there was no need whatever for him to go on doctoring, sir. He was making it a kind of hobby."

"Quite so," Wharton said. "But what I'm wondering is who he was going to leave it all to. Any friends who visited him here?"

The housekeeper remembered none in particular. An occasional colleague, perhaps, but none to whom he had referred as friend. As for his money, she had heard the doctor hint that it was going to charities and museums. She had no idea who his lawyers were.

"I expect we shall soon find that out," Wharton told her, and again caught Travers's eye. This time when Travers came back the General was in the act of dismissal.

"A pleasure to talk to someone as sensible as yourself," he was saying. "We may have to trouble you again but I'm sure you won't mind that. A pot of tea, for instance, might be very acceptable later on."

"Why, certainly, sir," she said. "And something to eat with it, sir."

Wharton dismissed her roguishly.

"Thou shalt not muzzle the ox," quoted Travers. "Personally I'm amazingly hungry, having fed last at one o'clock. But before the meal—what?"

Wharton shook his head. "Heaven knows. Routine work, I guess. I might get hold of that lawyer if Norris has found who he is." He grunted. "Don't know, though. I think I'll ring up the nursing home and find out if he went there yesterday evening. That fool of a woman may have got things all wrong. Hampstead's the suburbs, isn't it? Dangerous enough to drive out there in the fog?"

Then he thought of something else.

"If doctors of the Wimbeck Street class have nursing homes, aren't they usually just round the corner in one of the Squares? Hampstead's a fairish way off."

"It's not too far," Travers said. "Besides, Bendall wasn't the conventional Wimbeck Street type. He was a wealthy man, as you've heard, who regarded this end of his profession as a kind of hobby. The nursing home was the main preoccupation."

He went back to the surgery. Norris had utilised couch and table and was docketing the papers from the desk. Lewis seemed to be folding the dead man's clothes for dispatch to the Yard.

"I've got the lawyers all right, sir," Norris told Travers. "And the private address of two of the firm. Hillyer and Crove."

"I know them," Travers said. "Broad Street, aren't they?"

All at once Lewis was calling across the room.

"Here's a letter of some sort in his inner fob pocket." He was unfolding it with a somewhat sheepish grin. "Shouldn't half have been for it if Menzies had found it first."

He took a quick glance, and threw it over to the print men with a "Check up on that, will you?" Then he went on explaining. "Sort of folded up and tucked away in the corner of the pocket. And look at this, sir. You can hardly see the pocket, let alone anything in it."

"You want to be a bit more thorough," began Norris with a heavy reproof that brought from Lewis no more than another grin. Then in came Wharton.

"He wasn't at the nursing home," he said to Travers. "He was there morning and afternoon as usual but he left at half-past three. The matron says he told her he had an appointment out of town but he didn't even hint where. Only two patients there now, she says. One appendicitis convalescent and another under observation."

Lewis came over from the print men with the sheet of note-paper in his gloved hand.

"This has got the doctor's prints on, sir. And these two smudges are a hundred to one on being those of the one that did it."

Wharton shot him a look, then put on his gloves.

"It was folded up in the doctor's inside pocket," Lewis told him casually. "That was why it was passed over, sir." Then he gave an apologetic cough. "If I may suggest so, sir, it looks like a letter the murderer wrote to him."

Wharton shot him another look at that, then began reading the neatly written words. Travers peered over his shoulder.

Have it your own way. Expect you without fail to-night (Tuesday) at Garrod's Heath at 6:00 sharp by horse-trough on Common.

Wharton, mouth agape, looked up at Travers. Travers, mouth agape too, was already fumbling for his glasses. Lewis, wondering what it was all about, was gaping at the pair of them.

CHAPTER IV
SEALS AND CROWNS

WHARTON'S EYES fell.

"Garrod's Heath," he said slowly. "Garrod's Heath." Then he left it at that but his ears were alert for what Travers would say. And Travers was hooking on his glasses again.

"That bonfire wasn't two hundred yards from the horse-trough. Palmer had the car drawn up right against it."

Wharton smiled deprecatingly. "Surely you don't think—?"

"I think what you do," Travers told him dryly, "only I utter my thoughts aloud."

"Just a minute, sir," broke in Norris. "What is all this about Garrod's Heath? As far as I'm concerned you're talking double-Dutch."

"You explain," said Travers, and Wharton did the explaining. He also added what Travers did not know, that the bonfire body was probably by that time being post-mortemed by Sir Barnabas Craig.

"Now I get you, sir," Norris said. "You think there's more than a chance this Doctor Bendall went to Garrod's Heath last night and did the cutting up. A nice clean job, was it, sir?"

"A long way from it," Travers said.

"Just a minute," broke in Wharton, who had been studying that sheet of paper again. "There's one pretty sure way of finding out about last night. Lewis, you take the Underground and go straight to Garrod's Heath station. Find out if anyone saw him come through the barrier, then whether you have any luck or not, find out any taxi-driver who picked him up. Well, what're you waiting for?"

"To find out about his clothes, sir. What ones he wore last night."

"Ask the housekeeper to come then," Wharton told him. "I'd like to see her myself."

The doctor had been conservative over clothes and there was little trouble in finding out what he had worn on that supposed trip to Garrod's Heath.

"Those close-ups will be ready in the morning if you have no luck to-night," Wharton told Lewis at the door. "Ring up here as soon as you know anything."

Then he had a ghoulish smile for the housekeeper.

"This house is remarkably snug and warm, Mrs. Keepage. How on earth do you manage it?"

"That's the central heating, sir."

"Why, of course," said Wharton and chuckled at his own lack of observation. "And me so interested in it too." His face straightened. "You have a boiler, I take it?"

"In the basement, sir."

"A capital place," Wharton said. "Drives the heat upwards where it's wanted. I wonder now if . . . but I don't want to trouble you—"

"You'd like to see it, sir?"

"Well, being so interested, perhaps I would," Wharton told her.

Norris was back in the surgery at work on the patients' book.

"I've been through this once already, sir," he told Travers, "and I don't remember any mention of Garrod's Heath and there wasn't anyone of the name of Scott. Still, I reckon I'd better go over it again."

Travers drew on a pair of gloves and began a systematic search of the papers from the desk. It was ten minutes before Wharton came back.

"Had a good look round everywhere," he told them mysteriously. "Never a sign of a bone or anything in the clinker; no buttons from clothes or anything."

"A doctor wouldn't need to burn the head and hands," Travers said. "He could make out to anyone who happened to blunder on them that they were dissection pieces. He'd have them at the nursing home where his operating theatre is."

"But he didn't go back there last night," Wharton said. "The matron was sure they saw nothing of him after half-past three." Then his face took on an expression of comical dismay. "Wait a minute, though. He might have brought them home here and taken them there this morning."

He did five good minutes' telephoning before he reluctantly consented to be satisfied.

"He didn't go back there last night and this morning all he brought was his usual attaché-case and she saw there was nothing in it but some papers. Not that there aren't ways and means."

"His bedroom?" Travers suggested.

"I've been there," Wharton told him. "I asked to see the daughter's photograph again. I've had every drawer and cupboard open."

"Mind you, gentlemen," said Norris, looking up from his book, "I must say it seems to me that we're taking a lot for granted. There's ten thousand people in Garrod's Heath, to say the least of it."

"To put it most frankly," Travers told him, "your idea is that the connection of Doctor Bendall with the Garrod's Heath affair is a pretty wild leap in the dark."

"Of course I may not know so much as you," Norris said. "All I say is that from what I know there seems no reason to connect a highly respectable and well-off man like the doctor with a dismembered trunk found at a Garrod's Heath bonfire— even though it's proved that he was there at the time that fitted."

"Better be safe than sorry," Wharton told him. "Other things fit, don't they? Isn't that letter a fishy one, however you read it? The *have it your own way* and the rendezvous for about the loneliest place in the district."

"The doctor was a big man and strong for his age," added Travers. "He could have carried that corpse to the bonfire as easy as you'd carry a sack of coke. Which reminds me rather startlingly of something, George. Remember that conversation I had with Mott? How I put it to him that the last thing a medical murderer would have done would have been to sever the joints scientifically? That corpse was hacked about and no one could ever imagine it the work of a surgeon. It was in fact rather too hacked about."

"Well, sir, I'm always ready to be convinced," said Norris. "In fact, the more I'm convinced the better I like it. Now may I put something to you, and to you, sir. Take all the evidence we've got and also assume Doctor Bendall did the Garrod's Heath job. Then the facts are these. Yesterday morning —we'll say—the doctor got the letter telling him to go to Garrod's Heath, and that letter was written by the man who murdered him to-night. Then who was the man the doctor saw and murdered?"

"All in good time," Wharton told him imperturbably. "But before Mr. Travers offers us a cast-iron theory—which I see he's just about to do—I might suggest that Guy Fawkes, who was the bonfire corpse, and X, who wrote the letter and murdered the doctor, were confederates in something. The doctor murdered Guy Fawkes to get himself out of some hole. X murdered the doctor by way of revenge."

He was giving an arch triumphant peer over his spectacle tops when there was a tap at the door. It was the housekeeper and the house-kitchenmaid whom Norris had not thought it necessary for Wharton to see. A space was cleared for the two trays.

"If there isn't everything you want," Mrs. Keep-age said, "just ring the bell."

She lingered for a moment after Wharton's copious thanks. Something was on her mind and at last she got it off.

"You don't think, sir, he was really a burglar and after the seals?"

Wharton stared. "Seals?" he said. "Seals?"

"The ones the doctor had."

Wharton stared some more. "You don't mean performing seals?"

It was the housekeeper's turn to stare. Then she smiled.

"Oh, no, sir. Perhaps I didn't explain myself sufficiently. Seals, sir, like people wear. The doctor collected them, and seeing some of them were gold, and what with everything gold being so valuable nowadays . . ."

Wharton took a deep breath. "Collected seals, did he? And where'd he keep them?"

"In the drawing-room, sir."

"Had a look to see if anyone's been in?"

She hesitated. "Well, sir, I have . . . but I'd rather you had a look yourself."

Wharton grunted, shot a reluctant look at the tea and sandwiches, and disappeared with the housekeeper. But he was back again in less than no time.

"Everything's in glass cases and not a sign of disturbance. Very interesting collection by the look of them."

He gave his tea an ample sugaring and stirred it round; peered at a sandwich as if about to caution it, and then took a bite.

"You know, sir," Norris was saying, "all this reminds me of something and I can't for the life of me remember what it is. Now you've got a marvellous memory. What do you think of when anyone talks about gold seals?"

"Gold seals?" Wharton said, the truncated sandwich suspended in the air. "Gold seals? Why, yes. There was something. Let me see now. Let me see."

A moment or two and he was shaking his head. "Nothing I ever handled personally. Yet there's something, though. Some inquiries or other."

'Another moment and he was giving a satisfied nod. "I've got it—or I think I have. Wasn't there a case at Porburgh-on-Sea?"

"That's it, sir." Norris gave a nod of his own. Then his eyes opened. "That was a doctor, sir; don't you remember? Collected seals and caught some burglars red-handed. His son-in-law was one of them and the Porburgh police asked us about him. We were after him for a con job. What was his name now?"

"Johnson," said Wharton calmly.

"That's right, sir," said Norris admiringly. "It'd be a goodish time ago."

"Eight years come February," Wharton told him, as if the feat of memory were nothing. Norris gave Travers a surreptitious wink, implying an awareness of the General's display, and an appreciation.

"But the name of that doctor wasn't Bendall," Norris said. "It was something like Collinson . . . or—" He clicked his tongue. "I nearly had it then."

Wharton's third sandwich was waving in the air and he was making trial noises. Then he had an idea.

"Carter, wasn't it? Wait a minute, though. Carberry. That's it—Carberry! A Doctor Carberry."

"It looks as if there ought to be some connection, don't you think?" said Travers. "There must be an extremely limited number of people collecting seals. When you imagine that two of them were doctors, it makes it still more interesting. Also the Doctor Carberry had a son-in-law, I gathered, which means he had a daughter. Bendall had a daughter."

"Possibly Bendall inherited the collection from Carberry, who was a relative," Wharton said.

"Perfectly feasible," said Travers. "But though the suggestion may sound far-fetched, mayn't it be a fact that Bendall and Carberry are one and the same person? The doctor came here five years ago and engaged a wholly new staff."

"Yes," said Wharton slowly. "Yes. There might be something in that." He leaned back in the chair with eyes closed, and began a reminiscent muttering. Words emerged from the sounds.

"Johnson got seven years—or was it nine? The daughter's said to be dead, and Johnson'd be out of jail."

He shook his head, then all at once was getting to his feet.

"There's one safe way of finding out the truth about Bendall. Get me one of those solicitors on the phone, Norris, will you?"

"While you're phoning, I think I'd like to have a peep at those seals if I may," Travers said, and pushed the bell for the housekeeper.

The drawing-room faced Wimbeck Street and Travers drew the blinds to see that the windows were protected by stout bars, and of reasonably recent date.

"The doctor had them put in when everybody was talking about gold," Mrs. Keepage said. "He had quite a scare, poor gentleman."

Travers was not surprised. Some of the heavier Georgian and Victorian specimens were of massive gold, and even they were eclipsed in value by specimens whose rarity was wholly new to him, for the collection was widely representative. Of all ages and tastes it seemed and as widely representative as that Pentecostal gathering that had ranged from Parthians, Medes and Elamites to strangers of Rome, and Jews and proselytes. Mahogany show-cabinets held most of it, but there were chests with nests of drawers which Travers at the moment saw no point in unlocking.

He came back to the surgery to find Wharton in a fine temper. The lawyer had refused to accept as evidence a voice over the phone, even when that voice claimed to be a big noise at Scotland Yard and was heavy with tales of murder. Wharton had apparently referred the reluctant speaker to the Yard itself and was impatiently awaiting the verdict—and the prospect of turning out at ten o'clock at night for a trip to Maidenhead in the fog.

"Red-tape and flummery!" he was saying. "Sparring for time, that's all he's doing. Getting hold of one of his partners to see how much they dare let out."

"Lawyers are a queer lot—and always were," Norris told him placatingly, as he rose with the patients' register. "That's twice

I've been through this book, sir, and there's no word whatever about Garrod's Heath, nor anyone of the name of Scott."

Wharton grunted. Then the phone went and he whipped the receiver off. In a moment his expression was miraculously changing.

"Oh, yes, Lewis.... Splendid.... Splendid.... That's right. Take a statement and get back soon as you can.... I know. I know.... Good, good.... The sooner the better.... Good-bye."

He gave the two a glance over the tops of his spectacles.

"Well, the guess looks a bit nearer to turning out true. He was there last night. Arrived about a quarter to six. Took a taxi to the Common, at the junction of the main Oxford Road and told the taxi-man not to wait. If he took a train back from Garrod's Heath station, then nobody saw him."

"They wouldn't be likely to if there was fog," Norris said.

"He'd have to go through the barrier, wouldn't he?" challenged Wharton. "Unless he climbed over somewhere in the fog, as you say. Which reminds me. Lewis says it's beginning to rain out there. He reckons the fog'll be gone by the morning. Make a note, Norris, about Garrod's Heath. Lewis should be there first thing with a couple of good men and work out where Bendall went and how he got home. The Marylebone end might be tried."

He heaved a sigh as he took out his pipe.

"Well, I suppose there's nothing to do now but wait for those damn lawyers. You and I might go through those cheque counterfoils and account books, Norris. In the morning you'd better collect everything there is at the nursing home."

They settled down to the job while Travers drew his chair up to the electric fire and watched. Somehow or other his thoughts went to that collection of seals, and suddenly he remembered something and his fingers went to his waistcoat pocket. Then they went to another pocket. His face took on an expression of apprehension, and all at once he was searching his pockets feverishly. Then he was on his feet and repeating the search.

"What's up? Lost anything?" said Wharton.

"At the moment—yes," Travers told him uneasily. "That coin I showed you. The Limerick Crown."

"You don't say!" Wharton came over and watched while Travers made yet another methodical search.

"It certainly isn't on me," Travers said, and frowned. "Now what on earth can have happened to it? Let me see now. I came in and sat down. Palmer came in and we . . ."

But after that review of his doings of the earlier evening he was positive that at the flat he had never as much as remembered the coin, let alone having taken it out.

"I had it in this upper waistcoat pocket," he said. "I remember showing it to you, George, and that's the last I remember about it."

"I gave it back," Wharton said. "I distinctly remember handing it to you and seeing you take it."

"Then I put it back in the same pocket," Travers said. "I'd do that by instinct. But there isn't a hole in the pocket."

"Wait a minute," said Wharton, who had been all concern. "We can't be sure I did give it to you. What's more likely, though, is that you thought you slipped it in your pocket—sort of absent-mindedly— but you didn't. It slid down your waistcoat and on the floor."

"Try your trouser turn-ups, sir," suggested Norris.

But the coin was not there. Wharton was most upset.

"Forty guineas is no joke," he said, and began a fresh thinking back. "Mind you, I'd swear I saw you take it. Tell you what, though. You get off back to my room and have a look. Wait a second and I'll write you a chit."

Travers said that as there seemed to be little doing, he would go back from the Yard to the flat. Then just as he was going, the phone shrilled.

"Oh, yes," said Wharton, and from the hurt dignity in his voice Travers gathered it was the lawyer at last. So he lingered on for the news.

"Another guess proved right," Wharton said as he hung up. "He changed his name from Carberry to Bendall just over five years ago."

Travers raised his eyebrows. "What about the medical authorities?"

"They were perfectly complaisant, I gathered," Wharton said. "There was family scandal and Carberry thought it as well to change his name and clear right out of Porburgh." He pursed his lips. "We'll see how things shape, but it might be worth while to rake up that Carberry Case. There're one or two things in it that look to me a bit fishy."

"But I gather that the Yard has all the prints connected with the Carberry Case," Travers said. "And you've just had a report that the Print Department doesn't know the prints of the man who did the killing to-night. The man Johnson, for instance, who might have been Bendall's son-in-law, and who got a long term of imprisonment; he couldn't have been the man who posed as J. Scott."

"Don't I know it?" said Wharton, and left it abruptly at that.

Wharton's room at the Yard was searched and every foot of the way Travers had taken through corridors to the outer door. It was eleven o'clock when he came back to St. Martin's again, and by that time the fog was clearing and the rain was spattering.

In the flat itself was no sign of the missing coin, and it was as he reviewed the events of the evening that he had a sudden hope. Wharton was rung at once.

"No luck so far, George," he said, "but I've got an idea. I think I was wool-gathering somewhat when you handed me back that coin. There's just the possibility I may have slipped it into my trouser pocket without thinking and given it to a beggar in mistake for half a crown. . . . Well, not a beggar, really. A decent sort of man who sells matches outside Piccadilly station. . . . Oh, yes; I'll see him some time in the morning."

"If the fog should clear, would you be prepared to run me down to Porburgh in the morning?" came Wharton's voice. "Say, for instance, I'm at your place at about ten?"

"Delighted," Travers said. "Anything new turned up?"

"Nothing much," Wharton said. "We did happen to find an old engagement book of last year with a memo scribbled in it. '*J out yesterday*'—that's all."

"J?" said Travers, then remembered. "The man Johnson, who got nine years?"

"That's him," Wharton said. "And he's why we're going to Porburgh—prints or no prints."

CHAPTER V
THE VITAL CLUE

Travers had no knowledge of the time at which that match-seller was accustomed to arrive, but he took a chance soon after nine and found him already on his pitch. Even then he hesitated before he approached the man, fearing to make himself noticeable to passers-by on the busy pavements, and finding a strangeness in attempting talk with a figure so utterly motionless.

So Travers coughed diffidently as he came up.

"Pardon me," he began, "but might I have a word with you about something personal?"

It was as if an automaton had sprung to movement, for the head swivelled in a flash and behind their glasses he knew the eyes were searching him.

"Nothing that matters a great deal," he went on, "but last night you may remember I—er—bought some matches and gave you what I believed to be a half-crown. Now there's just the chance that I may have given you in mistake a valuable coin; an old coin, I mean. A collector's piece, in fact, for which I'd be glad to reward the finder with anything up to a five-pound note."

The man was motionless for a moment, then he shook his head. His voice, when it came, was that of a man of education, though it had a kind of bitter brusqueness.

"Last night, sir, wasn't it? At about six o'clock?"

"That's it. A few seconds after six."

Again the man shook his head. "I'm sorry, sir, but it wasn't any special coin. It *was* a half-crown— and grateful enough I was for it."

Travers smiled with resignation. "Sorry I've bothered you then."

His hand was already in his pocket but the other spoke quickly.

"No bother, sir—and I'd rather you didn't."

Travers flushed, and out the hand came. Then he remembered something else, for though the fog had gone it was a raw morning.

"You're not wearing your overcoat."

"No, sir, but I thank you for it, sir. Your man told me it was you who sent it. I know you well enough, sir. You're one of my regulars."

Travers flushed again. "Well, it's nice of you to say so."

Somehow he knew he was showing to poor advantage, and all at once he was mumbling a something and moving off. A minute later he was analysing that queer shamed diffidence that had come over him, and knew it for a twinge of conscience for a peering behind the barrier of pride and quiet self-respect behind which that poor devil of a match-seller could still keep something of his soul. As for the Limerick crown, it would be best to wait a day or two in case it turned up after all. If not, the loss must be advertised. And if that produced nothing, then Ludovic Travers would be forty guineas out of pocket, and the Major's collection would confront him for ever with a condemnatory gap.

It was an hour and a half's journey to Porburgh-on-Sea, but with good visibility and the morning too young for overmuch traffic, Travers was expecting to do it in less. Wharton sat in front, with Palmer behind, and the General was between the twin horns of need for hurry and a nervousness at high speeds. It was he who did all the talking, maybe to conceal his qualms.

"I've been making quite a lot of inquiries," he said, referring to the Carberry Case. "The facts we've got don't tell us anything really. They're just facts, if you know what I mean. We want to get what lies behind the story. Nothing whatever emerged last night after you'd gone, and this old scandal looks like our only hope. Mind you"—and he gave a little laugh that was just a bit too carefree—"I'm like yourself. I know that though Bendall was at Garrod's Heath the night before last, it's almost ridiculous to associate him with the body in the bonfire. What I mean is that we shan't get any help from that end."

Travers chuckled inwardly but refused to be drawn.

"That's why I'm glad in a way we haven't got to deal with the present Porburgh police," Wharton went on. "It's a Superintendent Watts we're going to see, who was in charge of the case and now's retired and living at Billingham, about four miles away, as I told you. I reckon they'll have warned him by the time we get there. If so he'll be expecting us."

Travers remarked that that would be ideal.

"About the doctor," Wharton said. "Best thing to do is to keep on calling him Carberry. I got in a rare muddle once through calling a man two names, though they were his rightful ones." He shook his head. "I don't seem to be able to concentrate on anything this morning. All I can keep thinking of is that coin of yours. Now you're sure you didn't . . ."

Ex-Superintendent Watts was in his garden, building a bonfire for his two grandchildren.

"Well, we've come to talk about bonfires," Wharton said as he shook hands. Then he hastily corrected himself. "At least, we may have to before long. Mr. Travers—one of our experts."

The name of Travers conveyed nothing to the old super, though maybe the sight of the handsome car produced the profuse apologies for the humbleness of the sitting-room.

"If I'd a place like this when I got married, I'd have thought I was at the Ritz," Wharton told him, and settled himself in the chair. "And now keep well under your hat what I'm going to tell you— which is what we've come to talk about. A Doctor Bendall was murdered last night."

"Indeed, sir?" said Watts, wondering why Wharton was peering so curiously over his spectacle tops.

"Yes," said Wharton. "Stabbed in the back at his surgery in Wimbeck Street in London. And here's what you've got to keep under your hat, for nobody knows it—yet. Doctor Bendall was a gentleman of your acquaintance. He was, in fact, Doctor Carberry."

Watts's eyes bulged. "What—him that lived at Porburgh?"

"Yes," said Wharton. "The one who was concerned with the Carberry Case—which is what we want you to tell us about here and now. Tell us the whole issue: what happened, all the gossip and everything you can think of."

But Watts was shaking his head. "Murdered, eh? You can hardly believe it. He wasn't at all a bad sort. Really missed too when he went away."

"How do you mean?"

"Very generous in subscribing to things," Watts said. "People used to say he could have been among the top-notchers if he'd liked and if he hadn't too much money. He inherited no end from his father, old John Carberry, the brewer. Watkinson's brewery it is now."

But Superintendent Watts's story, duly edited, was this. Doctor Carberry had a high-class practice at Porburgh, itself a fashionable resort. He was a widower with an only daughter, Moira, who was apparently the apple of his eye and whose schooling and finishing had cost him a pretty penny. During the war she did hospital work in the town, while the doctor himself was kept busy with operations in the extemporised military hospital.

It was just at the end of the war that Moira announced her engagement to a man. Everything was conjecture and rumour as far as Porburgh was concerned, but it was known that the man was older than she was, that her father was in opposition to the marriage, and that after a violent quarrel she left home. Then came news of the marriage, but Carberry himself was tight-lipped about the whole affair. Soon it was known that the husband's name was Johnson, and Moira described herself to friends to whom she wrote as Mrs. Rolland Johnson. It was also rumoured, and rumour for once was true, that Johnson had come down to Porburgh to interview his father-in-law, and that there was some outward reconciliation, for shortly afterwards Moira herself paid a visit home.

Then came the first scandal when Porburgh read in its newspapers that a Rolland Johnson had been sentenced to twelve months for fraud. What he had been before the war no one knew, but at the trial it came out that he had been dismissed from his temporary job in the Service for embezzlement of naval funds. Since then apparently he had made a living by his wits.

So much for the preliminaries, which were long-winded only because Wharton insisted on full details and proceeding step by step. And so to the Carberry Case proper, the story of which is best told as a brief report of the trial.

Carberry said that early on the evening in question he received a telegram purporting to come from his daughter and asking him to meet her at the station, which was three miles from the house. So he started off but, after going a mile, remembered a most import something which made him return to the house. He let himself quietly in—it was the afternoon off for two of the staff and the third had been decoyed away—and became aware of intruders in his drawing-room where was kept his collection of seals. He slipped out of the house, found a policeman at once— and a second—and returned to the house with advice to one policeman to take the back and the other the front. Almost at once the policeman at the back apprehended a man—a Henry Luke—who was making his escape. Inside the house there was the sound of a shot. Johnson, it was, and he had been armed, but the doctor had tackled him and wrested the gun from him, and it had gone off and wounded Johnson in the shoulder.

Johnson admitted decoying away the maid and his father-in-law, but he vehemently denied the possession of the gun. He claimed that when Carberry recognised him he snatched a gun from a drawer and deliberately tried to kill him, with the idea of freeing his daughter of a rogue, and covering himself on the plea of self-defence. But his confederate, Luke, proceeded to swear that Johnson was always armed, and that he himself had warned him of the consequences if he was ever caught with a gun on him.

"You never saw a man so taken aback in your life," Watts said, "as Johnson was when he heard that. Since then I've had my own doubts about things, and I've done a bit of thinking. Still, the judge gave him nine years—he'd asked for two other cases to be taken into account—and as soon as he heard what he'd got, he just leaned forward deadly quiet: 'I'll get you two when I come out,' he says, just like that. 'I'll get you two if it's the last thing I'll do.'"

Wharton gave a gratified nod. "That's what he said, did he? And what did Luke get? Three years, wasn't it?"

Three years it was, the superintendent said. And Luke's case was interesting enough. He had been living in the town and posing as an upright, interested citizen, and at his arrest the flood of burglaries ceased with which the town had been for some time troubled. But the police found no proceeds of burglaries in Luke's small villa, for the same night before they arrived there it was burnt to the ground—and deliberately.

"There was a mystery I was never able to fathom, gentlemen," Watts said. "Burnt to the ground, the place was, and him in custody. If he had a confederate, then no one ever saw him. But what was reckoned at the time was that whenever Luke went out on one of his burglary trips he used to leave incendiary material and a burning candle or something so that the house should be burnt if he didn't get back."

"How did he and Johnson come to meet?" Wharton asked.

But in what underworld of crime the two had become acquainted, Watts was unaware. All he could add, in fact, was that Moira Johnson came home and within a year was dead. The doctor sold the practice and went away, and that was the last Porburgh knew of him.

"I had a fairish bit to do with Johnson, one way and another," Watts said, "and I've never quite summed him up. He was a gentleman, as they say, and yet he wasn't the ordinary plausible sort, same as you'd expect a con man to be, which had been his general line. I believe he had a screw loose somewhere. There were things that came out about him, and things that never got out, that proved it. Regular genius, they reckoned he was, in some things— how he planned jobs and so on, and then he'd go and do some damn silly thing a schoolboy wouldn't do. Take the job we've been talking about, for instance."

"You'll pardon me," said Travers, offering yet another of his best cigarettes, "but there was some mention of certain thoughts you've had since, about the gun episode. I wonder if you'd mind telling us them."

Watts gave a careless wave of the hand. "Only just my thoughts, sir. We're all entitled to our ideas."

"Certainly we are," said Wharton heartily, and reading him like a book. "Still, you tell us what you thought. In our job you never know. And of course it'll be in confidence."

"Honestly, gentlemen, it wasn't anything." Then immediately he was qualifying it. "I shouldn't have said anything about it in any case."

Travers smiled. "I imagine the superintendent is none too sure of the collusion."

Watts stared. "Collusion, sir? You don't say you knew all the time?"

Travers smiled even more disarmingly. "But that doesn't prevent my wishing to hear your own version—in very strict confidence."

"All right then, sir," Watts said resignedly. "Well, how I had my suspicions was like this. When the doctor went away I happened to discover that one of my men—the one who'd apprehended Luke—was living above his means. We have to keep an eye on that sort of thing; and then it turned out that the doctor, when he was going, had given him a hundred quid. Later on this man of mine left the force and I found out that the night of the burglary Carberry had asked to have a minute alone with Luke—unknown to Johnson and the other constable. Then I remembered how well the doctor had spoken of Luke at the trial, and I put everything together and made up my mind Johnson had been framed as far as the gun was concerned. I was just due for retirement then so I kept it under my hat. How you unearthed it, sir, is more than I can fathom."

Wharton got to his feet with a roguish, "Ways and means, old friend. Mr. Travers is a regular bradawl for information."

"You're not going, gentlemen?" Watts said in consternation. "Why, my daughter expects you to stay to dinner—such as there is."

"We haven't a minute," said Wharton, who had more information than he could ever have hoped, and was bursting to be off. "But if you'll be so good as to come to your local station with me, I'll make use of their telephone."

Then while Wharton sent an urgent message to the Yard that Johnson must be picked up within twenty-four hours, Travers was purchasing for Watts's two grandchildren a huge array of fireworks at the local shop, to soothe the old superintendent's ruffled feelings over the uneaten lunch, and as a propitiation maybe for the flippancies that had been uttered to Palmer in the matter of Guy Fawkes.

Palmer drove. Travers sat behind with Wharton and the General said would Travers excuse him for a minute or two while he wrote some notes. Out of the corner of his eye Travers could see that Wharton was on admirable terms with himself, for now and again he would give an arch peer over his spectacle tops at what he had written.

But at last he had finished and he turned to Travers with a sigh of hypocritical resignation. Travers loved Wharton's little antics. But for the grace of God and Scotland Yard Wharton might have ended his days in melodrama.

"Well, so far, so good," he said. "And what's your opinion of what we've gathered this morning?"

"I'm more fogged than ever," Travers told him.

"Fogged?" Wharton glared. "Why, the whole thing's plain as a pikestaff. Unless I'm very much mistaken there never was a case more on the surface."

Travers began a gentle polishing of his glasses and he spoke in reminiscent vein.

"Last night, George, I tuned in my wireless and was unlucky enough to find most of Europe in the grip of crooners. As soon as I'd given up my search for a less lachrymatory programme, I drew up to the fire in my chair and began involuntarily to meditate on those neo-castrati, the crooners. I came eventually to the *-heims, -steins* and *-vitches* who provide them, and modern England, with ballads. Isles of the Mediterranean, mid-European seats of high romance, the sloppier States of America and the sleepy South: these, I thought, seem the one passion and background of the man behind the crooner; but of Jerusalem, Jericho, or even Damascus—never a word. No invitations to return there, George. No lost loves left behind there—"

"What exactly *is* this you're talking about?"

"A minute," said Travers, "and I complete the argument. May not some future historian or student of economic history, thought I, fall in some far distant future into egregious error? May he not suppose from the above evidence that the aforesaid *-heims* and *-steins* were curiously unpatriotic, or marvellously modest?"

Wharton grunted suspiciously.

"All of which," said Travers with an airy wave of the hand, "is a fugitive, roundabout observation on the dangers of surface judgment. Nevertheless I'd be extremely interested to hear why you think the case is virtually over."

"I didn't go so far as that," said Wharton. "But take a look at this summary and then tell me where I'm wrong."

"Before I do," said Travers, "I'll give you something to be thinking about. The most interesting connecting link we heard this morning is that at the time of the Carberry affair there were a whole series of burglaries at Porburgh. You may remember the same phenomenon has been occurring for some months and is still occurring at Garrod's Heath."

Before Wharton could answer he began a scrutiny of the summary.

1. Carberry tumbled to Johnson from the first. He had made up his mind to shoot him by some scheme or other, hence the gun handy.
2. He undoubtedly framed up the charge of attack when Johnson unluckily gave him the unexpected chance.

3. He bribed Luke to side with him in double-crossing Johnson.
4. Carberry knew the reality of Johnson's threats after the sentence, which was why he hid his personality so that J. should not find him when he came out (N.B.—Note in engagement book—*J. out yesterday* .)
5. Johnson fulfilled his threat and tracked down both Carberry and Luke.
6. Luke was the corpse of the bonfire.
7. He had been blackmailing Carberry, having that old hold over him. Carberry killed him to silence him.
8. Johnson could not have killed Carberry because the prints were not his, but he engineered it with a confederate.

FIND JOHNSON.

"Find Johnson," said Travers, handing the summary back. "An excellent slogan and much may be said for it."

"And what against it?" fired Wharton.

"Quite a lot," Travers told him. "Why not concentrate on the actual one who killed Carberry—the man who called himself J. Scott?"

"Concentrate?" Wharton fairly shouted the word. "Aren't we doing it?" he snorted. "Trying to do it, I ought to say. He came out of the fog and disappeared in the fog and we haven't a thing to work on."

"I'm sorry," said Travers. "I realise that now. As you say, we've got to get hold of Scott through somebody else. But tell me something. Why are you so sure that Luke is Guy Fawkes?"

"I'm not sure—at least I'm not dead sure. But even if we never find the head and hands, we can still be sure—in one way that is. Records will have all Luke's measurements. There's enough of him left to check up by."

"Yes," said Travers, "I hadn't appreciated that. Records will also prove if Luke had any betraying marks on his hands, or deformity. Also if you go into Carberry's financial affairs most carefully you may be able to prove that Luke had been blackmailing him."

"That's right," said Wharton, but with just a shade less complacency. "Which brings us back to the only problem. Find Johnson."

"One moment," said Travers. "I hate to be disputatious, but I'd like to read precisely what's in your mind. Am I right, for instance, in saying that in your considered judgment the Wimbeck Street and Garrod's Heath murders have their sole spring and origin in this old Porburgh Case?"

"I think you may say so," Wharton told him.

"And that there are three sole protagonists—actors, if you like, in the tragedies?"

"Yes," said Wharton and pursed his lips. "The three are Luke, Carberry, and Johnson. Two are dead, and the one responsible—the one we've got to find—is Johnson."

"And there is no fourth man?"

His look was curiously intent but Wharton failed to notice it.

"I see what you mean," he said. "I did sort of hint that as Johnson didn't actually kill Carberry— the knife prints were somebody else's, as we know— then he might have employed a confederate. The man, for instance, who called himself J. Scott."

"Then you believe in an X—the fourth unknown," Travers said. "You call him a possible confederate of Johnson. Watts had ideas about him, too, because he also hinted at a possible confederate, though his confederate was a possible ally of Luke at Porburgh."

But what was slowly impressing itself on the dim background of Travers's mind was a new and startling connection between that fourth unknown and the burglary series that had once taken place at Porburgh and had recently broken out at Garrod's Heath. Then before those thoughts could arrange themselves and make a logical coherence, Wharton was brushing both difficulties and theories aside.

"What's it matter about details? Once we lay our hands on Johnson, everything'll sort itself out." Then as if by some queer telepathy he was harking back to something, head cocked inquiringly to one side. "Why did you think it so important that there should be burglaries going on at Garrod's Heath?"

One moment before, Travers had held in his hands the clue that was to solve the queerest case that he and George Wharton had ever tackled. But though intuition had now become a quiet insistence, all he was still seeing was a dim part of a dimmer whole. Besides, it was often Wharton's irritating way to hold up clues for the sake of mysterious climaxes, and for once Travers was resolved to make that orphan of a clue nobody's care but his own. So he side-tracked Wharton with a little irony.

"Is thy servant a dog, George? Why should I want to set up opposition theories? Besides, when I do theorise all I meet with is ribaldry—"

"Come, come now." Wharton found the small riposte much to his liking. "That's only my little joke. But what about a quick lunch in town and a flying trip to Garrod's Heath before it's dark?" He chuckled again as he stoked up his pipe. "Garrod's Heath—where the burglaries are."

CHAPTER VI
KNOWN OR UNKNOWN?

IN WHARTON'S ROOM at the Yard there was a queer ten-minute meal that might have been late lunch or early tea. Norris was there for a quick report.

Lewis, he said, had been at Garrod's Heath since breakfast, and the latest heard from him was that at last he was picking up a trail. Norris would arrange for him to report to Wharton direct at Garrod's Heath police-station.

Norris himself had spent the earlier morning at the Hampstead nursing home but had found nothing that had the slightest bearing on the case. He had also placed two men on a second thorough overhauling of the papers and was awaiting an interview with the bank.

"Go into the money matters pretty closely," Wharton said. "We're none too sure there hasn't been blackmail."

"One thing I might call attention to," said Travers, "is that the doctor may have been frequently paid in cash. The blackmail would have been paid in cash."

"That's right," said Wharton. "Audit all his accounts if you can and try to find a leakage."

Norris said he would put two special men on it. Then when he had received the briefest resume of the morning's discoveries, he was getting into his overcoat again.

"Have Sir Barnabas's report ready for me when I get back," Wharton said. "And get from Records the details of a man named Henry Luke, a confederate of the man Johnson, who got three years for housebreaking at the same time."

He explained the full import of that as they went downstairs. Palmer had departed and Travers himself pushed the car on hard, but few minutes of daylight remained when they drew up by the horse-trough at Garrod's Heath Common. Wharton stood for a moment or two getting his bearings.

"I hadn't any idea there were houses on the other side of the road facing the Common," he said.

"Nor had I till now," Travers told him. "It was the fog and the fringe of trees that put me off, and yesterday afternoon, of course, I wasn't exactly worrying about the houses. They stood well back from the road too."

Then all at once he whipped round and was talking out of the corner of his mouth.

"Don't stare, George, but that curate coming out of the gate there is the one I told you about—Ropeling, who found the body."

In a moment Wharton was peering round. The curate had apparently not recognised the Rolls for he was tripping blithely along. At the same moment Travers became aware of another building he had not previously noticed—a church in brave new slate and stone, set back among the trees in the middle distance.

"That will be St. Elfrida's—that church," he told Wharton. "Palmer said there were two churches in Garrod's Heath, the parish church and that. I don't know where he unearthed the information, but possibly from Ropeling himself."

"Slip over the road," Wharton said, "and have a squint at that house he came out of. I reckon it's where he lives. If so it's remarkably handy."

Travers strolled over as directed and came back to report that the name of the house—or detached villa—was The Rockery. It looked just the least bit too expensive for the curate's home, unless he had private means.

From the horse-trough, ten steps took them out of sight behind the gorse. At the bonfire there was a surprise, for the area was roped round and a constable was instructing a small group of curious arrivals to move on. He recognised Travers from the previous afternoon.

"Funny thing to me, sir, people haven't got anything better to do. All I've been doing all day is clearing them away from here. And it ain't as if there was anything to see, as I keep telling them."

"The Common was searched this morning?" Travers asked him.

"All that part from there, sir." He indicated the area. "Best part of fifty men on the job. And never found a thing—least, that you could be sure was any good."

Wharton agreed when he had his first sight of the now wholly ruined bonfire, for there was nothing for the most morbid to see. All he could do was to get the lie of the land. Then he rather surprised Travers by showing that in his few spare moments he had done some hard thinking about the Guy Fawkes affair.

"We won't call him Luke at present," he said; "we'll just keep him at Guy Fawkes. Whoever he was though, I've come to the conclusion the murder was done locally, and for this reason. People might say that he could have been killed anywhere—a hundred miles away, for instance—and the body transported by car. They'd say it was a foggy night, which made everything simple. I say just the opposite. That dismembered body would probably be in the dickey of the car. Who would want to drive any distance at all on a night as foggy as that? That fog was stretching right across the Midlands. It'd have taken an hour to do four miles— and with the risk of a collision every second. And that's the real point. A collision or any kind of accident would have meant the risk of the discovery of what was in the dickey."

Travers agreed.

"And what about the sacking?" asked Wharton. "Very little blood on it, wasn't there?"

Travers agreed again.

"Then he died from a crack on the head," Wharton said. "And I'd give a fi'pun note to have a good look at that head."

"It's the hands that intrigue me," Travers said.

"Why?" fired Wharton.

"Personal predilection," prevaricated Travers, "and infinitely less horrible."

Wharton called the constable over and introduced himself.

"You were here yesterday, Mr. Travers tells me," he said, "and we've come to the conclusion that I may have to see Mr. Ropeling who discovered the body. Where does he live?"

The constable said it was in one of the new houses on the old Uxbridge Road, next to the cinema. Not two hundred yards from the police-station, it was.

"We just happened to see him coming out of a house over there," Wharton said, "and that's where we thought he lived."

"He was doing a bit of visiting I reckon, sir," the constable said. "You always see him in and out of houses round here, specially afternoons."

Dusk was heavy in the sky as Travers parked the car alongside the station wall. Mott was inside waiting, and Lewis with him.

"Any luck, Lewis?" Wharton asked.

"Not so bad, sir," Lewis told him.

"Right," said Wharton. "I'll see you in a minute and then perhaps Mr. Travers will give you a lift to town. Now, Inspector, let's hear what there is to hear."

"Your message just missed the Chief," Mott told him. "You and him probably passed each other on the road. He's gone to the Yard for a conference."

"I'll get him at once," Wharton said. "But tell me. What luck with this morning's search?"

"None at all, sir," Mott said. "We picked up a thing or two that might have been dropped by anybody. Perhaps you'll run your eye over them when you have a minute, sir. Then we couldn't keep all that quantity of men away from duty so there wasn't a chance to hunt the district for disturbed ground where anything might have been buried."

"One rather foolish question," broke in Travers. "Those burglaries you've been pestered with here for the last few months or so. Have they stopped now or not?"

"One the night before last," Mott said, and Wharton could not resist a waggish grin. "Big house broken into belonging to Colonel Pinch, who's churchwarden at St. Elfrida's. About half-past six, when the family had just gone to the pictures. Some rare valuable jewellery missing and some silver. We've sent out the list."

Wharton did some phoning, then devoted himself to Lewis, whose two men had already gone.

"I don't reckon you'll be any too pleased, sir," Lewis said, "because as far as I can see, everything's different from what it was expected. It looks as if what that housekeeper said was right after all—or what he told the housekeeper."

"Well, get on with it," Wharton told him impatiently.

"Right, sir. The first thing we did this morning was to try Marylebone with the close-ups and we ran down the ticket collector there who'd let him through on the homeward journey. He remembered him because the doctor couldn't find his ticket for a bit. What seems almost certain is that he walked on from here along the road to town and took the next station, but we haven't been able to try that yet. You see, sir, we had to waste the whole early afternoon because we hadn't a thing to start on. We had to find someone who might have seen him about, and all we could do was to tackle various houses round about the horse-trough—people we thought might have come back from town, or servants sent out on errands. That didn't produce anything till we tried the Maidenhead Road."

"Where the taxi-man set him down?"

"That's right, sir. But that's a posh sort of private road. Only three places in it and all with huge gardens. Still, I tried one myself and had a bit of luck at once. The doctor actually called there and asked for a house in the Maidenhead Road called The Towers. The gentleman said there wasn't such a house, but the doctor reckoned there was because he'd been asked to come there on a professional visit. Also the man who rang him up—rang him up, you'll notice, sir—should have been waiting for him where the taxi set him down. The gentleman said, 'Well, there are two more houses in the Maidenhead Road, which you say is the road you want, so if I were you I'd try them, in case the phone wasn't any too clear and you mistook the name of the house.' And that's what the doctor did, sir, for I tried the two houses myself." He pulled out a paper. "While I was waiting for you, sir, I worked out the times from when he left the last house and when he arrived back at Marylebone and when he finally reached home. It all fits in to a quarter of an hour, which is what it would take him to walk on as far as the next station."

"Capital," Wharton told him. "Now you get your things together if you have any and stake your claim to a seat in Mr. Travers's car."

He stood for a good minute, frowning away and pursing his lips.

"Don't like it," he said at last. "Things don't look nearly so easy. Somebody lured him out here and made a fool of him. Why?"

"There is just the other side, George," said Travers. "The whole thing might have been elaborate camouflage on the doctor's part. And yet I don't know. Lewis says the times fit in. Apparently he had no time available for doing a murder and hacking the body about. However quickly he worked, he couldn't have done that in less than a quarter of an hour. And a quarter of an hour is a long time for Lewis to be out in his calculations."

"Yes," said Wharton, "but he mayn't have walked on to the next station. That would find the necessary quarter of an hour." He nodded. "We'll call there on our way back and Lewis shall make inquiries. And yet, as you say, I don't know. Why should the doctor have gone out of his way to make an elaborate advertising of his presence in Garrod's Heath? Was the whole thing part of some highly intricate alibi which he'd worked out to the last detail? He was a clever devil by all accounts. Watts said so, and you admitted there was something a bit suspicious about him."

He had a final word with Mott and then the party at once moved off. Travers went the roundabout way to the end of the Maidenhead Road, reset the speedometer and drove straight to Shenfold station. He made the distance one mile and three furlongs exactly, which meant twenty minutes' walking, at just over a four-mile pace. Lewis insisted that the doctor could have done it.

The man on duty at the barrier was doing a full week's shift and it was he who should have admitted the doctor that foggy night. But he persisted in his denials that any such man had gone through.

"Well," said Wharton, when the car set off again, "it strikes me there's too much of the element of chance in all this. We all know a man at a barrier leaves his post for a second or so. I've walked through barriers unchallenged many a time, and so have we all. There's no reason whatever why the doctor shouldn't have gone to Garrod's Heath station and through the barrier there when the man had his back turned or was off for a chat. Tedious work hanging about in the fog when a train isn't actually coming in. There'd be nothing doing to keep him at his post on a foggy night except chance travellers *to* town. In the intervals of the trains *from* town, that is."

"And, of course," said Travers, "there is no reason to suppose that—" He broke off. "Tell me, Lewis. Did he make inquiries from any of those three houses about the quickest way back to town?"

"He certainly didn't, sir, or they'd have mentioned it."

"Exactly," said Travers. "We have no reason to suppose that the doctor knew his way about here. Surely he ought to be classified as a comparative stranger, which is putting it generously.

Why then should he prefer the devil he didn't know to the devil he already knew?"

"Devil, sir?"

"Mr. Travers is being poetical again," Wharton said. "He means that on a foggy night the doctor would have gone home from Garrod's Heath station, because he knew the way back there."

"Precisely," said Travers. "Which leaves us with one simple question. How much forrader are we?"

Rain had long been threatening and it was coming down in torrents when they reached the Yard.

"Come in for a bit," Wharton said. "There's half an hour before that Garrod's Heath conference. Norris might have some news."

Norris was not yet in but the Craig report on the bonfire corpse was waiting. Out of the mass of technical detail which Sir Barnabas would inflict on the jury, Wharton gathered the essentials with considerable ease.

> *a.* From personal habits the dead man seemed a member of the lowest middle classes.
> *b.* It is the custom of such classes to have tea between the hours of five and six. From the content and state of the digestive organs, and assuming the deceased had his tea between the times stated, then he died between six fifteen and seven fifteen on the Tuesday night.
> *c.* Death was from shock, and supervened within three minutes of such shock. A violent blow, or a series of blows, seems highly probable.
> *d.* Age of deceased was about fifty-five. Height —five feet four inches. Weight about one hundred and fifty pounds.

"Satisfied?" asked Travers.

Wharton gave a sideways nod and began hunting the desk for Records' report on Henry Luke.

"Here we are," he said. "Now we'll see where it fits. Date? Eight years ago, which is about right. Age, forty-seven, which fits in." Then he gave a look of dismay. "But his weight! A hundred and thirty. That's about a stone and a half difference!"

"Weight's a variable quality," Travers told him reassuringly. "What a man weighed eight years ago bears no relationship to what he might weigh now."

"That's true enough," said Wharton. "But the height. Five feet six." He paused. "Don't like it at all."

"Even Luke, by taking thought, couldn't have taken off two inches from his stature." But the old General was looking so disconsolate that Travers was glad to remember something, however ludicrous. "Yet I don't know, George. Think of the advertisements about adding to your height. Besides, when Luke had his measurements taken he might have adopted some device or other."

Wharton began nodding, then with a sweep of the arm he laid the papers contemptuously aside.

"The age was right and the weight might be. About the height, as you say, there might have been some jiggery-pokery." He got to his feet. "I've got it fixed in my mind that Guy Fawkes was Luke and it'll take more than a few words on a sheet of paper to make me change it. He *must* have been Luke."

Travers nodded. "I expect you're right, George. But just one little thing. Anything in his records about disfigurement to Luke's hands?"

Wharton reached out for the sheets again and ran his eye over them with much pursing of the lips.

"Nothing here," he said. "But what's it matter? All these records state is what he was eight years ago. A score of things might have happened to him since he came out of stir. He might have blown half his fingers off, and how were we to know it?"

"I quite admit it," Travers said. "Maybe I'm hard to please, but I'd like a bit more evidence. One of his hands, for instance, to show his prints." Then he suddenly stared. "But that's one thing that's been cleared up for us now. *There needn't necessarily have been any deformity to the hands.* They were removed so that we shouldn't be able to know who the man was. It was his prints the murderer really removed." His fingers went to his glasses and then moved away. "I suppose that I therefore ought to be finally convinced that Guy Fawkes was really Luke. Perhaps I am."

"He's Luke all right," chuckled Wharton, now in high good humour. "And that's one in the eye for you poets."

"Poets?" said Travers vaguely.

"Weren't you quoting poetry at me to prove that Guy Fawkes was a prince or something?"

"Oh, yes," said Travers, and smiled. "But not a prince, George, except by analogy. A personage, I think, was your own adaptation of the quoted words."

"Well, a personage."

"And wasn't I right?" said Travers genially. "Wasn't Guy Fawkes a personage? Hadn't he achieved sufficient notoriety to have his own indices in the Criminal Record office? And to have his hands cut off so that we should never be aware of the fact?"

"Well, yes," granted Wharton, and rose as Travers made his preparations to go. "But honestly, did you ever know a case that now looked so straightforward as this? Call it a drama, if you like, with its three actors. Two of them wronged the third and they're both dead, just as the third promised them. I tell you it must be right."

Travers smiled and held out his hand.

"Well, ring me up later if anything happens. If not I'll be along here at about nine in the morning."

At the door he turned. "Just a good night thought for your waking hours. Not three actors in the drama, George, but four."

Wharton shot him a look.

"The man you called the confederate of Johnson," went on Travers. "The man, in other words, who sent Carberry the wild-goose letter and later killed him."

Wharton grunted.

"And what do you call him?"

"I?" said Travers, and shook a dubious head. "For the present I call him X—the Great Unknown, the Keystone of the Arch, and the Vital Necessity."

"What is this? Astrology?" Wharton drooped a sarcastic lip. "And why all the extracts from Old Moore?"

"I'm not sure," Travers told him. "But the Garrod's Heath burglaries principally."

"Damn the Garrod's Heath burglaries," exploded Wharton, and looked up to find that Travers had conveniently gone.

CHAPTER VII
THE PENITENT THIEF

Travers had almost finished breakfast when Wharton rang him up.

"Don't be later than nine," he said. "We've got Johnson marked down—so I'm told."

"You mean, you're not sure?"

"Oh, yes," Wharton said. "What I meant was that I don't know a thing about it myself, and shan't till my informant gets here."

That was the gist of the news. Travers gathered in addition that a detective-constable had dropped a hint to his sergeant, who had passed it on, that if no trouble ensued he could give Johnson's whereabouts. Travers further gathered that Wharton had refused to grant the suggested immunity, but was willing to cast a sympathetic eye if the mysterious offence were not too flagrant.

So at nine o'clock both Travers and Norris were in Wharton's room, and the three looked up with considerable interest when the plain clothes man was ushered in.

"Yawlings, isn't it?" said Wharton.

"Yes, sir. O Division."

"Sit down there," Wharton said, "and don't look as if you're going to be hanged. . . . Now then; tell us all you know about Johnson."

Now Yawlings was new at the game and had all the enthusiasm of the beginner who had made up his mind to make good. Apparently his scanty leisure was spent as an inquisitorial—but perfectly lawful—Nosey Parker. He was, in fact, always on the lookout for the suspicious.

"I was in Piccadilly," he said, "going along towards Leicester Square, when I saw a man selling matches, with a card round his neck saying he had been an old Navy man, or words to that effect."

A wave of something like horror came over Travers as he heard that astounding opening. He knew that Wharton had given him a quick questioning look, but he kept his own eyes averted.

"I've got two brothers in the Navy myself, sir," Yawlings was going on, "and both of them older than me. All the same I don't quite know why it was, sir, but I stopped and had a word with him. You know, sir—asked him what ships he'd been in, and I slipped him a tanner too. He thanked me for the tanner that I'd given him for the box of matches but tapped his ears as much as to say he was deaf. Then I moved on as far as the Square and happened to come back and what should I see but the same man talking to an old lady who'd apparently been sympathising with him, and there he was telling her the tale, so I reckoned, and hearing plain enough what she'd got to say. That made me suspicious, and something told me he was a fake. Then I had an idea, sir, and I did what I shouldn't. I had a lovely set of prints on that box of matches he'd given me, so I made out to my sergeant they were someone else's and had them sent here—just on spec. When the information came back, my sergeant nearly had a fit, seeing they were whose they were, so to speak, and I had to make out I'd seen Johnson under suspicious circumstances and lost sight of him.

"You see, sir, as far as I could make out he wasn't doing anything wrong; I mean, he was going straight. Yet I was right, sir, to be suspicious about him—partly. He'd been in the Navy all right, during the War, but he'd been kicked out for embezzlement.

Anyhow, sir, something told me I'd better keep my mouth shut, which I did, till word came round that he was wanted urgent."

Wharton peered at him over his spectacle tops. "Well, your enthusiasm certainly led you a bit too far—so some people might say. And how long ago was this?"

"Last June, sir."

"And you've had no dealing with him since?"

"Well"—he hesitated—"not what you might call dealings, sir."

"Well, what did you have?" fired Wharton. "Now you're here you'd better get everything off your mind."

Yawlings shook his head. "I did something I oughtn't to have done. Next time I was that way, sir, I drew up alongside him and said, 'Good-morning, Mr. Johnson,' just to see how he'd take it."

Wharton gave a quick frown. "And how did he take it?"

"He looked startled out of his life, sir. You could see he'd never expected to be recognised. But he didn't say a word. He let on he hadn't heard. I didn't say anything else but just walked on. Once or twice since then I've just had a look at him when I've gone by."

Wharton pursed his lips, frowned and looked impressive. Then he grunted.

"You strike me as the sort of young officer who's likely to get on—but by only the right methods. Chivvying a man who's going straight—or comparatively straight—isn't one of the methods, and carrying out private investigations under false pretences isn't another. Whether you'll hear anything more about it, I can't say, but perhaps you won't. Stick to your job and stick things out—that's the way to get on; do you hear?"

"Yes, sir."

"That's all then. You can go."

The door closed on him. Wharton's face beamed.

"Smart fellow, that. Got a bit of push and initiative. Now you know what to do, Norris? Go and fetch Johnson in. Be civil and courteous. Invite him to come here as a favour to us. Say everything'll be without prejudice, and no statements—

and we'll be delighted to pay his out-of-pocket expenses." He winked. "You know what to do. *But bring him in.*"

Why, he hardly knew, but he felt a distinct sheepishness as he turned at last to Travers.

"Curious coincidence," he said, "your knowing that man?"

"Yes," said Travers, already on his feet and fingering his hat.

"You're not going?"

"I think perhaps I'd rather," Travers said. "You see, I've been in the habit of—er—buying matches from him whenever I've passed. The other evening Palmer and I set him up with a thermos flask and an overcoat. Whatever he is and whatever he's done I can't let him come here and think that what I've done was to spy on him on a pretence of charity."

"You're far too scrupulous," Wharton said gushingly. "Why worry your head over what a rascal like him thinks? I didn't tell Yawlings so but you know as well as I do that the man's been a rogue and still is. That label round his neck is enough to get him convicted of taking money under false pretences. *Cast off by the sea,* wasn't it?" He snorted. "You think about the righteous for once, not the ungodly. That's right now. I'll make it clear to Johnson why you're here."

"Well, since you put it like that," Travers said, and shook his head. "I'll own up I'd like to see him in mufti—as it were. He's intrigued me all along, and I've never been quite able to fathom why. But he didn't kill Carberry. I can swear to his alibi."

"Don't I know it?" Wharton protested speciously. "They weren't his prints on the knife."

"Then what do you want him for? If you think he had a hand in it, you're surely never expecting to get him to divulge anything? Besides, the whole attitude of the man runs counter. There he is, at his post where anyone can find him. He knows the law—in the person of that very obvious detective, Yawlings—is aware of him. But he's stuck it out. He hasn't run away. His is the attitude of a man with nothing to fear and nothing to conceal."

"Maybe," said Wharton, with an irritating wave of the hand. "Still, all in good time. And if he's got nothing to conceal, all the better from our point of view. There'll be a possible suspect eliminated. One less rogue to keep an eye on."

"But he's eliminated already," insisted Travers.

Norris himself ushered Johnson in and closed the door on him. Wharton's manner was a cross between a police court missionary's and that of a man of the world. There was to be much pondering and gravity and nodding, sympathy and appreciation.

Johnson, still wearing those dark glasses, had an appearance of honest poverty, to which the blue overcoat—palpably shortened—made its contribution. That muffler of his was now beneath his trim, torpedo beard, and Travers saw the mouth was thin and hard.

"Come in, Johnson, and make yourself at home," Wharton said. "Sit down there, will you? Most informal all this, and we're very grateful you've come to try and help us. This is Mr. Travers, the eminent author, who happens to be helping us over the murder of Doctor Bendall. You've seen that in the papers, perhaps."

At the sight of Travers, Johnson suddenly stiffened. His mouth drooped to a quick sneer.

"I never read the papers," he said.

"Sensible man," Wharton said. "But you may have seen it on the placards."

He leaned back in the chair and, like one who approaches a distasteful subject, ran briefly over Johnson's career as known to the police. More than one interruption was suavely stifled. Then at the end he gave Johnson his head.

"It's all lies," Johnson said, and his lips had that hard bitterness again. "I'm no real crook, and never was. I was always too trustful of people and got let down. All my life I've had bad luck—" Wharton raised a hand. "Why go into all that? It's past and gone. Right or wrong, you've paid, and the law doesn't go raking up the past. But I wonder if you'd care to tell me something." He leaned forward. "Why did you choose your present way of making a living?"

"A pittance, you mean."

"All the more amazing then," Wharton said. "You're a man of great abilities. You've been well educated, and you've held—with some distinction, I trust—His Majesty's commission. Yet when you came out you decided to be a match-seller. You and know that's only a legal form of begging."

Johnson had his answers pat. He had decided to become a kind of lone, honest wolf. All his life his association with others had brought trouble. Now he was getting to be an old man and had decided that the straightest path was the best. Nothing was left but begging. Even there the police had been after him.

Wharton assured him he was wrong. Scotland Yard had been quite unaware of his whereabouts. Then he again leaned forward.

"You've had trouble with your eyes?"

Johnson said he had, and the glare of the pavements had made the eyes worse. Who would employ a man with bad eyes? And a man of his age? Besides, if by some miracle he found work, the police would trade him and inform the employer.

"That's a lie and a gross libel," Wharton said with some heat. A deep breath or two and he recovered his equanimity. "Still, let's leave the past wholly out of it and come to the present, and where you can help us. I was referring to the murder of a Doctor Bendall. Would it surprise you to hear that Doctor Bendall was really Doctor Carberry—your own father-in-law?"

Johnson stared. Then, strangely enough, he took of his glasses and blinked his eyes. Those eyes were hard as the mouth, and a steely blue. There he sat with the glasses in his mittened hand, and at last he looked up at Wharton.

"Carberry, you said?"

"Yes, the man you threatened to kill."

The mouth tightened and be shook his head.

"If I'd ever found him I think I would." He shook his head again, and again was looking up. "You want me to tell you the truth, don't you? Well, all the time I was cooped up in that hellhole, I used to console myself with what I'd do when I got out, though it remained hanging. Then when I got out I began to see things a bit differently. I own up I tried to find him, but I couldn't—so I gave it up."

"And if you had found him?"

"If?" He smiled wickedly. "I'd have got these two hands round his throat and made him own what he'd done to me. Then I'd have had him in jail—and Luke too—and got compensation from the law for unjust punishment."

"Yes," said Wharton slowly. "Yes. . . . But you mentioned Luke. Would you be surprised to hear he's dead too? And murdered?"

The mouth gaped and the eyes stared. "Luke . . . murdered!"

"Yes," Wharton said, and again leaned forward. "Did you by any chance look for Luke when you came out?"

He shook his head. The lips drooped to a hard sneer again.

"Why should I? He knew I was coming out. He'd take care to hide where I'd never get these hands round his throat."

"You can't help us then?"

He shot a quick suspicious look. "How do you mean?"

"Well, if by any chance you had run across Luke again, you might have told us where. What he was doing, and so on."

There was an awkward silence for a moment, then Wharton cleared his throat and began afresh.

"You're a lucky man, in a way. You threatened Carberry and he was murdered. That might have made things most uncomfortable for you till you'd proved your innocence. Yet Mr. Travers here has been able to prove that innocence—of direct complicity." He waited for a moment but there was no rising to the bait of that innuendo. "You have an alibi and it's fortunate for you—it has saved you a considerable deal of trouble, shall we say?—that you have."

He got to his feet. "Well, as I said, we're sorry we had to trouble you, and sorrier still you can't help us. But would you care to give us your address in case we want to get in touch with you again?"

"You know where to find me," Johnson said. "I've got nothing to fear from you. The doss-houses are my address. They're all I can afford."

"You're going on with your present line of business?"

"Yes," Johnson said. "It keeps body and soul together—and it's safe."

Wharton gave a benevolent glance over the top of his glasses as Johnson rose and was hooking those dark spectacles on again.

"Then in return for the favour you've done us in coming here, may I give you a bit of advice. Alter the wording of that card you wear. There are people not so tolerant as we, who might consider it sufficient for a charge of false pretences."

He maintained the same benevolent peer till the door had closed on him and Norris. Then he gave a dry chuckle.

"Amusing, but hardly instructive. Yet I don't know." He turned on Travers. "Well, what's your opinion of him now?"

Travers shook his head. "He's not the man I thought he was. I think I wouldn't have minded if he'd been plausible or 'umble. There's something cold; sort of fishlike about him—poor devil."

"Why the pity?"

"I don't know," Travers said. "But shouldn't hate and bitterness be pitied the same as any other disease? And I honestly think he was double-crossed. No wonder he kept harping on innocence."

Norris came back then. "He's gone all right, sir. Wouldn't take a penny though."

"That's his funeral," Wharton said. "And what was your opinion of him?"

"A cold-blooded one that," Norris said. "One thing I'll say for him though. He didn't tell any great amount of lies, and he didn't make any bones about how he felt. Did you notice how he looked when he was talking about getting his fingers round Carberry's neck?"

"Frightening—positively frightening," Travers said.

Wharton chuckled. "He won't frighten me. Besides, anyone can talk as big as he when his neck's safe. But what have you got to say in his favour?"

"I don't know that I've got anything," Travers said. "I thought it was a good point you made about why he took up match-selling. It seemed as if he were trying to force a sincerity when he answered you. I didn't believe him somehow. Yet I don't know.

It's a hell of a life, standing there in all weathers. If it wasn't for the reasons he gave, why on earth does he do it?"

"The fact of the matter is, sir," broke in Norris, "he's been making quite a good thing out of it. That Peeping Tom of a Yawlings reckons he knocks up a steady ten bob a day."

"The public are generous," said Wharton, with a smirk at Travers. "But now I'll surprise the pair of you. What would you say if I received information last night through the prison governor that he received some money—beyond the normal—at his release?"

He was peering amusedly at the astonished faces.

"Two hundred pounds, in fact, from the estate of his dead wife. She left it to him and he duly received it. Now then; why should he have to beg for a living?"

"Lord knows," said Travers. "Except that you can't live out a lifetime on two hundred pounds. But why didn't you challenge him with the knowledge?"

Wharton shook his head. "I didn't want to catch him out in lies and antagonise him. Besides, he'd have said that was his final nest-egg against sickness and old age. Liars like him are never caught out."

"But what are we doing about him?" Norris asked.

"You're putting two first-class men on his tail," Wharton said. "They're to find out his lodgings or the doss-house he frequents. All the good he is to us is to lead us to the man who killed Carberry— Mr. Travers's famous X, the Great Unknown."

Travers was shaking his head with a kind of amused diffidence when all at once the telephone went. Wharton took the call, eyes lifted to the ceiling. Soon the eyes were staring. From the abruptness of his tone, Norris knew there was something in the air.

"Certainly, at the earliest possible moment. Ought to have been here before. . . . Here, to me, Superintendent Wharton."

He snapped the receiver back.

"Norris, try to get hold of Sir Barnabas and see if he's free. One of the sewer-men has just found a hand, cut off from the wrist."

CHAPTER VIII
TRAVERS PROPHESIES

Wharton was like a punter who has backed a certainty, and watches his horse come into the straight. Yet certainties have been known to come unstuck and the end of a race isn't always the winning-post; so though Wharton rubbed his hands and professed a fine optimism, there was an underlying uneasiness that betrayed itself in talk.

"It *must* be Luke's hand," he said, and the uneasiness lay in the hint of inquiry that accompanied the assertion. "There couldn't be any other missing hand, cut off from the wrist."

Travers cheered him up. "Of course it's Luke's hand."

Wharton nodded. "The luck has held so far. Take how we found Johnson, for instance. Every one had lost sight of him after he came out. Nobody would have recognised him in that beard he'd grown and the glasses, and then we have the luck to blunder on him because Yawlings had two brothers in the Navy."

Norris came back with the first damper.

"We've forgotten something, sir. Just as I was getting Sir Barnabas I remembered he'd be at the Garrod's Heath inquest this morning. He'll be on the way there now—body and all." He coughed apologetically. "But you were intending to be there yourself, sir, weren't you?"

"Didn't I say so?" fired Wharton. Then he nodded. "All right, Norris. I'll take that hand with me. See a car's ready in half an hour. And something else. What about keeping Johnson under observation all day?"

"Might be as well, sir. He might be in the swim with somebody."

"There's that little high-brow café above Hall's, the outfitters," Wharton said. "They'll accommodate us all right. Put a couple of men on, then if anybody suspicious gets in touch with Johnson, one can follow and the other can still keep an eye on Johnson."

"Funny case this," Wharton began, as the door closed. "In most cases you get the trimmings and work up to the essentials. Here we've got no real trimmings but we've got the essentials plain as a pikestaff." He shifted uneasily in his seat, picked up his pipe and put it down again. "It *must* be right. Carberry and Luke did the dirty on Johnson. Both of them are dead. The only association they had was through that Porburgh Case, therefore Johnson's mixed up in it." A new glow of optimism came and he rubbed his hands. "Wish they'd hurry up with that hand. You heard me tell them to get a move on."

Next he was buzzing through to Records and asking for Luke's prints to be sent up by one of their men. Best to have everything ready so as to waste no time. Then he began a restless prowling about the room till Travers quietened him by asking about the discovery of the hand. Wharton said it had obviously been dropped down a drain under cover of the fog. Some of the gratings were as wide as two inches and the hand was pliable and could be pushed through. It would lie in the trap till flushing took place or there were rains like those on Guy Fawkes' night. Those sewer-men tramped about with waders and had an instinct for valuables and whatnots that had been flushed down. The other hand might turn up at any minute. The head would have been too big for the drain, but his idea was that it and the clothes had been dumped in the Thames, which was near enough to Garrod's Heath.

Steps were heard in the corridor, then at long last in came Wharton's small parcel and the sergeant from Records. Wharton fell on the parcel like a vulture.

"Must have been a bit messy," he said, as he had a look at the stump. Travers had a quicker look and wished to see no more.

"Take the prints," Wharton said, and the sergeant duly pressed the dead fingers down. Then there was a silence and Travers saw the sergeant making his scrutiny and comparison. He shook his head.

"This hand isn't Luke's, sir."

"Not Luke's!" Wharton fairly bounded on the sets of prints and peered through his own glass. He straightened himself and scowled. Then he grunted. There was a smile in which was contempt and annoyance. Never was man more pigheaded when obsessed with an idea. Guy Fawkes was Luke, and Luke he should continue to be till the final proof.

"Then that's a perfectly simple explanation," he said. "This isn't the hand we want. This is some other hand. This isn't the one that came off the bonfire body. And now I come to think of it I never ought to have thought it was. Why should one hand be brought all the way from Garrod's Heath to town on a foggy night and dropped down a drain? Where's the other hand and the head?"

The sergeant avoided the challenge as if to say mildly that neither answer nor fault were his.

"Wrap it up again," Wharton said, "and see it's in my car. And while you're about it, take the prints and see if you've got them in the office. Let me know when I get back."

The last thing in Travers's mind was to do any pulling of legs, but Wharton slurred with a quick dexterity over that anti-climax of the hand.

"Well," he said, with an air of supreme indifference, "I suppose we'd better be pushing on to that inquest. Not much sense in taking the hand, really. We know it wasn't off the bonfire body— which was Luke's. Might as well get Sir Barnabas to have a peep at it, though."

"Yes," said Travers, with a crocodile sympathy. "And since it's not the hand from the bonfire, it'll mean a wholly new case for Sir Barnabas."

"Exactly," said Wharton, and grunted a thanks as Travers helped him into his overcoat. "Some young devil of a hospital student been playing a trick—more like it. Now we'd better hurry. I don't want to miss any of that evidence."

He stamped off down the corridor, Travers at his heels. Travers felt a quick glow of affection and smiled to himself at his tricks and subterfuges and special pleadings and how, in spite of the thrust of hard fact, he refused obstinately to abandon the obsession that Guy Fawkes was Luke. Then all at once his face sobered, for the thought had come to him whose that severed hand must be. It came strangely and for a moment was miraculously clear. Then a doubt came and small confusions, so that the thought emerged into others and was blurred. But in the brief second before it went it was as if he had looked through the opening of drawn curtains and had seen the dim figure of a man—the man whose hinted existence could excite the risibility of Wharton; the man whom he himself had vaguely and yet pretentiously described as X, the Fourth Unknown.

Wharton was a chastened man on that journey to Garrod's Heath. The horse might still lead the field but somehow he knew him for a loser. So he poured the peculiarities and difficulties of the case into Travers's sympathetic ear again.

"Funny we can't trace any blackmail payments. Carberry must have been a goldmine for Luke when he'd done his three years."

"If Johnson never found Carberry, then Luke didn't," Travers said. "Johnson wanted him badly enough, and he had many times the brain of Luke."

"I don't see why you should claim that," Wharton said, but with far from his old aggressive challenges. "Luke had brains enough to keep up a double life and swindle all Porburgh."

"Luke seemed a burglar pure and simple," Travers said. "He hadn't the wits to be a con man —even to get caught at it. I have a great respect for the intelligence of Johnson. I don't know that I'm not in agreement with Watts. Remember what he told us. He said Johnson was a genius who could make the most childish mistakes to spoil his own elaborate calculations. I think if we look at him from that angle—the angle of having a mental kink—we shall understand several things about him. The paradox for instance, of why a man of agile mind and active habits should take up and stick to the queer, static job of selling matches."

But Wharton had been busy with an idea of his own.

"Isn't it funny that neither Johnson nor Luke has had a relapse since coming out? Luke, of course may have been doing the Garrod's Heath jobs recently, which would fit in with his being killed there, but isn't it safer to say that he hasn't been up to any of his old tricks? What I'm getting at is that if he hasn't lived by crime, he's had to live somehow. Isn't that an argument in favour of his having blackmailed Carberry?"

"A very sound argument," Travers said. "And as I told you, a leakage in Carberry's accounts may be extremely difficult to trace."

Wharton rose on the buoyant waves of optimism again.

"We shall be all right. I'll lay a new hat that the hand doesn't belong to the body. Besides, Mott has scoured the district for advice about missing men, let alone all the Press publicity there's been."

They arrived five minutes before the inquest was due to begin. Sir Barnabas was there and Wharton made a bee-line for him, clutching the grisly parcel. Travers kept momentarily in the background, having no mind to view the main corpse again. Up at the front where witnesses were ranged he caught sight of Ropeling chatting with a little old gentleman with greying whiskers and a scholarly stoop. As he drew nearer he heard the surgeon's voice.

"I have no need to fit it, as you call it, my dear Wharton. That's one of the missing hands and there's no doubt whatever about it." He shrugged his shoulders. "If you would care to see for yourself, however?—"

On a trestle table in the far corner was something covered with a blanket. Travers turned his head away and waited for Wharton's return. Sir Barnabas caught sight of him and nodded and smiled. Wharton came back, looking as if he had suffered a personal loss.

"He's right," he said, and licked his lips. "The hand belongs and it isn't Luke's. What're you going to make of that?"

Travers shook a sympathetic head. He might have said that he had expected it; that in fact his own vital clues would have ceased to be such had the body indeed been Luke's.

"That queers things," Wharton said. "We'd better have the whole inquest modified. We'll make it formal and have a month's adjournment. Where's that fellow Mott?"

Mott was coming across. Travers left the hurried conference to itself and made his way out to the open air. Once more he had caught a glimpse through the drawn curtains, and now he saw things more clearly, and there were theories he wished to work out. So he took the road towards the Common and so to the Oxford Road, and turned back when he judged the inquest would be nearing its end.

It was as he turned towards the town, at a hundred yards from the horse-trough it might have been, that he ran full into Ropeling, and with him the elderly gentleman with whom he had been conversing in the inquest room. Ropeling's face lighted up immediately, and while Travers was courteously saluting him he had stopped.

"Ah, Mr. Travers. How are you? Very pleased to see you again."

Travers judged that he was his old robust pinky self. The afternoon of the bonfire he had been yellow about the gills, but now he exuded health and confidence.

"I'm very well," Travers said. "You've been at the inquest?"

"Yes," the curate said. "A purely formal affair and quite different from what we'd been given to understand." Then to Travers's quick look of inquiry: "This is Mr. Mathison, one of our sidesmen, and a very old inhabitant."

"Indeed?" said Travers, and smiled.

"Not so old, my boy," chuckled Mathison. In spite of his stoop and his greying hair he seemed spry enough and a bit of a fly-by-night.

Ropeling was waving his hand round. "I meant compared with myself. Your house too, compared with most of these. Mr. Travers," he explained, as if partly responsible, "is the famous author."

"Is he really?" said old Mathison, and looked a bit awed. "It's a pleasure to meet you, sir. I don't often meet famous people like authors."

Travers switched the conversation hastily round.

"So you're comparatively new here, Mr. Ropeling?"

"Yes," Ropeling said. "I was doing missionary work in West Africa till my health broke down. This is a kind of holiday for me before I return. Some time in the autumn, I hope."

"Let's hope you'll be quite fit," Travers said, and held out his hand. "Good-bye to you, and to you, Mr. Mathison. If I'm down this way again I may have the pleasure of seeing you."

"It'll have to be soon," Mathison said. "I'm getting too old to worry about housekeeping. I expect to be going to a niece of mine up North."

"But you're not going yet," Ropeling told him amusedly.

"I don't know," he said. "I may take it into my head to go any time. I'm not going to be bullied."

Travers smiled, left the two to their playful bickering and moved off. Soon a new amusing line of thought was presenting itself as for yet another time in his inquisitorial career he knew the folly of too suspicious a mind. Who could be more on the surface than the curate? And yet because he had made it his own business to fetch the police instead of sending one of the Scouts, at once he had become a suspect. As well claim the two Scouts as suspects. Had they not cringed at his approach through the gorse? Or old Mathison—a gay old dog that, or Travers was much mistaken—why shouldn't he and the curate have done the murdering and dismemberment between them? Who more respectable than a sidesman at St. Elfrida's, and who therefore more apt to be classed among the snakes in the grass?

Then Travers looked up from his speculations to become aware that he was at the place of inquest and Wharton's car was drawn up ready for the return journey. Mott came out of the door and was promptly hailed. Wharton, he said, was having a short conference with his own Chief and Sir Barnabas Craig.

"That's all right then," Travers said. "I feared I was late. As a matter of fact I met Mr. Ropeling and an old boy named Mathison, and they kept me talking."

"Mathison?" Mott raised his eyebrows, then smiled. "Oh, yes. Him at The Rockery. Keeps a rare good glass of port. An attempted burglary at his place a night or two ago. Bit of an old rip in his time."

"He looks it," Travers said. "He may be a sidesman but he seems to me to have a roving eye."

Mott didn't quite gather that.

"You know, the sort that hands round the plate on Sunday mornings and reads the divorce cases all the afternoon."

Mott enjoyed that bit. "And between you and me, sir, there's many a worse way of spending a Sunday afternoon." Then he deemed it time to assume more of a dignity. "How're things shaping your end, sir?"

"Bit early to judge yet," Travers told him guardedly.

"Yes," Mott said. "And that other business—about Bendall—doesn't make things easier; not if the two are connected the same as the Gen—as Superintendent Wharton seems to think."

Travers made suitable faces and admitted the difficulties. Then Mott, who had obviously been burning to get something off his mind, came to the revelation point. His voice lowered.

"Keep it to yourself, sir, because nothing may come of it, but I shouldn't wonder if there's a surprise from this end. You won't mention it, sir, will you, because we don't want to make fools of ourselves, which we should be if there wasn't anything in it."

Travers nodded gravely. "I understand. But who's the *we?*"

"The *we,* sir?" He made a wry face. "Well, sir, I'd rather not say for the moment—if you follow me. It's being taken out of my hands—if you know what I mean." Then recognising apparently that he was tying himself in knots: "You'll know soon enough, sir. Some time to-night, if there's anything in it."

Travers had an idea that he might have imparted all the secret but Wharton came out then. With a wink of tremendous import Mott sheered off.

Wharton had a grievance, and as soon as the car was clear of the town he came out with it.

"Would you believe it but I couldn't drive into their heads that there must be a connection between their case and the Carberry one? If nothing turns up we're having a conference in the morning."

"I'm not so sure that they're not right—partly," Travers said. "I wouldn't like to bet a penny either way but something tells me we've hardly begun this case yet. As far as I can see we're not dead sure of a thing—except two murders."

"What do you want? John the Baptist's head on a charger?"

Travers chuckled. "That's more like yourself, George. But I don't even want Luke's head on a charger. All I want to know is whose the head is. I don't care if it's Napoleon's so long as I know whose it is."

"Now you're getting poetical again," Wharton said. "Not that you aren't partly right. Facts, that's what we want—facts." He clicked his tongue annoyedly. "Funny, isn't it? It's just like one of those trick toys where you have to get three little balls into three little holes."

"Four holes, surely." He went on hastily. "It looks as if Luke isn't Luke, if you know what I mean, as Mott says. If Guy Fawkes isn't Luke, then Guy Fawkes is the man we're looking for—the Fourth Unknown."

Wharton glowered. "Who's looking for him? There oughtn't to be a fourth. I'll bet every penny I've got in the world that these two murders arise out of that old Carberry Case. Carberry, Johnson and Luke make three. There's no necessity for the fourth."

Travers smiled patiently. "Haven't you yourself admitted there must be a fourth? Johnson didn't kill Carberry, therefore a fourth man did."

"Oh, my God!" burst out Wharton. "Arguments like that drive me mad. How can Guy Fawkes be the fourth, if the fourth killed Carberry? Guy Fawkes was dead long before Carberry was!"

Then he remembered something. "Talk about your Fourth Unknowns, what about the man who did kill Carberry? The man who called himself Scott? How're you going to fit him in?"

He was so desperately in earnest that Travers had a twinge of conscience. Besides, the question of fitting in that shadowy person J. Scott was something he was always shelving and thrusting cowardly aside.

"I wouldn't worry if I were you, George," he said. "I'm prepared to bet something too—that before to-night's out we have a lot more information than we have now. That question of who J. Scott was may solve itself then."

"Information?" said Wharton. "Such as what?"

Travers shook his head. "Just an intuition."

"Oh, no," Wharton said. "I can always read you like a book. There's something you've found out."

Travers shook his head again. "You're wrong. But I'll tell you what I'll do. I'll make a wild guess and write down what I think we shall know within an hour of getting back to town."

Wharton shot him a look, then grunted.

"All right. Write it down in this book of mine and choose your own page."

Travers wrote and handed the notebook back. "I haven't done much disfiguring, George," he said. "Only half a dozen words."

Wharton buzzed down for a couple of fragmentary lunches to be brought to his room, and began going through the papers on his desk with the hope of finding something new. There was nothing but a message from Norris to the effect that he would be reporting at two o'clock, which was ten minutes from then. Before Wharton could make a comment there was a knock at the door.

"Come in!" bellowed Wharton, expecting lunch.

But it was the sergeant from the print department who entered, and he was carrying some papers.

"Sorry, sir, but can you spare a minute?"

"Why not?" Wharton told him.

"It's the prints, sir," the sergeant told him mildly. "Those off the hand and these ones here."

Wharton adjusted his spectacles, picked up his glass and bent down over the sergeant's pointing finger. Travers was watching with a curious intentness. Wharton all at once was drawing himself up, and on his face shone a wild hope.

"Why, they're the same! You don't mean to tell me they're Luke's after all?"

The sergeant shook his head dolefully.

"No, sir. These are from the hand found in the sewer and these are the last ones we had in—the ones that came off that knife that killed the doctor at Wimbeck Street. And they're the same!"

Wharton stared. For a moment he was speechless. A deep breath and he was off.

"You can't be right. It's impossible."

Once more the sergeant shook his head. "There's no mistake, sir. They're the same prints."

"Leave 'em here," Wharton told him curtly, and scowled down at them for a long minute. Then suddenly he looked up as one might do when a clock has stopped ticking. Travers had made no comment.

"What was that you wrote in that book of mine?"

Travers flushed faintly.

"The wildest of guesses, George. You'll find it somewhere in the middle."

Wharton whisked the pages over. Six pencilled words were there as Travers had said:

The dead hand held the knife.

CHAPTER IX
A FRESH START

"Held the knife?" Wharton said. "How could a dead hand hold anything?"

"Sorry," said Travers. "I wasn't trying to be enigmatical. You were just the least bit impatient when I was writing—hence the economy of speech. But a dead hand can hold anything if a live hand guides it. My firm belief is that Carberry would never have been killed but for the dead hand. If you prefer it another way, Guy Fawkes was killed for the sake of his hand—the hand which would give an alibi to the man who controlled it."

"I've got you," said Wharton. Norris slipped in then in his usual unassuming way, and he collared him.

"Here's something to make you think a bit. What would you say if I told you that the sewer hand belonged to the bonfire corpse after all?"

Norris shot a quick look at Travers. "It wasn't Luke then, sir."

"No," said Wharton. "You can take that for gospel. For all we know, Luke's walking about alive and healthy. But what about this? These prints come from that sewer hand. These are of the hand that killed Carberry. Both are the same!"

Norris stared, then grinned sheepishly. "You're laughing at me, sir."

"And why?" queried Wharton with immense patience.

"Why, sir? Well, if a man was killed on a Tuesday night, and his head cut off, how could he stab someone else twenty-four hours later?" Then his eyes went wide open. "I see, sir. Someone got hold of that hand—"

"Why not say the one who killed him?"

"Well, the one who killed him—the one who called himself J. Scott—cut off the hand and used it to fake prints on the knife and the chair." He nodded to himself. "They were right-hand prints and that was a right hand."

"Mr. Travers has apparently been of that opinion for some time," Wharton said, and it was plain that he was harbouring a grievance.

"You're wrong, George," Travers said. "I made that wild guess of mine only when we knew the hand fitted the body."

Wharton grunted. "Well, how did you arrive at it? Tell us the processes."

"Well"—he smiled diffidently—"that's rather an invitation to blowing my own trumpet and deprecating yours. But as I saw things, there was some vital reason for cutting off the head and hands. We assumed it was for the purpose of concealing the identity of the body, but as soon as we knew that the prints of that body were not in the Criminal Record office here, then the whole situation changed. The hands were not cut off to conceal the prints, but for some other reason. From that I proceeded to argue thus. Here's a hand transferred all the way from Garrod's Heath to town, and a right hand at that. Between the time of its cutting off and the time of its discovery in the sewer, Carberry was murdered. Immediately after Carberry's murder there was no rain, but there was a fog which facilitated the dropping of the hand down a drain. Then the rain came and the hand was washed to where it was found. The chronological sequence is perfect. To sum up, the dead hand was used to establish somebody's alibi. If the hand had never been discovered we should have gone on hunting for a person who had no real existence."

Norris had been listening almost rapt. "That's right, sir. And what's worse, we should have paid no attention to the one who did it. Whoever he was, prints don't lie, and they wouldn't have been his."

"Yes," said Wharton, and was suddenly raising his hand. "But do you know what else is cleared up? Carberry didn't tell his housekeeper a lie. He *was* inveigled out to Garrod's Heath at the time to fit in with the murder. That note in his pocket—the wild-goose letter as you called it—carried the prints to the dead hand. It was prepared sometime during the Wednesday and slipped into his pocket by the murderer—the fake patient who called himself Scott. It was a trap and we fell into it."

"Well, there's no great harm done yet," Norris said. "We know exactly where we are now, sir, and that's one good thing."

"Oh," said Wharton ironically. "And where are we, pray?"

Travers waded in to the rescue.

"Mightn't it be as well, George, to write down just how we stand? Why not pool our ideas for a minute or two?"

The minute or two turned out to be half an hour, with the eating of the scratch lunch making for leisured thinking. What evolved was this:

MAIN LINE OF APPROACH

Assuming that both the Garrod's Heath and Wimbeck Street Cases are bound up with the old Porburgh Case, then:

1. The pivotal point becomes Henry Luke. Since Carberry may have been paying him in cash—always safer

than by cheque for both parties—then there is no reason why evidence of the blackmailing transactions should ever come to light. It is no argument to say that Luke would not have killed Carberry— the goose that was laying the regular, golden eggs. The probability seems to be that Carberry was refusing to go on paying. Luke had been raising his price and it had grown to an amount which made Carberry take a stand. Luke sensed the new attitude and suspected some trap in collaboration with the police.

2. Henry Luke must therefore be found. Both methods to be employed at the same time, viz.:

   a. Directly.

   b. Through Johnson, with whom he may be reconciled and in partnership.

ALTERNATIVE LINE OF APPROACH

This will only be used when above has failed. It assumes that there is no connection with the old Porburgh Case, but that Carberry was murdered *for* reasons arising out of events subsequent to that case.

SUBSIDIARY PROBLEMS

Who is the man of the bonfire? Immediate and extensive broadcast and press publicity, with description, for missing men who conform. The probability is that he was a casual acquaintance of Luke, killed by him for the purpose of obtaining the hand. What relation to both is the fake patient Scott?

Norris said he already had two doss-houses that Johnson had occasionally frequented, but information received was that he was never accompanied by anyone or known to be friendly with any other inmate.

"We'll hang on Johnson's tail if it's from now till judgment day," Wharton said. "He's my hunch and I'm going to give myself a treat. Now we'll set things in motion to get every bit of information we can about Luke. We can try to pick up his tracks after he came out. We can broadcast a description with the usual *anxious to get in touch*. And we can get Records to get in touch with Porburgh and work back from the old case."

"Curious, his description being not too unlike the bonfire body," Travers said. "Both men below the average height and the age corresponding as well. Still, you can't get away from the two inches in height."

"Why keep theorising?" said Wharton. "Luke wasn't the bonfire body, as we know by everything. Luke's alive and kicking. The bonfire body was some poor devil Luke killed for the sake of the hand."

Then he had a last dig at Travers. "There was a certain poetical theory that you had about the bonfire body. First he was bound to be a personage; then when you were harried from that you fitted it in with saying he was notorious enough to have his records with us. And now he turns out to be an utter nonentity, what hole are you going to bolt to?"

Travers laughed. "None at all. You say Johnson's your particular hunch. Well, the bonfire corpse is mine. I still hold there's truth in the original theory. He certainly isn't Luke, but he's no nonentity. Money talks, and I'll back my opinion for a modest sum." He got to his feet. "No takers? Then as you're all going to be very busy, I'll leave you to it for a bit."

The telephone went then. Norris thought the call might be his, and took it.

"Right," he said. "Report here if you can," and hung up as quickly as that.

"Johnson's just moved off," he said. "It's Saturday afternoon and he wouldn't be staying as late as usual."

"Better stay and hear what happens," Wharton said to Travers. But Travers said there were things he must do, though he might drop in at about five. Dusk was near as he came out to the Embankment, and the night gave promise of frost. But there was no hurrying of pace as he made his way along Whitehall, his mind preoccupied with the intricacies of the case.

Somehow too, all that talk with Wharton and Norris seemed of little significance now he was out of their company. More and more he felt an urgency in that clue that Wharton so amazingly was refusing to consider—the clue of the unknown man. Maybe the bonfire body was that of the unknown man or J. Scott might be that unknown man. Indeed it was with that last problem that Travers had been preoccupied, and by the time he had reached the flat his mind was made up.

Garrod's Heath was the vital spot, for it answered most questions. Its burglaries helped to solve the problem of Luke's way of life since he came out of jail. By the simple answer that there had never been any blackmail it settled the question of why no evidence of such had been found among the doctor's papers. It made a link with Porburgh—and yet it was a theory that to Travers's mind Wharton would regard as untenable, for it was built upon an occurrence which was itself capable of different explanations.

So as soon as he reached the flat Travers made some phone inquiries and at last got through to that little shop where he had bought the fireworks. He recalled himself and asked if as a great favour Superintendent Watts could be fetched. In five minutes the Superintendent was there, his puffings plainly audible.

"Hallo, sir," he said. "Were you wanting me?"

"Yes," said Travers. "About that fire that burnt out Luke's house the night he was taken at the Carberry burglary. Who was responsible for the theory that it was started mechanically? You know, with a candle and combustibles."

"The place was insured, sir. The insurance experts did all the inquiry in case Luke should bring an action for recovery when he came out."

"They actually found a candle?"

There was a kind of chuckle. "Well, sir, the place was gutted so they couldn't have done that. They reckoned there'd been a lot of paraffin used though."

"And why do you reckon the house was burned down?"

"Well, sir, if the police had got their hands on what was in it there'd have been enough to connect him with sufficient jobs to have given him ten years."

"Lived alone, did he?"

"Yes, sir, except for a woman who did for him. If I remember rightly, she used to come every day and go about tea-time."

"And no one in Porburgh has ever clapped eyes on him since?"

"You bet they haven't, sir," said Watts, and chuckled.

Travers smiled too, maybe because for most of the Superintendent's answers he had answers of his own that fitted quite as well.

At five o'clock he was tapping at Wharton's door and entering. Then he withdrew, for a man stood in front of the desk and Wharton was questioning him.

"Come along in," Wharton called. "This is York, who's been following up Johnson. Begin all over again, York, so that Mr. Travers can hear."

"Well, sir," York said, "as soon as we saw him put his matches in that little attaché case he has, we knew he was going, so while Peters got through to here, I nipped off down. He went quite slowly, Johnson did, and right through to St. Martin's, where Peters overtook me, and when Johnson mounted a bus and went on top, I went on top and Peters inside. It was a Wapping bus, sir, and nothing happened till we got to the Tower, when he shifted his seat right to the back behind where I was. I thought he was going to get off so I got up too, but I made it all right by having an argument with the conductor, about thinking we were at Wapping.

"At Wapping Stairs he got off and turned back along the River. He only went about two hundred yards, sir, and then something happened. Peters had passed me, and him too, and had gone right on as far as the first opening, so as to overlap him, but Johnson stopped right under a lamp-post against where there's a ten foot wall. I was in a passageway, and I saw him give a look or two each way and then he pulled a piece of chalk out of his pocket and wrote something on the wall. This is what it was, sir. I went up as soon as he'd gone, and copied it down."

Wharton took the paper, frowned, and handed it to Travers.

Travers blinked. "What is it? Some secret sign? Or thieves' code?"

Wharton shook his head. "First time I've ever run across it. Carry on with your story, York."

But York had come to the anti-climax and was looking ill at ease.

"That's all there is, sir."

"But what about Johnson?"

"Well, sir, I drew along cautiously so as to get in touch with Peters again and I couldn't find him for a bit, and when I did he was looking for him himself."

"He'd lost him?"

"Well, sir, he says it was just as if the ground opened up and swallowed him. He followed him from behind and all at once he was gone. It's dark round there in those alley-ways, sir. A regular warren it is all along there by the River."

Wharton nodded grimly, knowing that district well enough.

"Carry on," he said. "What happened then?"

"Well, sir, we set a time and place to meet and both scouted round for a bit but we didn't get any luck. The pubs weren't open but we looked in an eating-house or two, and that doss-house in Clarion Street, and then we gave it up. I told Peters to keep an eye on that mark on the wall—"

"Pardon me," interrupted Travers, "but how large was that circle?"

"Just over a foot, sir." A fleeting smile. "Peters called it a hot-cross bun with a question mark."

"Yes, yes," said Wharton impatiently. "You told Peters to keep an eye on the mark."

"Yes, sir. I thought if the one it was written for was to come along to collect the information, then Peters could follow him and so get taken to where Johnson was, or else get hold of something fresh. After that I came straight back here, sir."

Wharton and Norris exchanged glances. The latter took over.

"All right, York. You'd better get back to Peters and take turns about. Report here if anything happens and see it gets passed on to every constable on that particular beat. Knock off at daylight and then report here."

As soon as the door closed Wharton was examining York's copy of the marks. Norris had a good look and said he had a vague idea he'd seen something of the sort before.

"Do you know Flanagan at Aldgate?" Wharton said. "Of course you do, though. You send it along to him with a chit. He knows more about rogues' shorthand and underground slang than any man alive. And why not have a couple of extra men tomorrow somewhere near the spot where Johnson disappeared?"

"Monday, sir," Norris said. "He won't be at his pitch on a Sunday."

The buzzer went and he lifted the receiver. It was the A.C., and something to do with the Garrod's Heath end.

"Don't you go, sir," Norris told Travers. "He'll be back in a minute or two."

So Travers sat on for company, and watched while Norris worked. The letter was dispatched to Aldgate and there was a draft to prepare for the Porburgh inquiries.

"You're not going away this week-end?" Norris said, for it was Travers's habit to spend his weekends in the country.

"Not for once," Travers said. "I shouldn't like to miss anything that happened. The Wimbeck Street end is going slow, isn't it?"

"It's hopeless," Norris said. "Nothing you can get your teeth into. Take that J. Scott who did it. Who was he—what about him? Not a thing. Don't even know where to start." Then he gave Travers a shrewd look. "What about that Fourth Man you've been talking to the Super about, sir?"

Travers smiled. "You mean my obsession. He is just someone who belongs to the old Porburgh days and now belongs nowhere." Then he changed the subject. "But about that sign Johnson made on the wall. Haven't tramps and beggars a sign-language like that?"

"Nothing as elaborate as that, sir," Norris said, and between the intervals of writing gave him a few details. Then just as Travers at last rose to go, Wharton came back.

"We've got something at last," he said. "And I had to give Garrod's Heath a bit of my mind."

No time had been lost, as he admitted, but procedure was procedure and discipline discipline.

"There was I at Garrod's Heath and never a word said or a hint dropped. They found what they thought were blood marks on the pavement there, and Mott says they didn't report to us because they mightn't have been human blood. Might have been dropped out of a butcher-boy's basket and pretty fools they'd have looked. You all right for the morning, Mr. Travers? Leave here at nine?"

Travers expressed himself as ready and delighted. But he was still somewhat hazy over what it was all about.

"Yesterday morning, it was," Wharton said; "not long before we got there. One of Mott's men caught sight of a red blot or two on the pavement and reported it. Mott had their man scrape them off and make a test. He's a good man apparently and reckons it's mammalian blood. Sir Barnabas is going to check."

"And where was this particular pavement?" Travers asked.

"That," said Wharton, "is the interesting thing. Imagine you're coming from Oxford towards town and you arrive at the Common. There's a house with green railings, which belongs to a wholesale draper with his business in town. Then there's one plot not built on—"

"I know it," said Travers. "All overgrown with weeds and used as a surreptitious dumping ground."

"That's it. And then comes that house where we thought Ropeling lived—The Rockery. That has two gates. One's plumb in the middle of the palings, leading to the front door; the other's a kind of private gate leading to the rock garden and a sort of summerhouse. I ought to say there's a tradesmen's entrance in the back road."

"And where exactly were the blood marks?"

"Just past the side gate. Where the vacant plot begins."

"Yes," said Travers, and nodded. "All of which is near as nothing to the horse-trough. I don't know quite why, but somehow I'm rather glad I didn't go away for the week-end."

CHAPTER X
SPATS AND LINOLEUM

IN THE NIGHT the wind changed. The Sunday morning dawned cloudy, with a mist that looked like turning to rain. Travers, driving his Rolls towards Garrod's Heath, remarked to Wharton that Nature seemed in lugubrious sympathy with the work in hand, especially digging up that vacant plot of land for a buried head and hand.

Wharton grunted, being in none too sprightly a humour. That morning he had already had a nil report from York and Peters, and Flanagan had sent word that the sign of the hot-cross bun and question mark was one he had never run across or heard of. Then as the car was within half a mile of Garrod's Heath Common, and Travers slowed down where the road had been narrowed for a long stretch of repairs, he all at once shot out a hand.

"Go dead slow along here, will you? I want to try and pick up where the men were filling in, the first time we came this way. Do you remember how far they'd reached on that Wednesday afternoon when you came by?"

"I don't," said Travers. "As a matter of fact I don't think they'd done much filling in. I seem to remember pipes being still stacked all along here."

"I reckon we could always find out to a yard or so from the foreman on the job," Wharton said. "It just occurred to me that here's a remarkably handy place for burying anything. The road was up for a quarter of a mile and a traffic man at each end only— and it was foggy, that Tuesday night. If the cutting was open, all you'd have to do would be to sneak in from behind and dump in whatever it was you had to hide, cover it with some of the soil from the side, and there you are. Next morning the men wouldn't know anything'd happened. They'd just go on filling in from where they'd left off."

Travers thought the idea a sound one. If everything else failed they might have the culvert reopened. Once find the head and the identity of the bonfire corpse would be infinitely easier to ascertain. Wharton cheered up at that.

"Heard no more about that missing coin of yours?" he said.

"Never a thing," Travers told him. "I've given you people full details and advertised in most of the papers."

"It's worried me a lot," Wharton said. "But there's nothing we can do. We've circularised the description and given your address, so if it turns up anywhere the police will let you know."

They called at the police-station first to pick up Mott and one of his men. Wharton advised no digging the plot till it had been well scrutinized.

"I don't see why he should have taken the body in there to cut it up," he said, "when he had the whole Common at his disposal. We'll just go over it this morning first."

They parked the car by the plot itself, a rank, sodden piece of ground hemmed in, as were the neighbouring gardens, with towering elms. Its wooden palings were green and mildewed, and here and there one was missing.

"There isn't a gap big enough for a man to get through," Wharton said. "And what was the point in hoisting the body over when all the Common was open, as I said. However, let's see the spot where the blood was."

That side, private gate of The Rockery had its clapping post clean against the untidy hedge that separated the vacant plot from The Rockery. The paving stone where the blood had been was dead in a line with the hedge itself, and the spots of blood had been nearer the palings than to the curb.

"What's that?" said Wharton, pointing to one of the palings. "Something's scraped the green off it."

He spread a newspaper, got down on his knees with his glass and made an examination.

"You have a look, Mott," he said. "Tell me what you make of it."

Mott said something had fallen against it with enough force to tear the fibres of the wood.

"That's what I made it," Wharton said, and shook his head. "The devil of it is you can never be sure. Anything might have done it. On the other hand our friend Guy Fawkes might have received a crack on the skull with some jagged weapon just here, and have fallen over with his head here. That'd account for the blood and the scrape. There'd be no blood to talk of from a crack on the skull. Also his hat would be on at the moment of impact."

Somewhere away in the town a clock chimed a quarter past ten. Almost at once there was the sound of bells to the west as St. Elfrida's began their Sunday morning peal.

"Don't think we shall be here long," Wharton said, doubtless with a thought for church-goers. "There's no sense in trying a reconstruction if you've nothing solid to build on. All we can guess is that the murderer followed Guy Fawkes—he was wearing rubber-soled boots, I imagine—as far as here and judged the fog dense enough and the place lonely enough to catch up with him and give him that crack on the skull."

"He wasn't a stranger, sir, if he knew the lie of the land," Mott said.

Wharton gave a shrug of the shoulders. "What's the point in arguing at all? Why shouldn't Guy Fawkes have come here with the murderer in a car? Soon as he stepped out to the pavement, then he was struck. That fits in, doesn't it? So would a dozen theories more."

"I don't know, sir," Mott said doggedly. "Now I come to think of it, it might have something to do with that man Mr. Ropeling was telling me about." He broke off. "There is Mr. Ropeling now, on his way to church. Catch him, Smith, and ask him to be so good as to come over for a minute. He's got plenty of time."

"What's this about a man?" Wharton said.

"Someone Mr. Mathison saw under suspicious circumstances—and what looked like attempted burglary on the night of the murder."

Wharton took a prodigious breath and let it out again. "Then why in God's name didn't you mention it before?"

"How was I to connect it, sir?" Mott challenged him. "We'd been making inquiries about the burglaries and we had dozens of reports about people supposed to be suspicious. Nearly run off their legs, my men were. What reason had I to associate it with the murder, sir? We hadn't an idea where it took place—not till we found this blood."

"Maybe you're right," said Wharton, and shaped his face to an official smile at Ropeling's approach. Mott did the talking.

"Morning, Mr. Ropeling. Sorry to trouble you but would you mind telling Superintendent Wharton here what you told me about that man on the Tuesday night?"

Ropeling looked about him with a quick appraisal of the circumstances. Then he gave a startled look.

"You don't mean it took place here?"

"There's more unlikely things than that," Mott told him enigmatically.

Ropeling told his tale with a due appreciation of the dramatic. Just after tea—at half-past five to be exact—he had come as arranged to spend an hour or two with Mr. Mathison. Cribbage was the game they were accustomed to play and they had a very comfortable hour at it in the living-room—the one with the bay window on the left from where they stood talking. Wharton had to crane his neck to look over Mathison's hedge to see the house front.

"It was about seven o'clock," Ropeling went on, "and we were having a last end, as Mathison calls it. I ought to have been away earlier but he persisted in playing just one more. We were very quiet—concentrated on the game—when all at once we heard the noise of breaking glass. Mathison looked scared to death, because there shouldn't have been a soul in the house, and the noise seemed to come from inside. 'What's that?' he said. Then we heard it again and it sounded to me like the other room—the one he uses as a workroom, corresponding to the living-room. I hopped up and grasped the poker as I went." He gave a deprecating smile. "I did it by instinct, really. I mean, I'm a pretty tough customer to tackle—or I used to be. But the thing is I had the door of the room burst open in a jiffy and turned the light on, and just then I saw a man . . . well, I hardly know how to describe what I saw, but it was as if he was scared by the light and I caught a glimpse of him as he disappeared in the fog. Then when Mr. Mathison came in we saw the window was broken just underneath the catch."

"My sergeant came along," Mott told Wharton, "but there weren't any prints."

"You saw anything of the man at all?" Wharton asked the curate.

"I wouldn't swear to anything," Ropeling said. "All I thought at the time was that he seemed a fairly big man. And I'd almost swear I caught a glimpse of a beard. Something whitish there seemed to be as he turned. I wouldn't swear to it though, as I said."

Wharton nodded. "The living-room. It was closely curtained?"

"It was," Ropeling said. "Mr. Mathison has a horror of draughts. I have too, for that matter, and it was a very raw, foggy night."

"But the other room wasn't curtained?"

"The curtains weren't drawn," Ropeling said. "The room's never used except as a kind of workroom. I'd never been in it before and I don't remember a thing about it. I believe there was a fire on, though, as if Mr. Mathison had been working in it earlier."

"Thank you, sir," Wharton said. "We hope all this may lead to something. Perhaps we'd better hear Mr. Mathison's own account."

"He'll probably be coming out in a moment," Ropeling said. "If you'd like me to, I'll fetch him."

He went through the centre gate. Wharton gave a nod or two.

"A burglar, breaking into what he thought was a dark, empty house. Curious, though?"

"And why, sir?" asked Mott.

"Because at about the very same time there was another burglary happening here. A Colonel Somebody-or-other, while he and his family were at the pictures. Quite a distance from here, if I remember rightly, which means two distinct burglars."

"Yes," said Mott, and it was plain enough that the point had never struck him. Then he was craning over the hedge, for over the side gate there was no view since the crazy paving path to the summer-house was winding and obscured by tall shrubs.

"The old gentleman's just coming," he said.

The party moved on to the front gate. Mathison was dressed as became a sidesman, with top hat, black silk muffler, velvet collared overcoat, kid gloves, plaid trousers and spats. Ropeling's report had evidently alarmed him for he was talking away furiously.

"I tell you I won't stay a day longer," he said. "First the burglars and now this. It isn't safe for anyone."

"Now, now, now," said Ropeling soothingly. "That's what the police are here for—to put everything right. You tell them about the man you saw."

"I *have* complained, haven't I?" said Mathison, with a glare at Mott. "I said there'd been a suspicious character about there on the Common, and I'd seen him from the bedroom window. All the police did was to come when it was too late."

Mott bestowed a quick wink on Travers, which meant, if it meant anything, that Mathison was a terror.

"I don't think you ought to say that, Mr. Mathison, sir," he said. "Soon as you complained, we kept a lookout, and we didn't see any man."

Wharton broke in then and his voice was a positive purr.

"The man you saw, sir. Could you give any description of him?"

"How could I when it was foggy?" His voice had lowered from that first shrill petulance. Then he gave Wharton a look. "You're not one of the local police?"

"No," said Wharton genially. "But about the man you saw. Could you give any description at all?"

"He was a tramp—and he looked like a rogue." He muttered something to himself. "A big man he was. All muffled up, what I could see of him. He kept looking up to my windows."

"Thank you, sir," said Wharton. "We won't trouble you any longer."

He might have saved his words for Mathison was through the gate and moving off. There was a kind of growl. Ropeling looked back with a sheepish sort of farewell nod and caught the old man up. As the two moved on there was the sound of his voice administering a scolding.

"Regular bantam-cock, isn't he, sir?" said Mott to Wharton. "A good plucked 'un for an old 'un, I lay."

"Old?" said Wharton. "You don't call him old? He's not a day over sixty. And but for that stoop he'd look younger." He peered each way along the road. "People turning out for church. We'd better get inside here, the four of us, and go over the ground."

Mott ripped away three or four of the rotten palings and made a gap. The four moved off to the far end of the plot and a line was stretched across. Then for an hour they went methodically over each square foot, until at last it was certain that there had been no recent digging, and there was never a sign of blood.

"Well, that's the end of that," Wharton said with an ironic patience. "If anyone has anything to suggest I shall be uncommonly glad to hear it."

"I think if you were to tackle him alone, sir," Mott said, "you might get more out of Mr. Ropeling about that man he was supposed to have seen."

Wharton gave a shrug of the shoulders.

"He'll be coming right by the station, sir—or should be—on his way home."

"Well, we'll see," said Wharton, and Travers at once drove the party back. But there was still a quarter of an hour before matins would be over, and Travers had a sudden desire to question old Mathison out of the curate's company. So he made his way on foot to the neighbourhood of The Rockery and waited in a convenient side lane till he should come in sight. And when he did appear, a stranger was with him, and the two chatted for a minute or two at the fork of the roads. Then Mathison came on and Travers timed the distance for a perfect meeting at The Rockery gate.

"Well, what have you found out?"

There was a certain amount of frowning and glaring as he fired the question. Travers smiled, knowing Mathison for a sheep in wolf's clothing.

"As far as I'm concerned—nothing," he said. "It's a great pity though that nothing was done about that burglar of yours."

"Too independent, that's what the police are. Who pays 'em? That's what I ask?"

The indictment came to a sudden end. He looked up with the comical dismay of one who realises he has dropped a brick.

"I didn't mean you, of course—"

Travers smiled. "But I'm not the police."

"Then what are you doing here with 'em?"

Mathison was now inside his own gate and he looked like shutting it.

"I'm a kind of apprentice," Travers told him. "You see it's rather hard for authors to get a living nowadays. Remarkable piece of work, that rock garden of yours. Did you design it yourself?"

Travers had switched the conversation so violently that Mathison took a moment or two to readjust his thoughts.

"Course I did it myself," he said. "I'm not so old as all that."

"Must have cost you a goodish bit," said Travers, trying to look like a boy who surveys an autumn orchard from the wrong side of the fence, "having all that earth carted in, and the rocks—must have been pretty expensive. Delightful little summerhouse you've got there too."

Mathison closed the gate. "You can come and have a look at it some time," he said. "Come in the spring when the flowers are out. There's nothing to see now." And then he too changed the conversation abruptly round. "You don't tell me you've been here all this time looking for that man who tried to break into my house?"

There seemed a cunning in the question, and a certain hostility. Travers decided to drop the fooling and talk as man to man.

"Well, perhaps we haven't. You see there was blood found on the pavement outside that side gate of yours."

"Blood?"

"Yes. It's not too preposterous to think that that poor devil whose body was cut up and hidden in the bonfire was killed outside your very door—so to speak."

But something surprising was happening. Mathison had stared, and his cheeks had literally begun to wobble. A fear and a horror were all at once in his eyes and then he turned and was making his way to his front door.

"I say, Mr. Mathison—"

But the door closed on him and Travers was left in mid-air. A shake of the head and he too was moving on, and with the knowledge that he had made a mess of things. And then something began to puzzle him. Capable it might be of the simplest explanations but for the life of him he could not fathom why the old man should have given that display of childish fear at the mere mention of the bonfire corpse. He had spoken in the same strain to the curate and had mentioned last straws and putting up with no more, and going away.

But by the time he was back at the station, Travers was in a more tolerant and understanding mood. Old Mathison was a fidget. He had made his money in business and had come to Garrod's Heath for rest and quiet. People at his age were irritable and selfish, and as for the fear there was an excuse for a man who spent his evenings alone and who, but for the happy presence of the curate, might have been tackled in his house by a burglar, while at almost the same moment the body of a murdered man was being hacked about practically on his doorstep.

But something else emerged from Travers's thoughts, and he put a question to Wharton on the way back to town.

"Might there be any connection between the man who tried to break into Mathison's house and either the murdered man or the murderer, do you think?"

"You mean, was the burglar Guy Fawkes or the man who killed him?" Wharton shook his head. "I don't see the connection, except in the matter of time."

"And the fact that the blood—some blood—was found near Mathison's house."

"A coincidence, surely." He clicked his tongue. "What's the use of speculation, as I told that fool Mott? There's nothing definite to go on. Nothing to get our teeth into. Mott's bungled the burglaries and he's bungled everything from the start. If I'd had him I'd have had that coat of his off his back."

He rumbled on for a bit. Travers began telling him about Mathison. But so that there should not be a new eruption on the General's part he gave the information which he had obtained from Mott without mentioning Mott's name.

"He's a Cockney, apparently," he said. "A retired draper, so they say."

"He's an irritable old fool—that's what he is," said Wharton.

"He'd be all right when you got to know him."

"Who wants to get to know him?"

"I do," said Travers blithely. "I like all cranks and fools. Besides, he can't be so bad if he's a gardener. There's a special kind of humanity about gardeners, as there is about anglers."

Wharton grunted.

"Curious, though," Travers went reminiscently on. "Most retired drapers would have a garden with roses down the front path, charming and utterly rickety arches, and beds of geraniums and blue lobelia cut in the lawn. I must ask him some time why he thought of concentrating on a rockery. The most difficult branch of gardening—so my sister always says." He smiled. "I might also pull his leg about having linoleum on his summer-house floor."

"Linoleum on the summer-house floor?" repeated Wharton. "Why shouldn't he?"

"I don't know," said Travers. "But have you ever seen a summer-house floor other than bare boards?"

Wharton pursed his lips, then grimaced. "If he and I ever get acquainted, I shall ask why he wears spats."

Travers chuckled. "I love you, George, when you're in ironical vein. But I have a perfectly good theory for both spats and linoleum. They were part of the unsold stock when he retired."

Wharton had not been listening. An uneasy stirring on his seat and he was making an announcement.

"It's nearly six years now since Luke came out of jail. I wonder if it'd be any use getting authorities to have a look back at any burglary epidemics in their areas since then? Lags like Luke always play the same tricks. We've got an excellent description of him, and suppose there were burglaries anywhere, and a certain respectable citizen suddenly disappeared—"

"Or his house was burnt down."

"Exactly," said Wharton, and began discussing ways and means.

CHAPTER XI
THE LAST LAUGH

For at least a day or two, according to Wharton, there would be no developments. Possibly by the Monday night there might be information about Henry Luke, but till he was picked up or some informatory connecting link was found, the case would mark time. So on the Sunday afternoon Travers slipped down to his sister's place as usual, and it was towards seven o'clock on the Monday evening when he called in at the Yard on his way to the flat, having phoned Wharton early.

Wharton was soberly optimistic. He might not have his teeth in a beef-steak but there was a smell of cooking in the air. Things were coming in about Luke, he said—or it looked as if it were Luke. There had been two replies to the SOS, and the first was from Bournemouth.

"Norris is still down there, making inquiries," he said, "but the facts as supplied seem to be these. Five years ago they had a small crop of burglaries down there, including two jewel robberies. A certain man was suspected—name of Courtney, but that would be an alias—but he turned out to have a perfect alibi and the police down there very nearly landed themselves in trouble. Shortly afterwards he left the district, and he gave the police to understand that they'd made scandal about him which was turning people against him. He left everything in order when he went—paid the rent for the little furnished house and everything—and that was the last Bournemouth heard of him. The curious thing is that he bore a very exact physical resemblance to Luke."

"What about prints?"

"Ah!" said Wharton, "they never got so far as that. What happened was this. There was a robbery and someone saw a certain person coming in a suspicious manner from where it took place, though he didn't know till later that a robbery had taken place. He didn't say a thing to the police, but a day or two later he saw the man and rushed up to a policeman and said there was the man who did the robbery, or something like that. It turned out to be absolutely wrong, as I said, but the informer still swore blind he was right."

"And what about the second discovery?"

"Ah!" said Wharton again, and his jaws clamped together. "There's some more of our friend Mott. Four years ago there were two cases of robbery at Garrod's Heath. In one, a Hatton Garden man who lives there was knocked on the head and his pockets rifled. He claimed a loss of five thousand worth of stones, though what he was paid I don't know. Just before that there was a burglary at a house about a mile out of the town, and a lot of stuff including some rare old silver went. Both took place within a month, and then there weren't any more till just over a year when this series started, and they've been going on spasmodically ever since. I've worked out this tentative time-table. Have a look at it and tell me if it conveys to you what I think it conveys to me."

Travers had a preliminary look. "I notice you assume that Luke is the man concerned throughout."

"That's right. Merely an assumption."

'27. Porburgh burglaries. Luke sentenced.
'30. Luke out (June).
'30. Bournemouth burglaries (Oct.).
'31. First Garrod's Heath affairs (March).
'35. Second Garrod's Heath series begin.

Travers hooked off his glasses and began a dubious polish.

"It's obvious," he said, "that all these affairs are connected, at least as far as the first Garrod's Heath affairs. On the same ground of argument I think you're justified in ascribing them to Luke. They're all robberies that were worth while, I gather—jewellery, and so on. Then there's the zigzagging."

"That's it," Wharton said. "Porburgh first, then clean on the other side of England—the South Coast. Then right away from there to the London suburbs. Then an unfilled gap." He pursed his lips. "That's what I can't quite account for. Over three years before he appears again. And he wasn't in stir or we'd have had his prints."

"Mightn't he have been in America, disposing of that collection of rare silver?"

"You've got it!" Wharton's fist smote the table. "He may have stayed on there till it got too hot to hold him. We'll send his prints straightaway."

Word came that York was waiting with an urgent report. Wharton scribbled a hasty chit and then had him in.

"Well, what tricks has he been up to to-night?"

York grinned. "We've got him pinned down tonight, sir. He's in a doss-house in the Whitechapel Road. Peters is there and we're getting a man inside as a down-and-out."

"He didn't go to Wapping, then?"

"No, sir," York said. "We had the two men planted down there and all for nothing. Soon as he knocked off at six o'clock, he walked through to the Strand and took a bus to Liverpool Street, and he didn't seem in a hurry, sir; he just sauntered along. Then he got off outside Liverpool Street station and we almost lost him there on account of the traffic crowds. Then we picked him up against the Liverpool Street Hotel. It isn't quite so well lighted there, sir, and it stands a bit back and when we saw him he was just going away, so while Peters was on his tail I slipped in to see what he'd been at, and what do you think I found, sir? Another one of the hot-cross-bun signs, just the same as the last." Then York shook his head. "But he nearly had me, sir. He must have turned right back, Peters said, and I had to pretend to be doing up my bootlace as he came right by, and Peters tailing him. Then he crossed the road and turned back into Bishopsgate and through to Whitechapel."

"Right," said Wharton. "Get a report from the man who's inside, and pick him up again in the morning. Anyone watching the Liverpool Street Hotel?"

The second of the now spare men from Wapping, so York said, and left with quite a genial smile from Wharton.

"This sign business beats me," Wharton said. "I don't like it somehow. Do you?"

"I don't know that I do," Travers said. "It strikes me as so utterly flamboyant. It's as remote from experience and real life as a boy's game of Red Indians."

"That's just it," Wharton said. "I don't know whether to treat it seriously or not, but the trouble is we can't afford to miss chances."

"But why does he make use of doss-houses at all?" asked Travers. "He's got plenty of money to pay for a decent lodging. He's a man of education and some breeding, and he's known the best. Then why deliberately get down to the gutter and stay in it?"

Wharton shook his head. "He's got me beat in some ways. I'm beginning to agree with old Watts. He's mentally unbalanced. He does things there's no accounting for."

Travers smiled thoughtfully. "Let's say that is so, George. If he's two-sided—incredibly sane and hopelessly mad—then all the things we can't explain, and there seem to be a whole lot of them, can be put down to the mad side of the ledger. But what about the other side? Watts claimed a marvellous brain for him. Well, what evidence of it have we seen? Where's that other side of him?"

"Don't know," Wharton said. "Maybe it's gone since the days when Watts knew him. He's spent years inside, brooding over that dirty trick that Carberry and Luke played on him, and he's come out merely one-sided. He's harmlessly mad." He laughed. "He's gone miserly. That's why he's saving his money and putting up at doss-houses."

"Maybe," said Travers. "But there's no reason why one of his history shouldn't have gone mad the other way—spent his substance on riotous living and had a few weeks' blind at the Hotel Palatial."

Wharton chuckled. "For all we know that's what he may have done already. Now he's in the gutter paying for it."

Next morning when Travers arrived, Norris was in conference with Wharton over the Bournemouth burglaries. Norris seemed dead certain the man had been Luke.

"He posed down there as a man who'd made a little money in Canada and had come home to spend it," Norris told Travers. "He had the accent, and a game leg which he said he got from a fall in the Rockies. Very popular among the Baptists, he was, and gave a lecture once about his adventures. But he bested the police all right over his alibi, or else he didn't have anything to do with that particular burglary."

There was a tap at the door and a sergeant came in with the usual interview form. Wharton raised his eyebrows.

"Right," he said. "Show him in."

"Well," he said, "if that doesn't beat cock-fighting, what does? Who do you think it is? Johnson! Wants an interview urgently."

Johnson came in with a dignity that was somewhat stilted.

"What favourable wind blows you here?" asked Wharton genially. "Got some information for us?"

Johnson quietly refused the proffered chair.

"What I've come to ask you, sir," he said, and Wharton pricked up his ears at the sudden courtesy, "is why I'm being victimized."

"Victimized?" said Wharton, and looked unutterably shocked. "Why, who's victimizing you?"

"The police are, sir," said Johnson, doggedly.

"But, my dear man"—Wharton raised hands to heaven and cast appealing glances round the room— "you must be under some unfortunate misapprehension. Why on earth should the police be victimizing you? And how are they doing it? What form does it take?"

"I'm being followed about," Johnson said. "The police watch me wherever I go."

"That's rather an amazing statement to make," said Wharton, unblushingly. "Why on earth should the police want to follow you?"

"That's what I'm here to find out, sir."

"I should think so—if it's true." He gave a magisterial peer over the top of his glasses. "What grounds have you for bringing this charge against the police:"

Johnson maintained that queer immobile dignity.

"May I ask you a question, sir?"

"By all means," said Wharton heartily.

"And you'll give me a plain yes or no?"

"Why not?" said Wharton. "That is, if it's something you're entitled to ask and me to answer."

"Then this, sir. Have you ever seen it before?"

He was placing a sheet of paper on the desk beneath Wharton's eyes and then drawing back. Travers, casting a quick look, saw on the sheet nothing but that sign of the hot-cross-bun and question mark. Wharton was pursing his lips, wondering how to wriggle clear. Then he decided on a counter-question.

"And suppose I have?"

Johnson nodded. He had stood his small attaché case by his foot and now he stooped and picked it up as if the interview, as far as he was concerned, was over.

"That tells me all I want to know, sir. We caught a spy in Malta like that, during the War."

Wharton stared. Then he leaned forward with a tremendous patience.

"Would you mind telling me just what you're talking about? Spies in Malta, wasn't it? And what have spies in Malta to do with what you've come here for?"

Johnson took off his glasses, gave his eyes a rub with the back of his hand, and put the glasses on again. It was as if the talk had gone off the anticipated track and he was hunting for words.

"I'll tell you, sir," he said at last, and there was never the slightest rancour in his tone. "I put a mark in certain places last night and Saturday night because I had an idea I was being followed. It doesn't mean anything, as far as I know, but it's how we caught that spy in Malta. Soon as I'd scrawled it up a police spy was on it—both times."

Wharton might purse his lips and frown, and Norris might wear a look of incredulous innocence, but the room had a gaping silence. Then Wharton gave a nod or two.

"Well, Johnson, there's plenty of people who wouldn't believe this yarn of yours, but I'm not one. If you'll give me details as to where these occurrences took place, I'll have the divisions concerned hauled over the coals."

"Thank you, sir," said Johnson, and Travers had the uncanny feeling that while his manner was that of the quarter-deck, his jaws and belly-muscles were shaking with triumphant laughter. So the farce was played solemnly out, and Johnson departed, attaché case and all. Wharton was the first to speak.

"Well, that's that, then."

The shamed uneasy silence lingered for another moment about the room, then Travers and Norris each spoke at once, and a sort of confidence came back with the talk.

"Beg pardon, sir. You were going to say something."

"Nothing much," said Travers, fumbling for his glasses. "I was merely going to remark that it might be as well to admit that

Johnson has the laugh on us, and he might as well be written off at once as a bad debt."

"Oh, no," said Wharton, and got to his feet. "You keep up the day supervision, Norris. He hasn't tumbled to that yet. Let the other go for a bit."

"Rather risky, don't you think, sir? If he was to make a complaint in a certain quarter, we might have trouble in explaining things. I don't altogether mean us, but suppose, for instance, he was to write to *Old England?* A nice case they'd make out, sir. *Police victimize ex-convict who's been going straight,* and all that sort of stuff. Somebody'd go and ask questions in Parliament."

"Let 'em," said Wharton grimly. "You keep that day lookout, and I'll take the consequences." He grunted. "He didn't catch me with all that tomfoolery. I told Mr. Travers it was all damn nonsense."

"All the same, sir," said Norris dryly, "I don't think we'd better let on to Flanagan about it."

"Flanagan," said Wharton contemptuously, and fidgeted with the papers on his desk. Then he handed Norris that list of dates back on the supposed movements of Luke. "See what you think of that. As for Johnson, he'll will find himself in Queer Street if he isn't careful. He's got a screw loose. That's what's the matter with him. He's gone childish."

"Ex ore infantium," said Travers quietly. "What disturbs me is that I feel the cleverness of it—for it was clever, that trapping your two men, George— and yet there isn't any method in it. Why couldn't he have confronted the men and told them pointblank who they were?" He shook his head. "Watts was right. He's a mass of queer intricacies. Everything about him is just specious enough to be taken for normal—and yet it isn't."

Norris had been frowning away over Wharton's paper. Wharton told him what he was doing about Luke's prints, and why. Norris suggested sending them also to Quebec, in view of the Canadian accent of the Bournemouth suspect. Wharton said both should be telegraphed at once.

"Now I'd like to put something up to you, sir," said Norris. "It looks promising to me and it'll clear up the Johnson difficulty. I'd like you to follow me carefully, sir, if you will. Now this paper of yours, which it's concerned with. It reads as if you assume the one all through was Luke."

"Yes," said Wharton, and waited.

"Well, there were no prints ever taken at either Bournemouth or Garrod's Heath, and therefore you can't be dead sure. Is that correct, sir?"

"Carry on," said Wharton.

"Therefore the Bournemouth man and the one who did the two jobs years ago at Garrod's Heath mayn't be Luke after all. But he wasn't all that far off his build, and his age, that he needn't have been something like him. And so was the man whose body was found in the bonfire. Therefore why shouldn't the man you refer to all the time in this paper have been the bonfire corpse and not Luke at all?"

Wharton pursed his lips.

"I'm quite in agreement so far," said Travers.

"Then I'll go a bit further," said Norris. "This bonfire body—Guy Fawkes, as we call him—we can approach another way. The burglaries at Garrod's Heath seem to be over for the moment. Until they do break out again we can act on the assumption that they're over. Now why should they be over if not for the very good reason that the burglar has been eliminated? He wasn't scared off by the police. I hold he was eliminated. That, in so many words, he was Guy Fawkes."

"That's interesting enough, and it's logical," said Wharton grudgingly. "But why was he eliminated and by whom? Tell me that. All we've been relying on is that Guy Fawkes was killed for the sake of his hand. Now you're saying he was a wholly new character—the Garrod's Heath burglar, in fact. You're leaving out Luke and all connection with him."

Norris shook his head. "That's just what I was coming to, sir. Mind you, though, we now begin to get a bit sort of—"

"Hypothetical," suggested Travers, interpreting the vague wave of the hand.

"That's it, sir. Hypothetical, and it's to do with Johnson. His last job was burglary and there isn't any reason why he shouldn't have taken it up again in a quiet sort of way when he came out. Now why shouldn't he have been in partnership with Guy Fawkes? There was a burglary at Garrod's Heath on that very Tuesday night, and why shouldn't Johnson and Guy Fawkes have been mixed up in it and then Johnson have done in Guy Fawkes for the sake of the swag?"

Wharton merely raised his eyebrows.

"Johnson had a first-class alibi for the Wednesday night," Norris went on. "We know he didn't kill Carberry, and the more we handle the Carberry Case the less it has to do with the Bonfire Case. So what I ask is, *Where is Johnson's alibi for the Tuesday night?*"

Wharton nodded knowingly as if anticipating what was to come.

"Test the alibi for its own sake," Norris concluded. "But it also gives us another handle. If Johnson tries to make trouble for us over being unwarrantably shadowed, we can claim that we had every right to, because we had him in mind for the bonfire job." He gave Wharton a wary look. "Or better still, sir, if you agree, why not spike Johnson's guns beforehand and get to the right quarter with your information first?"

Travers smiled quietly. "A good effort, Norris. There were gaps in the argument but there was a tremendous deal of sense."

Wharton's fist smote the table.

"I'll square the tailing, Norris. You go and see Johnson at once and take a witness with you. Where's Lewis?"

"On the Wimbeck Street end, trying to find out something about J. Scott."

"Well, take someone else. Give Johnson his option of being questioned somewhere there—in a tea-shop, for instance—or coming here, and make sure everything's according to the book of rules."

And then, in the very moment when the sound of Norris's feet died away down the corridor, he saw the fallacy in all that long argument, and his hands rose despairingly to heaven.

"Doesn't that show you how my brain's going round in circles? I can't even think." He glared at Travers. "How could Johnson have killed Guy Fawkes? Guy Fawkes was killed for the sake of his hand, so that Carberry could be safely murdered. And Johnson *didn't* murder Carberry. That's one of the few things of which we're absolutely sure." He grunted. "Wind and blether—that's all that talk of Norris's was. Theories! Any fool can theorise. Facts are what we want—facts!"

"Such as?" interpolated Travers.

Wharton stared amazed. "You stand there and ask a question like that?"

"Yes, but what vital fact?" persisted Travers. "When one knows the essential thing wanted, then there can be a concentration of search."

Wharton pursed his lips in thought for a moment, then glared again.

"Well, what about the truth of a half fact? J. Scott was flesh and blood, wasn't he? None of your fourth unknowns. Who was he? Where's he disappeared to? How's he fit in?"

"Lord knows," said Travers. "As far as my private arguments go, he's someone who oughtn't to be in the case at all. Which is why I can't fit him in."

It was some twenty minutes later, as Travers rose at last to go, that the phone bell sounded. Norris was ringing up to say he was coming back at once and everything had gone off without a hitch.

Wharton was uneasy. Norris, he said, was merely meaning that Johnson had made no trouble, but most likely he had refused to open his mouth. But Wharton was wrong. Norris had tested Johnson's alibi.

"He didn't make a murmur," Norris said, "so the three of us adjourned for a nice cup of coffee all by ourselves. He reckoned he'd nothing to conceal and all he wanted was to be let alone. Nobody could have been more decent than he was. 'The Tuesday,' he said, 'now where was I on Tuesday evening? And what time Tuesday evening?' I told him from six o'clock to half-past would do. Then he began thinking and running over the names of what he called his regulars."

"That'd be regular subscribers," said Wharton bitterly. "Like Mr. Travers."

Travers merely chuckled at the jibe. "My alms are for the love of Allah, George. But carry on, Norris."

"Well, sir, he thought of one, a young lady typist who works right above his pitch. She always knocks off round about six and always tips him a penny. We tested her a few minutes later and she'd swear to him on the Twelve Apostles. Then he remembered the chap in the tobacconist's shop and we adjourned there. We made out to him it was something to do with a third party, but he swore all right to the time. Just about a quarter to six it was when he slipped Johnson a cup of tea, and when he took the cup in again Johnson was still there."

"Right," said Wharton, and let out a breath. "It looks as if Mr. Travers was right. We'll have to write him clean off the books as a bad debt. I can't see a loophole in his alibi."

"It's more water-tight than what I told you, sir," said Norris. "At least he said if I wasn't satisfied he'd have a word with one or two more of his regulars when he thought of them during the day."

"All right, all right," said Wharton impatiently. "We've heard enough." Then all at once his eyes opened wide and he began licking his lips. "Wait a minute. What about his alibis for Saturday and Sunday?"

"What've they got to do with it, sir?"

But Wharton was thinking. His legs shot out beneath the desk, then shot him upright again.

"There's more ways than one of testing alibis. We won't go begging Mister Johnson to be so good as to give us his alibis." His fist smote the desk. "I'll do it! I'll take a chance for once."

He peered over the top of his antiquated spectacles as if challenging contradiction. Travers put in the leading question as expected.

"Do what, George?"

"Listen to me a minute," Wharton told him, "and you'll think the way I do."

CHAPTER XII
OUT GOES JOHNSON

"First of all," Wharton began, "I'd like to say perfectly frankly that I'm tired of trying to fit things in. We've tried things that seemed to make sense and simply wasted time, so now we'll have a go at some that don't make sense. For instance, Johnson killed nobody, but he may have a pretty good idea who did. He may even have been behind the scenes and engineered the whole business. He had two hundred pounds to spend, hadn't he? So don't ask me to explain things that don't appear to make sense. Just listen to my idea, which is this: Mathison said he saw a man behaving suspiciously in the neighbourhood of his house, which is the same as saying the neighbourhood of the bonfire. We're not going to ask Johnson to give us his alibi for that. We're going to test it ourselves. And in this way. We'll get Mathison to walk past Johnson to see if he identifies him."

"He'll never come," Travers said. "He's a pigheaded customer and Mott seems to have set him against the police."

"Mott!" said Wharton, with infinite scorn. "But you hear all I've got to say. Norris is going to Garrod's Cross and Norris is going to handle Mathison as if he were egg-shell. Ropeling's the secret."

"Ropeling?"

"Yes," said Wharton. "And for two reasons, one of which is sensible and the other sheer lunacy. The sensible part is this. Ropeling can handle the old boy, so he'll be induced to approach him on behalf of the law. Norris, in fact, will see Ropeling first. That's where the mad part comes in. Ropeling caught a glimpse of the burglar that Tuesday night, and he mentioned a big man and something that resembled a beard. That recalls Johnson." He raised a quick hand. "I know what you're going to say—that whether Johnson had an alibi or not for the vital times that

Tuesday night, he's got people who can swear that he has, which is the same thing. I know I'm mad, but you just let me have my way for once. This is a hunch and I'm following it up. You see, even though Johnson's alibi is correct, Ropeling won't know a thing about that. So Norris will see Ropeling first; then both of them will go along and persuade Mathison."

Norris seemed satisfied. Travers simulated an enthusiasm he was far from feeling.

"We'll run no risks and we'll mention no names to either Mathison or Ropeling," Wharton said. "The whole thing has got to be a favour to the police, and unofficial. Play up to the idea of doing a public service for the citizens of Garrod's Heath. We won't even have one of our cars. The ideal thing would be for Palmer to drive Mr. Travers's Rolls."

Travers smiled there, for in less specious moments Wharton was accustomed to describe the same car as a hell-wagon.

"The private chauffeur and the very fine car will flatter both Ropeling and Mathison, and make it unofficial. They'll be taken right home to their own doorsteps again as soon as the little favour's done."

Travers was willing. He would warn Palmer over the phone and go along with Norris and pick the car up at St. Martin's, and on the way give Norris a few tips about both Ropeling and Mathison.

"That's the spirit," said Wharton. "I suggest we bring them to half-way up the Haymarket. While you're away I'll take a chance and fix up with the tea-shop so that we can keep a watch on what happens. We shall have to get up by some back way. If Johnson saw us hanging about it'd put the lid on everything."

It was two hours later when Wharton rang up Travers at the flat and with a suppressed exultation reported Norris as on the way back. The two met at the Haymarket rendezvous.

"Everything's ready," Wharton said. "Lewis has got his men handy in case Johnson should do a bolt. Everything's fixed up at the tea-shop and you and I'll have a front pew."

When the Rolls drew up at the pavement he was the first to be at the door. His hand helped Mathison out, and his tongue had never been more sweetly oiled. Ropeling had been somewhat nervy at the strange prospect, but the General had him at his ease in no time, and Mathison was bathed in such a sea of unctuous thanks and flattery that he seemed as amenable as an old sheep.

"Inspector Norris has explained the simple routine," Wharton ended, "but I'll go over it just once more. First you, Mr. Mathison. You know where the suspect stands, and you couldn't miss him even if you didn't. All you do is walk quite naturally along the pavement, keeping to the inner side, and when you do see him you stop naturally and fumble in your pocket to find a coin—a penny'll do. That will give you time to run your eye well over him. Then you drop the coin in his box and walk on—still perfectly naturally. Take the first to the right and first to the right again and it'll bring you back to where we are now. Inspector Norris will be here to receive your report.

"And now you, sir. You do the same as Mr. Mathison, except that you don't fumble for a coin. You go right past the man and then come back as if you'd decided to give him something after all. Report to Inspector Norris, and then—as far as we're immediately concerned—the little job's over. Everything understood? Right then. Lewis, you'd better be opposite him on the other side of the road. Three minutes to allow Mr. Travers and myself to get upstairs, and Mr. Mathison can move off. Another five minutes and the job'll be all over."

With which heartening words he moved off. In two minutes he and Travers were at a table in the tea-shop window, and at Zero minute two cups of tea were on the table and they were glancing idly towards the Haymarket. Travers's heart was beating at a disturbingly rapid rate.

"Here comes Mathison!"

Wharton was facing the Haymarket way. Travers, with the tea-room almost filled with customers, was loth to draw attention to himself with a craning of the neck. His eyes were on the immobile Johnson, who stood with back to the wall and a steady hand that held the small tray of matches. Then from the corner of his eye he too caught sight of Mathison. Wharton's voice came with a hiss.

"My God! he's doing it fine."

Travers squinted again and now the figure of Mathison obscured that of Johnson. Mathison was hoisting his overcoat and getting to his trouser pocket, and then almost at once was putting a coin in the tray. So natural was it that Travers could almost hear the mumbled words that accompanied the charity. The eyes of Travers followed Mathison for a yard or two.

"Ropeling's coming!"

Travers's heart was racing again. He took a breath or two with closed lips.

"Bit soon, isn't he, George?"

"My God—look!"

Wharton was on his feet and the room was staring. Travers looked but saw nothing, and then an age after, as it seemed, he knew that where Johnson had stood there was a vacant space, but something was lying on the pavement, and people were running, and there was Lewis. . . .

In the same second Travers became aware that Wharton had gone. People in the room were rushing to the window, and Travers made his way through them and out to the pavement. Across the road was nothing but confusion. Lewis's men seemed to have come from nowhere and were forcing the crowd back. A constable in uniform was elbowing his way through, and Wharton's holler was heard, and in a gap of the crowd Travers saw the white collar of Ropeling.

"Move along there, please. . . . Come on now. Move along please."

Another minute and the crowd had thinned. Travers slipped past through a gap at the constable's back.

"Here you are then," said Wharton, and in the same second his eyes were on Johnson again.

"What's happened, George?"

"Had a stroke or something. A fit, more like it. Look at the corners of his mouth." He grunted. "Might have cracked his skull if the wall hadn't broken his fall."

There was a distant wail. A traffic policeman rushed to the road and the ambulance drew up. A quick word with Wharton and the men were lifting Johnson in.

"Just a minute," Wharton said. "What'd you see, Lewis?"

"All I saw, sir, was him on the pavement. He seemed to go down all of a sudden. First he was standing here and then he wasn't."

"Right," said Wharton. "You go to the hospital with him and explain who he is and no more." He craned up and whispered something. Lewis flicked a finger to his hat.

The ambulance moved off. Wharton looked round for Ropeling.

"Where's that damn curate gone?"

"Where you told him, I expect," Travers said.

Travers was right. Ropeling was standing by the Rolls with Mathison and Norris, and his tongue was going and his hands gesturing. Wharton's arrival came only as a momentary silencer.

"Whatever was the matter, Mr. Wharton?" the curate was going on.

"Don't know yet," Wharton said. "But about you, Mr. Mathison. Ever see him before?"

Mathison seemed unaware if he were on head or heels. Ropeling's truncated story had conveyed nothing. But he was positive enough about Johnson, whom he had never seen in his life.

"And you, sir?" asked Wharton.

Ropeling was far from positive that he had never seen Johnson before. Then he recalled the fact that his view of the burglar had been less than fleeting. At that Mathison remembered how the mist had obscured all but the faint form of the suspicious character that had haunted The Rockery neighbourhood, and finally the two came to the crucial issue that there was never the slightest reason for connecting Johnson with either loitering or burglary.

"That's all then, gentlemen," said Wharton curtly. Then he decided that nothing was to be gained by losing patience. "But I hope you'll allow us to show our gratitude by offering you some lunch."

Mathison, who seemed to be getting back to normal, shook his head somewhat testily and said he had to hurry home. Ropeling, more reluctantly, was of the same mind.

"A glass of something then," said Wharton. "Just a sherry or a cocktail to warm you up."

But Mathison was already entering the car. Ropeling followed and then withdrew his head again.

"Is there any explanation—"

But Wharton had a sudden deafness. He was helping the curate in, uttering more thanks, and making covert signs to Travers to get the car on the move.

"Thank Heaven they've gone," he said, when the Rolls glided off. "Bursting to know all the ins and outs—both of them. I hope Norris spins 'em a pretty yarn."

Travers shook his head perplexedly. "So am I bursting, George, if it comes to that."

Wharton pulled out his watch. "Hadn't better go along to the hospital to inquire yet. I'll pass the word on to one of Lewis's men and we'll slip in somewhere for a beer and a sandwich."

Travers was forming his own ideas. As soon as a corner was found for the scratch meal, he fired the leading question at Wharton.

"Do you think Mathison recognised Johnson?"

"Of course he didn't," Wharton said with a snort. "That's out of the question. I'll lay ten pounds to a peanut he didn't."

"Then it was the sight of Ropeling that made Johnson flop."

Wharton's eyes narrowed. He took a long pull at the beer, and wiped his moustache with ample gestures. Then the answer came.

"What had Ropeling got to do with it? We haven't anything against him, have we?"

"I don't know that we have," Travers said. "But it's not what we have against him. It's what Johnson might have against him."

"I get you," Wharton said. "If it was Johnson that night at Mathison's window, he was just about to reach in and undo the window catch when on went the light and there was Ropeling. Johnson in the dark must have seen Ropeling in the full light. He needn't have seen his face, but he certainly saw the white collar and knew he was a parson." He shook his head. "Parsons are common enough. Why should Johnson have had a fit when he saw one?"

"If there's any point in the assumption that Johnson saw Ropeling's face on the Tuesday night, then he might have had a fit," said Travers. "He might have been suddenly scared at the sight of him. If Ropeling were to spot him, then good-bye to a good deal. Johnson, when he saw Ropeling, saw the inside of another jail."

"Well, I can't say what it was," Wharton said. "My eyes were on Ropeling. I remember your saying Ropeling had followed rather quick on Mathison's tail and the next thing I saw was Johnson on the ground. Ropeling was about ten yards off him then." He gulped down the last of his sandwiches and finished the beer. "Might as well be getting along to the hospital now. They'll know what was wrong with him."

They turned into Wardour Street for a cut through, and Travers had never looked so lugubrious.

"We shall go crazy, George," he said, "if we go trying to build up theories contrary to all common sense. Why worry about Johnson at all? He has an alibi and that's the end of it. Mathison says he never saw him in his life, so there's no point in trying to connect him with Garrod's Heath."

"Maybe you're right," said Wharton gloomily. "For all we know Johnson may have been heading for a fit for weeks. The fact that he had it just now doesn't make it more than a coincidence."

Travers halted at the hospital door.

"Aren't you coming in?" Wharton said.

Travers shook his head. "I don't think I'll wait about. You ring me up some time later and tell me what they say."

It was strange entering the flat and Palmer not there. And it was queer, thought Travers, how unreal that world seemed in which Wharton and he talked and theorised. Always when he was alone he felt a curious oppression of thought, such as comes when something vital has been forgotten and lies behind the memory and batters at a fast shut door. But there was no forgetting what was in his own mind, and what haunted it whenever he had spent an hour in his own company.

The Unknown Man—he was the vital clue and the connecting link. Yet that was an incomplete name. The Unconsidered Man or the Unidentified Man—either would be better. Watts had mentioned him and had not been aware of the fact. Wharton had heard the mentioning and taken the contrary for granted. Or when Wharton thought of a fourth man—to the unholy trio of Luke, Carberry and Johnson—he thought of fantastic, unreal people, such as accomplices of Johnson who did the murdering of Carberry, and put notes in dead men's pockets. Even J. Scott had never seemed to Travers so shadowy and unreal.

But the new tragedy— as Travers now was seeing it—was not only the failure to find and identify the Unconsidered Man, but the fact that the more Johnson was tested, the less he seemed to be in any way implicated. In other words, not only had no fourth been added to the trio, but the trio had been reduced to that pale cast of Luke—the bonfire body —and Carberry—*two dead men*. But someone had killed them, and as Travers faced again that circling problem, his long legs drew up from the fire and he sat with head in hands. And there he sat when the phone went and Wharton was calling him.

"Johnson's all right," Wharton said. "Just a fit —of the epileptic kind, I gather. They're keeping him under observation for a day or two."

"Did they say what might have brought it on?"

"I didn't get any real information," Wharton said. "I asked if a shock might have caused it, and they said of course it might, and that was that."

"I may inquire myself later," Travers told him. "And what's the programme now as far as concerns yourself?"

"Getting things in order for opening a certain trench out Garrod's Heath way," Wharton said. "I'll find that head if I dig up half the country."

It was strange, thought Travers, how lop-sided those twin murder cases had become. The Carberry Case, which had promised endless scope for inquiry, had proved a dead end; while the Garrod's Heath affair, that had seemed barren of all clues beyond the naked body, had become the one source of inquiry and the one hope. But Travers kept his thoughts from murder for a while, though after dinner, he drew along to the hospital. Then a house-surgeon whom he knew went by the waiting-room door and Travers hailed him.

"What are you doing here?" the doctor asked.

Travers told him.

"Don't stay there," the doctor said. "Come along in here. It's more private. And you're inquiring about Johnson, are you?" He smiled. "He'll be out again in a day or two. At the moment he's sound asleep."

"Pardon me," said Travers, "but just why did you smile when you mentioned his name?"

"Did I?" He smiled again. "The fact is he's been giving us a bit of trouble. He came round normally enough and had a sedative, and then all at once he began kicking up a fuss about a body-belt arrangement we'd taken off him when he was put to bed. He was told it'd be all right but he made himself such a damn nuisance that we had to let him have it. Shouldn't be surprised if he's got it tight round his tummy at this moment." He caught Travers's intent look. "You don't think there was anything fishy about that belt? It looked to me stuffed out with something."

"It'd be his money—poor devil."

"Of course," the other said, and then all at once was looking interested. "By the way—without being personal and all that—isn't your name Luke or something?"

Travers was startled. "Good Lord, no! Ludovic, if you like. But why'd you ask that?"

"Well"—he smiled—"I was putting two and two together. I remembered your name was something like Luke—it is, you know— and then it looked to me as if you were a sort of friend of Johnson; might have known him in his school days, or something; then I remembered how Johnson was muttering about someone called Luke when he came round. He was sort of mumbling it."

Travers got hold of Wharton at once.

"Johnson keeps all his possessions in a belt on him. He was most anxious it shouldn't be seen by anyone else."

"That'd be the two hundred quid he took over when he came out," Wharton said. "Plus what he's made out of the match-selling game. Find out anything else?"

"Yes," said Travers. "When he came to, he kept muttering the name Luke."

There was a quick grunt from Wharton.

"Luke, eh? . . . Well, that's not unreasonable. He had Luke on the brain for eight years when he was inside. Luke and Carberry were his obsessions. I'll wager if they'd listened close enough they'd have heard him say Carberry as well."

CHAPTER XIII
THE DROPPED WALLET

OF ALL THE innovations introduced at the Yard by a certain Chief Commissioner, the most admirable was the internal information bureau, which classified and multiple indexed all news receipts. When Lewis therefore, as liaison officer for the Garrod's Heath and Wimbeck Street affairs, happened to observe the word Wapping, he looked the matter up, made certain inquiries on the spot and reported to Norris. At half-past eight the next morning Mr. Solomon Frisch was in Wharton's room, with Norris and Lewis.

"You came here yesterday as a result of an appeal made by us for missing men," Wharton said. "What exactly is your information, Mr. Frisch?"

Frisch, an elderly, crafty-looking specimen, went warily from the start. His chief idea, he said, had been to do the right thing in the eyes of the police. His tenant had disappeared and when he left had tried to burn down the premises.

"You informed the police?"

Frisch shuffled a bit. "No, sir. Not the real police. You see, I want to make no troubles."

"Not the real police, eh?" Wharton smiled somewhat dourly. Frisch had clearly been concerned in his time with more than one fire, and his information would need careful checking, if it happened to relate to Johnson, though that was a wild shot indeed, whatever the opinion of Lewis.

"Describe this tenant of yours," Wharton said.

He was a big man, Frisch said, about the size of Wharton himself. When he first took the room he was clean-shaven, but since then—which was last December—he had grown a beard, so Mrs. Frisch said.

"You haven't seen him yourself then for best part of a year?"

Frisch said that was so. He had let the room to the man—name of Harrison—for six shillings a week. Regularly on a Monday morning Harrison would call at the house in Weekes Street, Wapping, and drop the money wrapped in paper through the letter box. Frisch himself was never in then, and on occasions when he had looked in at the room, it had been shut and the tenant had been out. Moreover the tenant had said from the start that he wanted no spying or interference.

"You didn't think that suspicious?" Wharton said.

Frisch shrugged his shoulders. His motto, one understood, was live and let live. Besides there is nothing reprehensible in a wish for privacy.

"Wore glasses, did he?"

Frisch said his wife had never mentioned the fact.

"Spoke like a gentleman?"

Frisch said, and as if he were a capable judge, that the tenant had always been accepted as a gentleman. He was an old ship-captain, fallen on hard times.

Frisch was asked to step outside for a bit. The room agreed that he was probably Johnson's landlord.

"Some filthy hole or other, this room of his," Wharton said. "Six bob a week, and secrecy. You know what that means."

"If the room is Johnson's—" Norris began. Lewis broke in.

"I'm sure it is, sir. I had a good bit of talk with him before he came here and it's right against where York and Peters lost him that night."

"Well, we'll say it is," Norris went on. "That makes Johnson out to be a liar, because he told us he had no lodgings. That makes him liable to be looked after."

"He'll be looked after all right," said Wharton. "As soon as he leaves the hospital we're going to keep him under our eye. There's a money belt he's very attached to, which I'd like to have a look at; and there's that little matter of babbling about Luke in his dreams. Still, what about Frisch? We'd better go along and have a look at that room of his, don't you think? You come with me, Lewis, and bring Johnson's prints."

In the car Frisch gave details of the room and the yard where it was built. He had up till recently been in the old iron and lumber business, and the room was really a converted shed which had been a foreman's office in the palmier days when the yard had been used by a builders' merchant. Wharton made a wry face us they passed that wall on which Johnson had chalked the first sign of the hot-cross bun, and then Frisch was asking for the car to stop, and out the party got.

It was a raw, misty morning and that drab fringe of the river had a squalor that depressed even Wharton. But that small yard with its back on the river mud had a squalor unspeakable, with its grimy refuse, rotting timber walls and dumps of rusted metal. The brick-built shed stood at the far corner at the end of a rutted cinder path, foul with weeds and water.

"Handsome exterior," said Wharton ironically. "If only the inside's as good, you're a philanthropist, Mr. Frisch."

But the inside was none too bad. It was watertight and had a brick floor, with a stove whose pipe ran through a cemented hole clear of the low roof. The furniture was a camp-bed, an old wicker chair and a rickety chest of drawers. Frisch said he supplied them to the tenant's orders and they were all he wanted.

Lewis had been sniffing the paraffin. Wharton had seen the heap of shavings and papers by the dry woodwork that ran by wall and window, with an old lamp artistically turned over ready to be found when the fire had burnt out. A candle had been set and why it had gone out was hard to say, but the hundred to one chance had supervened and all that remained was evidence of arson that had never materialized.

"Get going for prints," Wharton told Lewis. "That's the only reason he wanted to burn this highly desirable residence. He didn't want us to prove him a liar."

"The less you say about this place the better," he said to Frisch. "If the sanitary authorities and a few other people knew about this, you'd be in an awkward spot." He gave an ironical peer over his spectacle tops. "But what I'm wondering is if you'd do the law a favour."

Frisch was only too eager to do anything.

"In a day or two," Wharton told him, "I may ask you to take a walk past a gentleman who may bear a remarkable resemblance to your missing tenant—Harrison. You want to lock this place up again, I suppose? You don't? Right. Then you can go now and we'll let ourselves out." He gave him a last look at the doorway. "We'll leave the fire in case the sanitary authorities might like to use it."

"What a hell-hole!" he said to Lewis. "What brought Johnson here is beyond me altogether. Mr. Travers is right about him. First you think he's mad and then you think he's as full of brains as a jelly-fish is full of water. You've got something, have you?"

Lewis had enough prints for proof. Johnson, it appeared, had wiped prints off here and there, for where they should have been there were none. Then, as Lewis worked it out, he'd decided to *do* the job thoroughly and burn the place down.

"For which he ought to have been thanked," Wharton said. Then he stooped with a "Hallo, what's this?"

There were two or three newspapers in the small pile among the shavings. Wharton drew them gingerly out and, still wet with paraffin as they were, unkinked them and flattened them out.

"Never read the papers, so he said. *Evening Record,* eh? And the latest on the Carberry affair. And the first break of the Guy Fawkes story."

He stood for a long minute scowling into space, then shook his head knowingly.

"You think I'm an old fool, but I knew I was right. I said all along it was that Porburgh Case. I tell you Johnson's mixed up in it."

Lewis nodded dubiously. "The thing is, how're we going to prove it, sir. You can't get away from cast-iron alibis. Johnson didn't do Carberry in, and he wasn't near Garrod's Heath on that Tuesday night."

"It's no use talking about how," Wharton told him. "Our job's to find answers—not ask questions. Johnson's got the answer, and we've got to sit on his tail till he tells us. We've got to eat with him and sleep with him and think with him; do you hear?" He gave a grunt or two. "Wait till he comes out of hospital, then we'll see. Unless Mr. Travers takes one of his short cuts and finds this mysterious man of his." He gave a sardonic chuckle. "X, the Unknown, like you read about in the books."

He made his way the few feet to the rotting fence that separated the yard from the river, and stood for a minute or two surveying the desolate mud of the low-tide flats. Then he was shivering in his heavy overcoat.

"We'll get back," he said to Lewis. "Those seagulls give me the creeps. Which is something else about Johnson. Can you tell me a single reason— knowing as much about him and his circumstances as you do—why he should choose this hole to live in, if it wasn't because he wanted to hide himself like a rat in a corner?"

"They say people are like animals," Lewis said. "He might have felt like a sick rat when he first came out of stir."

"He had money, hadn't he?"

"I know, sir," said Lewis. "But there's something else. They say all old sea-faring men like to end their days in sight of the sea or the river."

Wharton shot a look at him to see if he were serious, then grunted contemptuously as he moved off.

On the stairs at the Yard he ran into Travers who was just coming down.

"They said you were at Wapping," Travers said, "so I thought I'd come in later."

"Well, come along up now," Wharton told him. "Heard anything about Johnson this morning?"

"Only that he's progressing normally. He should be out the day after to-morrow, unless anything happens to him. And now what's all this about Wapping?"

Travers was most interested. He thought Wharton was dead right about Johnson's having tried to get rid of prints by burning down the shack.

"Funny how all sorts of queer connecting links keep cropping up," he said, and blinked away as he polished his glasses. "Mind you, one has to be careful about attaching too much importance to coincidence, but take the matter of burnings—"

Then suddenly Travers came to a full stop. For a moment he was tempted to thrust upon Wharton a discussion of the clue of the Unconsidered Man— and then he thought better of it. He would hint obscurely at it, and if Wharton should see the point, then he would put all his own cards on the table.

"Porburgh, for instance," he said. "There a villa was burned down for the purpose, one imagines, of wiping out clues." As one last salve to conscience he put the question direct. "That was so, wasn't it?"

"That's right," Wharton said. "Watts reckoned he burnt enough stuff to have given him another seven years."

"Yes," said Travers, and shook his head. "And a certain body was to be burnt in a bonfire, so as to conceal certain things. Now we have Johnson burning the shack so that you could never prove he'd been in lodgings at all—though that's a fairly elaborate precaution to be taken by one so hard-boiled as Johnson, who oughtn't to trouble a hoot whether you think him a liar or not."

"Yes," said Wharton. "There has been a lot of burning. We might do worse than look into it. Now, if you'll pardon me, I'll run my eye over these papers."

But Travers sat thinking, not about the burnings, but about the one case—or maybe two—when nothing had been burnt. There had been that man at Bournemouth—Luke most likely—who had fallen under suspicion and then left, but he had not burnt down his house. Then there had been the two Garrod's Heath affairs that had come to a sudden end....

"This is extraordinary," Wharton was saying. "Perfectly amazing." He pushed the papers aside and was clicking his tongue exasperatedly. "This case is tying me in knots Listen to this, for instance. You knew of course that we'd telegraphed Luke's prints across the Atlantic. Well, we decided at the same time to send the bonfire ones as well, Guy Fawkes's, that is— and what do you think's happened? Neither New York nor Canada knows a thing about Luke. New York doesn't know Guy Fawkes's, but Guy Fawkes was thought to have been in *Canada* not long after that silver job at Garrod's Heath—which fits— and was wanted afterwards on suspicion of being concerned in a job out there, when they had his prints. He was thought to have slipped over the border into the States and there he was lost. Now what are you going to make of all that?"

Travers shook his head, not because he had no ideas, but because of too many.

"Guy Fawkes and Luke," Wharton said. "Men with no great physical resemblances and yet not too unlike, and of the same age. And connected through Garrod's Heath. Near enough alike to have deceived me into thinking they might be the same."

"But how connected through Garrod's Heath?"

"By the old Porburgh Case," Wharton said. "It's vague but it's always there. Luke, Johnson and Carberry; Carberry lured to Garrod's Heath and a dead man found there whose hand killed Carberry. By every rule of sense it ought to have been Johnson who killed him, but we don't want to rake up that."

Then Travers's long legs all at once drew in and he was bolt upright in the chair, but Wharton, frowning away, was noticing nothing. Travers leaned back with closed eyes. He thought of a certain room that was used as a workroom; he remembered a garden rockery and linoleum on a summer-house floor.

"George?"

"Yes?" said Wharton, suddenly becoming aware of Travers again.

"There's a certain woman I'd like to interview—"

The phone went and Wharton grabbed the receiver.

"Put him through," he said, and, "Oh, yes, Lewis. . . . But you can't. Inspector Norris is probably now with the county surveyor, on the way to viewing that excavation job we're doing to-morrow. There won't be a phone there. . . . In three minutes' time? Certainly. Bring him up. . . . Good-bye."

"Lewis has got hold of something queer," Wharton said. "He sounded a bit too excited to me." He frowned in thought. "He knew Norris was on that excavation job. . . . I see it though. He's got hold of something to do with the Garrod's Heath end."

"It's about time the Wimbeck Street end produced something," Travers said. Then he smiled queerly: "Or perhaps a house has been burned down."

"A house?" Wharton rounded on him. "What on earth makes you imagine that?"

"Curiosity," Travers said. "If a house has not been burned down, then I'd like to slip over to Garrod's Heath with your permission."

There were steps outside the door. A quick tap came and to Wharton's holler Lewis came in, and with him a plain clothes sergeant.

"Sergeant Johns, sir. I thought you'd better hear his story from him, sir. I've taken the liberty of phoning Garrod's Heath."

Wharton nodded, wondering quite what Lewis meant.

"Well, sergeant, what is it?"

"I was outside the Underground at Farringdon Street this morning, sir, round about half-past nine when I picked up Tubby Hughes, though he didn't see me—"

"Tubby Hughes," said Wharton, and gave a dry smile. The sergeant smiled too. Tubby, Travers decided, was evidently a character.

"I got on his tail, sir, and saw him take a ticket and go down. I went by the stairs and picked him up on the platform, and straightway as soon as a train came in he didn't take it but he made for the lift again with the crowd. I knew his game so I nipped back too and got in the same load. Wedged in like sardines, we were, and sure enough I spotted Tubby up to the game. I couldn't see just who he was frisking, but I thought it was an old gentleman he was wedged against, so the very minute the gates opened I darted forward and I had my hand on Tubby by the time he was at the curb.

"'Come on, Tubby, hand it over,' I said.

"Then he looked the innocent—you know him, sir—and started asking what I meant and all that, only I noticed he kept moving away. Right against a sand-box, he was, and he'd dropped a wallet down nice and handy to pick up again. So I slipped a bracelet on him, sir, seeing I was single-handed and not being actually on duty, and I just caught sight of that old gentleman who he'd been against, going down towards Clerkenwell, so I called to the newspaper man outside the station to run and fetch him back. While he went, sir, I had a squint inside that wallet and there were three or four of the finest bits of stuff inside you ever see. A ring with a step-cut emerald I reckoned was worth a few hundreds.

"Well, sir, the gentleman was caught up by the man and he came back. A little inoffensive old chap he was, and I showed him the wallet—just the outside, that is.

"'This yours, sir?' I said.

"He had a look at it and then he had a look at me, and I don't know how it was, sir, but I knew there was something fishy going on.

"'Why'd you ask me?' he said, as if he was sort of feeling his way.

"'Well, sir,' I said, 'our friend here took it from someone and you were the one he was against, so I reckoned it might be yours.'

"Tubby started swearing then how he never knew a thing about it, but the gentleman reckoned it was his and all he'd been wondering was how I'd come to have it.

"'Right, sir,' I said, 'I'll just trouble you to come along with me as far as the station, where we'll take particulars and then you can take your wallet, and that'll be all for the present. Name, sir?' I asked.

"'Ropeling,' he said, pat as pie. 'Frederick Ropeling. I'm a diamond merchant in Hatton Garden.'

"'That's all right, sir,' I said. 'We'll just walk along to Clerkenwell Road and there we are.'"

Then the sergeant smiled ruefully.

"That's where I lose him, sir—"

"What, Tubby?"

"No, sir—the old gentleman. I had hold of Tubby's bracelet and he wasn't coming along any too easy, and soon as we got to the corner he was arguing the toss and people started crowding round, and when I looked for the old gentleman, he'd gone. Soon as I got a chance, sir, I had half a dozen men after him and I reported here direct."

"You looked up the Hatton Garden end?"

"How could I, sir?" the sergeant said. "There wasn't an address. But this is what made me ask his name, sir, and why I didn't let him lay his hands on that wallet. Half a dozen cards were in it, sir, like this one."

MR. JAMES MATHISON
The Rockery,
Garrod's Heath.

CHAPTER XIV
UNDERGROUND WAY

WHARTON SPRANG to his feet. The visiting card flew towards Travers, who reached for it.

"What was that you said about ringing Garrod's Heath, Lewis?"

"Soon as I saw the address and the name, sir, I wanted to report to Inspector Norris as he was that way—"

"Hurry up, hurry up!"

"Well, sir, after I spoke to you I took a chance and got hold of Garrod's Heath and told them to watch out for Mathison and detain him, whatever he said."

"Good," said Wharton tersely. "But he's had an hour and a half's clear start. Get out there on a motor-bike yourself and try to pick up Inspector Norris on the way. I'll be along later. If Mathison's detained, keep him there. I'll ring up about that."

He peered till the door closed, then whipped round on the sergeant.

"Where's the wallet now?"

"Downstairs, sir."

Wharton reached for a phone and pressed the buzzer. The wallet was to be sent up, and any lists of missing objects from the Garrod's Heath burglaries. Then he got Records and was asking for Luke's prints and a man.

"All right, sergeant," he said. "You can stand by for a bit. That was good work of yours and I shan't forget it."

"We can't get away for a minute or two," he said to Travers. "We've got to make sure about one or two things."

"My car is outside," Travers told him. "We can make up for lost time."

Wharton remembered something then. "What was that you were saying about interviewing some woman? Mrs. Solomon Frisch, was it?"

Travers gave a diffident shake of the head.

"Mathison's housekeeper, or whoever looks after him." He smiled diffidently again. "Just a theory that seems to have worked out partly right—for once."

"You thought Mathison was Luke?"

"Well," said Travers, "I suppose that's what it amounted to. But I hadn't got to the point of certainty."

But Wharton was buzzing through to exchange.

"Get me Garrod's Heath station." His hand went over the phone. "Just thought of Ropeling. Don't know where he comes in—" Then his call was through.

"That Garrod's Heath? . . . Where's Inspector Mott? . . . I see. Well, note this as urgent. An eye is to be kept on Mr. Ropeling. I'll spell the name. . . . Oh, you know who I mean . . . that's it . . . . Most confidential. . . . Yes, good-bye." "Well, that's got that end fixed," he said to Travers. "Ropeling may be a relation of his and he may not. We're not taking any chances."

Then people began coming in. Wharton made a start with the wallet when he had fixed his gloves. There were two rings and a pair of ear-rings. Then came something the sergeant had missed—a small necklace of pearls about the size of a Woolworth string. The wallet and the rest of the contents were flicked over to the print man.

Wharton had started his earning life in a jeweller's shop and the Yard knew him for an expert. Now from that drawer where Travers had often expected even a rabbit or a steak-and-kidney pudding to be concealed, so chock-full was it with surprises, he brought out a jeweller's glass, a diamond gauge and a pearl gauge. Inside five minutes he had finished.

"Trade valuation about eleven hundred quid," he said. "I thought the pearls might be cultured, but they aren't. Now the lists."

It was the list of valuables stolen on the vital Tuesday night in which he was most interested, and he shook his head when he drew a blank. The next attempt was a winner.

"Here we are. A fortnight previous, to the very day. Philip Archment—that'd be the multiple-shop man." He mumbled away to himself as he made a check, then got to his feet.

"What about prints? Find a Luke one?"

The man's grin gave the answer.

"Right," said Wharton. "Take over everything and make a report. Not that we hadn't enough to hold Mathison by already. Pity we couldn't have picked up the Clerkenwell fence he was selling this little lot to."

At once he was buzzing through again for Garrod's Heath, and when the call came was hanging up almost at once.

"Nothing from there yet," he said, "so if you're ready we'll go."

Wharton bothered Travers with no talk till the main traffic was left behind and the Rolls was in the comparative straight of the Uxbridge Road.

"How'd you get on to Mathison?" he asked then.

"Can't say yet," Travers told him. "It's a line of reasoning that isn't complete. I'll know more when we find out if Mathison tried to burn down his house before he left just now."

"You don't think they've got him then?"

"I'm afraid you don't think it either," Travers said dryly. "Didn't you say that Garrod's Heath had no news?"

Wharton grunted, then gave a little chuckle. He was in his best humour for days.

"What was it then? One of your short cuts?"

"In a way," Travers said. "Perhaps I'll explain, complete or not."

The lights turned to green and he moved the car on.

"We were talking about the number of burnings," he said. "Let's suppose that Mathison didn't burn his house down, and the chances are very much that he didn't; firstly because if the house were now on fire you'd have been told so when you rang

Garrod's Heath up, and secondly because Mathison hadn't a second to spare when he got back there this morning. Which brings us to the case of X— the Unknown Man."

"Ah!" said Wharton, and shot him a look.

"The Unconsidered Man would be a better title," Travers was going on. "It'll pass the time away if I spin it all out somewhat. Tell me, for instance, what was the speciality of Luke—Mathison, if you like—in robberies?"

"Jewels and silver, by his record."

"So I gathered," Travers said. "Now go back to what Watts told us. He said that the night Luke was caught at Carberry's house, Luke's own house was burnt down, and in order to destroy certain evidence—proceeds of robberies he meant—that would otherwise have added considerably to his sentence. But why burn jewels and small pieces of rare silver? They're things you can hide anywhere. If Luke hadn't disposed of them, he could have hidden them somewhere where he could pick them up later. He knew the police would be in his house if he was ever caught."

"But he'd always left an incendiary mine laid!"

"You're obscuring the issue," Travers said. "You never believed surely that whenever Luke went out on a job he used to leave a pile of shavings and a burning candle in case he weren't home at a certain time; in case he were caught, in other words? You don't believe that?"

"And what if I don't?"

Travers smiled. "Well, you don't—and neither do I."

"Then why was the house burnt down, and how?"

"That's where the argument began," Travers said. "We'll leave Porburgh and go on to the next place in order of time, namely Bournemouth. When the burglar left there, the house wasn't burnt down. And why? Well, as I worked it out it was because the burglar was only under suspicion. He'd saved himself by an alibi but he was safe, and so he had plenty of time to rid the house of every print he'd left in it."

Wharton stared. "I see. So that's why the Porburgh house was burned."

"Exactly," said Travers. "That affair of Johnson's this morning suggested it to me in one way. A confederate of Luke's—and he was the Unknown Man Watts first told us about—burnt the house down that night at Porburgh as soon as he knew Luke was caught. In that way the confederate of Luke's stopped the police from ever finding *his own prints.*"

"I've got you," Wharton said, and clicked his tongue exasperatedly. "The man who burned down the Porburgh house was your X—the Unknown."

"The Unconsidered Man," Travers said. "The man we didn't take into consideration."

A traffic area was passed and he shot the car on. Wharton sat thinking things over.

"I haven't got all of it," he all at once said, "but I'm beginning to see."

Travers nodded. He had wanted Wharton to find the rest for himself.

"You've got it all right I expect, George. The confederate took everything of value he could carry from the house and then set fire to it to obliterate his own prints. Luke was inside for his spell of sentence, and when he came out X had set up house in Bournemouth, where Luke joined him. In the interval he had probably lived on the proceeds of the Porburgh series of burglaries."

The car was drawing near that single-traffic stretch and the road was clear. The two kept an eye out for Norris but he must have gone long since, for there was no sign of a soul way back where the excavations would begin. Then Travers let the car streak on and in a minute or two was drawing up at the curb outside The Rockery. A constable was on duty at the gate.

"The inspector's at the station, sir," he told Wharton. "I was to give you word."

"Right," said Wharton. "Anyone inside there?"

But the house was locked and Inspector Mott had the key. Wharton and Travers pushed on to the station. Mott and Lewis were out but Norris gave the news.

Mathison had come back to Garrod's Heath—and apparently all the way in a taxi. He had sent away the woman who did day work in the house on the plea that he was called away urgently for a few days.

"Got her address?" asked Wharton, and Norris handed it over.

Then all that had been seen of Mathison was the taxi outside Ropeling's house. Mott had questioned Ropeling, who said the call was a purely private one to do with church business. Wharton smiled sardonically.

"Where's Inspector Mott?"

"Gone to put a man on Ropeling's tail, as you asked," Norris said.

"And Lewis?"

"He's off on his motor-bike to try and pick up the route the taxi took. I've got through to the Yard for a general inquiry of all taxi ranks."

"Right," said Wharton. "Give me the key of the house and Mr. Travers and I will go along. If nothing happens inside the next quarter of an hour, get out a description of Mathison ready for circularising—with beard and without."

Travers had a word with the station sergeant who showed where Mathison's woman lived.

"Mind if we go and have a quick word with her first?" asked Travers.

Wharton was agreeable, and Travers moved the car off. He proposed, with Wharton's permission, to do the brief questioning. And the woman turned out to be chatty enough, though somewhat deaf.

"He had you out of the house quickly, did he?" Travers asked.

"Yes, he did, sir. In a rare hurry, he was."

"And did you have your own key?"

"No, sir. I used to be let in in the mornings."

"So I guessed," said Travers. "And Mr. Mathison had a special workroom, did he?"

"Oh, yes, sir. I never was allowed to go in there. Something special he was doing, he said, and I might have gone and broken something. Kept locked it always was."

"You had a yearly holiday? A free holiday, I mean?"

She shook her head dubiously. "No, sir. Not a holiday at all. Not that I wanted one."

"And how long were you with Mr. Mathison?"

"Nearly five years now, sir."

"Ever away at all?"

Her face lighted. "Ah, yes, sir, I remember now. My daughter hadn't been very well and I happened to mention it, so he fairly made me go, sir. Paid my fare and all. A fortnight I was away altogether and he paid my wages same as if I'd been here. A good one he was for things like that."

"I expect he was," Travers told her. "And when you came back you had a surprise?"

She stared.

"Didn't you come back and find that Mr. Mathison had made that fine new rockery and changed the name of the house?"

"Why, yes, of course, sir. How silly of me."

Travers smiled. "You just happened to forget, that's all. But did Mr. Mathison ever mention to you any relatives?"

She shook her head again. "No, sir. The poor gentleman was alone in the world; neither chick nor child as the saying is. He used to say sometimes he wondered what he'd do with his little bit of money."

Travers slipped her a half-crown, and with remembrances of the Limerick Crown had a good look at it before he gave it her.

"I feel easier now than I did, George," he said. "We'll drive slowly and I'll explain things to you before we get there."

"Who told you the name of the house had been changed?"

"I had to guess that much," Travers said. "The chances were a hundred to one on it. But do you mind if we go on from Bournemouth where we left Luke and X? They left Bournemouth, as we said, and Luke established himself here at Garrod's Heath, and after a time the two began the same old game. They had two affairs successful enough to keep them in clover for a bit and

X left for America to dispose of the silver. He got involved in some trouble with the Canadian authorities and after some time came back here. I don't know how he overcame the difficulty of getting out of the States —the difficulty of his papers, I mean but apparently he did. Perhaps he slipped back into Canada again for his getaway. Still, he got back here and then funds ran out and a new series of burglaries began. They continued up to the night when X was killed."

"I get you so far," said Wharton, and then Travers was drawing the car up at the curb again.

"The hardest part is just coming," Travers told him. "I don't mind saying I'd never have had the nerve to try it out if that woman hadn't told us what she did. Let's go to the side gate first. Sorry to be so frightfully mysterious.

"This is a newer gate than the front one," he said. "It must have been made to fit in with the rockery and at the same time. Notice those tall shrubs that mask all the view? Anyone coming from the summer-house along that crazy-paving path would be hidden from everywhere. The whole garden's hidden for that matter. No overlooking by neighbours, what with the trees and that vacant plot of land." He opened the gate. "Let's go along to the summer-house, shall we?"

But long before they reached it he was fumbling away at his glasses.

"The linoleum," he was saying, and hooked his glasses on again as they looked down at it on the summer-house floor. Then he smiled.

"See that, George? It isn't laid in one piece, though it must have been bought in one convenient roll. It's been cut shortways into three pieces. This one's tacked down. . . . So's this. . . . This one isn't. Lend the your knife, will you?"

It was not that third strip of linoleum that worried him, for it came away as he lifted it. It was the crack in the flooring at which he began prising. A square space all at once lifted slightly, and he hooked his fingers under and laid it back. It was hinged, and from the floor joist in the empty space beneath it went a ladder or a set of steps.

"My God!" said Wharton. "What is it? A cave or what?"

"There's a torch in the car pocket," Travers said. "If you'd be so good as—"

But Wharton had gone off like a streak. He came back to find Travers emerging from the hole.

"There's just room to move and no more," Travers said, "but it's all shored up."

"Let me try it," Wharton said. "My legs are shorter than yours."

He got down with the torch and Travers never lost the sound of him. There was a noise as if he were kicking woodwork or a door, and then he was coming back. Travers lent him a hand out.

"Let's get on inside," Wharton said impatiently. "There's a door somewhere under that wall. It's nailed up or something, and I can't break it down."

"Just a minute," Travers told him. "Let's get the lie of the land. The door will lead into that workroom which was always kept locked. That was the room the burglar tried to enter that Tuesday night. After Luke lost his confederate—"

He stopped suddenly and his fingers went to his glasses. Then his hand grasped Wharton's arm.

"Listen to this, George. The door wasn't locked on the Tuesday night!"

"Oh, yes, it was," Wharton said. "Didn't Ropeling say he had the door *burst* open in a jiffy?"

"You're sure?"

"Of course I'm sure; didn't I hear him say so?"

Travers smiled weakly. "That gave me a scare. But why weren't the curtains drawn?"

"Ask me another," Wharton said.

"Maybe that was a bit of carelessness," Travers said. "All the better in a way too. It may have helped to scare Mathison into realizing everything and making a bolt—that and our inspection of the vacant plot, and how we got him to try to identify Johnson. But don't be in a hurry, George. Let's see what happened that Tuesday night. Mathison, alias Luke, had Ropeling in to keep him company and provide an alibi—"

"You think that's all Ropeling had to do with it?"

"I don't know," Travers said. "But let's give Ropeling temporary credit for being a dupe. While the cribbage game was on, X slipped out through the underground passage. Wait a minute though. He may have been out already, which would account for the curtains not having been drawn. X did the burglary of the Tuesday night, but he was late and Mathison got Ropeling to stay on. But X never returned and I'll wager that Mathison took immediate steps to find out by some obscure questions about burglars whether the police had got him.

But Wharton had been jotting down quick notes.

"I'm none too clear about certain things," he said. "What exactly is all this rockery business?"

"The rockery?" Travers smiled. "While the woman was away, Luke, *alias* Mathison, and X made the underground passage. I expect they had a ton or two of earth carted here, but they had to do something with what they excavated, and, as the crooner would put it, that's how the rockery was born."

"Yes," said Wharton. "I've got it. They made the summer-house and path and gate and everything at the same time. But how do you explain the burglary? The workroom burglary of the Tuesday night?"

Travers shook his head. "I can't, George. It beats me absolutely. Unless—"

"Unless what?"

"Unless it was all a fake by Mathison and Ropeling."

"Ah!" said Wharton, and gave a triumphant leer. "Now you're coming to it. And you've come to my third question. Who killed X?"

Travers shook his head again. Wharton sniffed contemptuously.

"Isn't the answer the same? Just another fake by the same two?"

He whipped round as voices were heard. The front gate opened and Norris came in.

"Anything new?" asked Wharton, going to meet him.

"Something suspicious about Ropeling," Norris said. "That's all there is. What I was wondering was if I'd better rush this Mathison description to town before you'd heard about Ropeling or after."

"Get it off at once," Wharton told him. "Add—WANTED FOR MURDER."

Then he answered the unspoken question.

"Yes, for the murder of X—on the night of Tuesday, November the third. Now what's this about Ropeling?"

CHAPTER XV
THE LIMERICK CROWN

"He slipped out of the house," Norris said. "Mott was doing that job I told you about, and he followed him because Ropeling was taking a cautionary look or two down the road. Then he slipped round the back way by the cinema and down a side path to the station. A train was due in three minutes but Mott just had time to nip up and send his man down instead. This chap followed Ropeling, and instead of Ropeling going to town as he expected, he saw him get out at Westgrove North. He went straight to the post-office and used a public call-box, and Mott's man couldn't get near enough to hear a thing. Then he came out and sauntered round for a bit, and when the phone message reached us he was on a Garrod's Heath bus."

Wharton rubbed his chin. "I see the game. If Ropeling had phoned from here, we might have traced it. So he went along to Westgrove North where the automatic system begins, and he gave Mathison the news from there."

"That's how I worked it out, sir," Norris said. "What about you seeing him? I can have him along as soon as the bus gets in."

"Oh, no, no," said Wharton. "Let him have his head. The last thing we want to do is to let him think we're on his tail." He nodded. "You get a couple of our own men along here and put them on the job. Ropeling's the apple of our eye. He's the one who's going to lead us to Mathison."

Norris turned to go. Wharton called him back.

"Just a minute, Norris. Let's have a peep in the bathroom."

He unlocked the front door and the three sniffed the comfortable frowstiness. Norris switched on the light and then a landing could be seen at the head of the hall stairs. Wharton mounted with the others at his heels, and there was no need to open doors for the bath-room door was open and a towel lay just inside. Wharton peered round.

"He's been in here evidently. In a bit of a hurry too."

One look at the wash-basin and he was pointing to grey hairs among the lather.

"All right, Norris. You can get that description away now. He couldn't have shaved unless he'd trimmed that beard of his off first. But leave out that bit about murder. Just say—wanted. We don't gain anything if we scare him into suicide. We've *got* to land him alive and learn the truth about Carberry." He made for the stairs again. "Now, Mr. Travers, we'll have a look at the underworld."

But he had a peep into the living-room first. A fire was still faintly glowing in the grate and it was as if the room had been for no more than a moment untenanted. The door that faced it was unlocked.

"He knew we'd smash it down," Wharton said. "And see this? Where he had it repaired after Ropeling burst it?" Then he gave one of his contemptuous chuckles. "I'll give them credit for one thing. They worked that fake pretty thoroughly."

A kitchen cupboard of cheap, unvarnished wood stood in the corner, but it was locked and the key gone. Wharton glanced round and his eye fell on the poker, and he had the door burst open in half a minute.

"Dear, dear, dear," he said. "Tinned foods, eh? And plenty of tinned milk. And a little oil-cooker. And a folded camp-bed. If we don't find a few of X's prints there, I'm a Dutchman."

He turned his back on the cupboard and surveyed the room, with its few horrors of pictures, its one easy chair and old-fashioned couch. His eyes fell to the floor.

"More of that linoleum. And where'd the door be? About here, wouldn't it?"

Once more a strip of linoleum went back. Wharton's knife and the poker hoisted the flap and there were the short steps and the underground door. Wharton got down and had a look round.

"I reckon they carried some handy little contrivance for lifting the two flaps," he said. "Doesn't matter about breaking in the door. We can do that any time. Wait a minute, though."

He was fumbling in his pockets and Travers heard a chuckle. A flash of the torch on the lock and a minute's fumbling, and the door was open. Another minute and he was coming up again.

"That's the advantage of being old-fashioned. I always carry a hair-pin or two for my pipe." He gave himself a nod of approbation. "Nothing down there so we might as well close up again. Then we'll go through the rooms. His bedroom first, don't you think so?"

They had spent an unproductive ten minutes there and were still at it, when Travers all at once left the job in hand and gave a shake of the head.

"You had some questions to ask me, George. Things you didn't quite follow. I wonder if I might do the same."

"Ask away, my dear fellow, ask away," said Wharton amply.

"Well, I can't quite follow why Mathison—I'll still call him that because Luke's rather confusing —why Mathison reported to the police that he'd seen a suspicious character round here. Surely it was to his interests to have as little to do with the police as possible. Suppose, for instance, there'd been a local Nosey Parker, like that chap Yawlings, who'd taken his prints just for fun."

Wharton gave a chuckle as he went on rummaging in the drawers. Travers was supplying his own answer.

"All I can think is that Mathison did see a man and was scared. He notified the police because he guessed it might mean they had him under observation for the local burglaries and the man was tailing him. He had to make certain of that."

Wharton chuckled again.

"All part of the fake, that's what it was. There never was a man. If anything suspicious turned up about the murder or the fake burglary he'd planned, then he had a red herring all ready for the police to follow up."

"Well, yes; that may be so," said Travers dubiously. "But a question in much the same context. First I'll preface it by a statement, so as to make things absolutely fair. On that Sunday morning when we were here, when I happened to mention to Mathison that blood had been found outside his side gate, he went yellow about the gills and fairly bolted back to the house. For that there might be all sorts of explanations, but we'll say for the moment that he knew we were on his track. But the question's this. Just why should Mathison want to kill X?"

"When thieves fall out," quoted Wharton tersely. "Mathison was sitting cushy here and maybe the other man had become a bit of an embarrassment. There're a dozen good reasons."

"I'll put some more cards on the table," went on Travers. "You and I want to arrive at the truth, not worst each other in argument. About Mathison again. Say he did the murder. Say he had only the vaguest apprehension that we had him under suspicion. Wouldn't he have bolted at once? If a man's suspected of murder he doesn't stand on the order of his going—he runs like hell. What I claim is that Mathison's actions since the vital Tuesday have been more consonant with suspicion of burglary than with suspicion of murder."

"Nothing here apparently," Wharton said with a wave of the hand. "The other rooms can come later, so let's try the living-room. And what was that argument about Mathison not thinking himself under suspicion for murder? If you ask me, his conduct was exactly what you might expect. Crippen lived with a body for a bit, didn't he? So did others. They knew as Mathison did that it wasn't wise to bolt too soon. And didn't Mathison tell you the first time you saw him that he was going away up North somewhere to a relative? Wasn't he preparing the ground gracefully?" He snorted. "He wasn't fool enough to bolt till he'd made sure." Then he gave a smile amusingly hypocritical in its touch of deprecation. "Mind you, I may be wrong. I probably am."

Already he was examining the drawers of the living-room desk. Travers shook a dubious head.

"Well, George, I'm sorry to be a nuisance but just when did Mathison kill X? Let's assume that Ropeling was merely a dupe of some sort. Even then I don't think we can get away from the fact that Ropeling was actually here from shortly after five o'clock that night till seven o'clock. Craig says that X was killed between six and seven, which is when Ropeling was in this very room."

"Out of your own mouth I'll answer that," Wharton said. "The times laid down by Sir Barnabas depended on the hour when X had his tea. It assumed that he had it at the normal time of his class—round about half-past five. But if he had his tea at four o'clock—say—then he might have been dead before Ropeling arrived. When Ropeling left, and Mathison knew he wouldn't come back, all that remained was to dismember the body and stick the comparatively harmless main part in the bonfire."

Travers had to smile. "You know all the answers, George. But just one last thing, and this time—Ropeling. Cast your mind back to the Wednesday afternoon when I first caught sight of him. He was running like a madman—which might have been acting and pretence. But when I saw him—and mind you, he hadn't the least idea my car was behind him—he was white all round the gills and scared stiff. That's something you can't pretend."

"Funny, isn't it?" said Wharton. "You're the world's champion theoriser—and a most useful one —and yet you can't find answers to your own questions. Assume Ropeling was aware that X had been killed. That wasn't to say he was expecting to find the body in the bonfire? And hacked about?"

"Very well," said Travers. "We'll leave it at that. But just one more question and it's absolutely the last. How was X killed, and how could Ropeling be involved?"

Wharton pursed his lips.

"Well, that's where you can lend a hand. Just try working on a theory something like this. The workroom window was broken in some way and Mathison pretended to be assailed by a burglar, who, of course, was X, and X got killed. Mathison said, 'He isn't dead, or if he is we must keep it dark. We'll say there was a burglary.'"

Wharton pursed his lips again, and waved an airy hand.

"Of course that's only the beginnings of a theory. But you think about it and I'll wager you make it all fit in like a jigsaw."

His look was so craftily hopeful that Travers had to smile.

"All right, George, I will. And in the meanwhile —what?"

"I shall carry on here," Wharton said. "You never know when I might drop on something to tell me where Mathison's gone to."

There was a knock at the front door. The two looked at each other.

"I shouldn't be surprised if it's Ropeling," Travers said.

Wharton's lips clamped together and he moved off. The door was opened and Travers was aware that it was not Ropeling but some message for himself. From Palmer, it turned out to be, and forwarded via the Yard. "A gentleman rang up about the missing coin and wanted to be spoken to at once."

"That's good news," said Wharton. "I'm as pleased as if it was my own. What're you going to do? Get back to town?"

"I think I'd better," Travers said. "But about yourself. You'll get home all right?"

"I mayn't be home at all to-night," Wharton said, and followed Travers to the door to see him off. "And if anything happens here I'll ring you up. And don't forget that little theory we were talking about."

But Travers had no intention of working out a theory so untenable and indeed fantastic. Though Wharton would often boast to the same effect, it was he who could do the reading like a book. Wharton was still flummoxed and casting about for a chance catch, which was the reason his answers had paradoxically come so pat. And which was also why Travers himself had not had the heart to show the flaws in the foundations of Wharton's brave new structure.

Yes, those flaws had been plain. X had not been killed before the arrival of Ropeling, and for a reason which only Wharton's over-eagerness or prejudice could have missed. For if X lay dead in the house while Mathison and Ropeling played crib, *then who did the burglary that took place that same night between six-twenty and seven*? And if Mathison killed X, it must have been for the purpose of obtaining the dead hand. And therefore Mathison killed Carberry. And that, since his description was utterly unlike that of the mysterious and elusive J. Scott, was grotesquely absurd.

Night had long since fallen when Travers reached the flat. Palmer said the message had been wrongly taken, and the phone had been bad. What had happened was that someone had rung up asking for a Mr. Ludovic Travers. Palmer said he was out and explained himself. Then the voice said that the business was about a missing coin, and would Mr. Travers ring up Dockway 25.

"Dockway," said Travers. "That's right down the river beyond the Pool. How on earth did the coin get there?"

While Palmer was making a belated cup of tea he dialled Dockway 25. An official-sounding voice was heard.

"Yes, who's speaking please?"

Travers explained.

"Just wait a minute, Mr. Travers, will you?"

"Who are you exactly?" Travers put in.

"Just a minute, sir," the voice said suavely and then there was silence. A minute, and a new voice spoke.

"Are you there, Mr. Travers? This is Inspector Acton speaking, from Headquarters Riverside Police, Dockway. About that missing coin of yours. Could you come along and inspect it?"

"Now, you mean?"

"Well, sir, if it'd be convenient."

"Inside the hour then," said Travers. "But would you mind giving me some idea how you acquired it?"

"Found on a body taken from the river this morning, sir."

"Oh," said Travers blankly, and spoke into the phone again only to find it was dead.

Palmer came in with tea. He agreed with Travers that it was a most unexpected finding. Travers must have dropped the coin and some down-and-out had picked it up and found it of no immediately realisable value. Travers, as he munched his cake, made quite a tragedy out of it—some poor devil at his last extremity, the finding of the coin and the sudden joy, the failure to pass it and the new despair, and then the last watery leap to end it all.

But everything was to turn out vastly different from those cosy imaginings. The night was raw for one thing, and the drive through dim-lit, squalid, dockside streets, with the road often missed and long delays. There was the unpretentiousness of the station so that when he entered it he was afraid he had come to the wrong place. Then his name was taken with no sign of recognition and there was a long wait.

"Mr. Ludovic Travers?" he was asked at last.

The speaker was the Inspector Acton who had spoken over the phone, and in the presence of the station-sergeant he produced the coin.

"That your coin, sir?"

Travers needed only the briefest look.

"That's it," he said, and explained just why.

"Funny how we found it at all," the inspector said. "We might have dropped it ourselves and nobody ever found it. Only there was something peculiar about the one that had it. To cut a long story short, sir, it was in his boot."

"Good Lord," said Travers. "How on earth did it get there?"

"Now you're asking, sir," the inspector said. "Seeing it was in his boot, though, we shouldn't be far out if we said he was trying to hide it. And seeing he was trying to hide it, I reckon he stole it."

"That's interesting," Travers said. "But where should he steal it from?"

"Now you've got me, sir. From some other poor devil who'd picked it up, most likely. From his pocket in a doss-house."

There was something placidly funereal about the room, and the inspector, like an undertaker, consulting his book of records—or was it accounts?

"Lost by you on the evening of the fourth of November. That correct, sir?"

"That's when I missed it," Travers said.

The inspector rubbed his chin. "That'd be about when he got hold of it. I should say he'd been in the best part of a week when we pulled him out. Not that you can always tell to a day. He might have got caught up or something. Still, we'll know all about that after the P.M., which is coming off now. And about this coin, sir, it'll have to stay here till after the inquest to-morrow morning, when you can have it on signing the book. Just wait a minute, sir, and we'll pop it in this envelope and seal it and then it can go in the safe."

The formalities were complied with and Travers rose to go.

"Just one more minute, sir," the inspector said. "We'd like you to have a look at him to see if you can identify him."

Travers was horrified. "You mean, the—"

"That's it, sir. The one we found it on. This way, sir, and mind these three steps down."

From a cold passage Travers stepped down to a room that had something sinister in its icy chill. Something lay on a table, covered with a sheet.

"This is the first we've had for two days," the inspector said, and drew the sheet back as far as the shoulders. "You just take a peep at him and tell us if you've ever seen him before."

Travers peeped. The grey face looked old and worn and tired. It was clean-shaven but for the day or so's stubble of beard, and the staring eyes were a brown. A biggish man he must have been, and his hair a badger-grey.

Travers shook his head.

"Never clapped eyes on him in my life—at least to my knowledge."

"That's all right then, sir. You won't be wanted in the morning." He was about to throw back the sheet and then stayed his hand. His fingers closed on the hair of the head and drew it forward, and Travers, watching against his will, saw the discolouration at the back of the skull.

"That's the contusion that's causing all the trouble, sir," the inspector told him confidentially, and let the head fall again. "That's what they'll be after in a few minutes."

But Travers was moving away. There was the sound of the sheet as the inspector flicked it back, and then his cheerful voice.

"Not that you can always tell, sir. I've had 'em with the tops of their skulls regular stove in where they've fallen on something. . . . Mind the three steps, sir."

In two minutes Travers was in the car again and in some new, known world that was somehow warm and kindly. But he was glad when the mean streets had gone and the nearness of the river, and the thought of the grey, cold face. Then when he reached the flat he was all at once desperately tired. The case could look after itself and for one evening he would put it behind him.

"Any message for me?" he asked Palmer.

"One from Mr. Wharton, sir. I've written it down."

Travers made for it at once. But nothing had happened. All Wharton wanted to know was if Mr. Travers would care to accompany Norris in the morning to the excavation of the trench and the possible exhumation of the head, clothes and hand of X.

"Sufficient unto to-morrow are the horrors thereof," Travers said. "Which means, tell Superintendent Wharton, if he rings again, that I'll be seeing him in the morning. And if anyone rings or calls, I'm out."

CHAPTER XVI
TRAVERS DISCOVERS

Travers had just sat down to breakfast when Wharton rang him up. He was going to Garrod's Heath some time during the morning, he said, and he wondered what Travers would be doing.

"I don't think I'll go to the digging," Travers told him, "but I'd like to know what happens, if anything does."

"You're too squeamish," Wharton said. "If we find anything there'll be nothing unpleasant. That cold clay in the bottom of that trench will have been like a refrigerator. Still, you come along when you feel like it."

"Anything happened?" Travers asked.

"Not a thing," said Wharton. "Ropeling hasn't stirred out of the house except on his usual business. I'm going down there myself to finish searching the house. By the way, our friend Johnson's due out this morning all being well. He's been a bit broody, they tell me."

Travers made inquiring noises.

"Sort of sullen," Wharton explained. "You know, as if he had something on his mind. He's got a screw loose somewhere, that chap, I'll lay a ten-pun note."

"You're going to keep him watched?"

"Oh, yes," said Wharton, somewhat too casually. "I reckon he'll be back at his old job though. As soon as he is we're having Frisch identify him. That'll give us a hold-on for arson if we want it."

"Do you think he recognised Mathison?"

"Don't know," Wharton said. "I've been wondering about that myself. I don't see why he should have done; the old boy had made a good hand of disguising himself. And I'll lay a fiver Mathison didn't recognise him."

"You see," Travers said, "if Johnson did recognise Mathison, that might account for the flop. It'd also explain why, when Johnson came round, he began babbling about Luke."

"I know," Wharton told him. "I've been thinking all that out. But we're up against the fact that Mathison had gone by and Ropeling was coming, when Johnson did his flop. You there? Something I knew I wanted to ask you. Have you given any thought to that theory I put to you?"

"It was rather vague, you see," prevaricated Travers. "It'll take a good deal of working out." Wharton admitted that that was certainly so, added that he would be seeing Travers later, and rang off.

Travers finished his meal in peace, glanced through the papers and supposed to Palmer that he might as well be moving on to the Yard. Then the phone went again.

"Sounds like the gentleman who called you yesterday about the coin, sir," Palmer whispered across. Travers took the receiver.

"Yes, Travers speaking."

It was the official voice of the station-sergeant, and a request to stand by for a minute. Then came Acton. Would Mr. Travers, as a great favour, slip along to Dockway for a few minutes.

"Certainly, if it's urgent," Travers said, with a masterly reticence. But the details, for which the *if* had subtly angled, were not forthcoming.

"Thank you, sir. At about ten this morning would suit us best."

Travers was uneasy. That obscure affair of the drowned derelict looked like cutting across the day's programme. Some musty regulations of law might compel attendance at the inquest which Acton had mentioned, and might involve hanging about in that unsavoury Dockway neighbourhood for the best part of the day. The mention of a few minutes was merely a kind of trap to get him there. And then Travers thought of Wharton, a word from whom might mean quick release. But Wharton, when he rang, had just left the Yard.

It was then well after nine and Travers had to push the car on to reach Dockway in time. As he drew the car in below the steps that led to the tiny pier where the station stood, he saw a man whom he vaguely recognised. Then he knew him for Chief-Inspector Pettingford. Pettingford thrust out a hand and smiled at the sight of him.

"Been waiting for you, sir. How are you?"

"Still bearing my burdens," said Travers. "But what brings the great ones of the earth down?"

"You will have your little joke, sir," he said. "But come along in out of the cold. There's a nice fire in the room here."

They had the little room to themselves. Pettingford's face took on an official look as soon as Travers was seated.

"The fact of the matter is, sir, I'm down here for murder."

"Really?" said Travers politely. Then he stared. "Not that poor devil—"

"That's him, sir. The one you saw last night. Which is why we've dragged you over here, just to see if there's any little thing you remember which might help. Now about that coin, sir. Would you mind telling me exactly when you last had it, and how you think you came to lose it?"

"I was in Superintendent Wharton's room at the Yard," Travers began.

"Oh, yes, sir. You're in on that big job."

"Well, I wasn't then," Travers said. "But we happened to be talking about things and I'd given him the coin—a rather valuable one—to have a look at. He gave it back to me but I was most absent-minded at the time, so instead of slipping it into this waistcoat pocket here, I must have missed the opening. What happened then must have been that the coin fell in the turn-ups of my trousers, and when I left the Yard it must have rolled out."

Pettingford was ignorant of Travers's powers as a theoriser, and he nodded approvingly.

"You bet your life that's what happened, sir. That was on the Wednesday, wasn't it, sir, and a rare foggy night it was."

"That's right," said Travers. "The night of the Wimbeck Street murder."

"Now there's a funny affair," Pettingford said, hoping no doubt that Travers had some private information to impart. But none was forthcoming and he heaved a sigh.

"But to get on, sir. According to the doctor—and I don't mind telling you, sir, they're specialists down here about drownings—this man was in the water since the Wednesday night or the Thursday morning. In other words, sir, he acquired that coin of yours between the time you left the Yard and the following morning. Now, sir, a very important question. Was there any reason to suppose that the man would recognise the coin as valuable?"

Travers thought hard for a good minute.

"I'll give you the facts and then you can answer the question for yourself. Everything depends on the man. There are men—

specialists and collectors—who would recognise the coin as the rare Limerick Crown—"

"Pardon me, sir, but it's only the size of a half-crown."

"Exactly," said Travers. "Take the term for a collectors' one if you like. But as I was saying, if your man was a down-and-out specialist or collector or man of wide literary or artistic interests, then when he picked up the coin he might reasonably have secreted it in his boot, knowing he had something which, though it was worth fifty pounds or more might still be very hard to explain away if he were seen with it."

It was Pettingford's turn to think.

"I get you, sir," he said at last. "And I can answer the question. This man's hands aren't the sort you'd find on a scholar or a gentleman like you mean. Therefore I reckon he didn't know the value of what he picked up." He gave a shake of the head. "That's beginning to complicate things still more. Unless it's as Acton thinks. He stole the coin from someone else and slipped it into his boot. One thing's certain. He wasn't killed because he had it, or else whoever killed him would have gone over every inch of him, boots and all."

Ludovic Travers, most modest of men, was wholly unaware of the reputation that was his in the inner circles of the Yard. Pettingford, it would otherwise have been clear, had brought him there to pick his brains. Travers proceeded to make things easy.

"You talked about killing. Do I gather that the post-mortem proved he was murdered?"

Pettingford glanced up at the clock.

"We've got plenty of time yet, sir, and I'll tell you all about it. I reckon it's the most peculiar affair I've ever had anything to do with, and that coin of yours only complicates it still more. But about the post-mortem. It established that he didn't die from drowning. There were no signs of asphyxia, as we put it."

"In other words he was hit on the head and his body was thrown into the water."

"Wait a minute, sir." Pettingford wished to control the reins himself. "Because there weren't any signs of asphyxia, that doesn't prove he was killed. We've had cases here—a good few of them—where people have hit their heads in falling, and then gone into the water. A man might fall from a rigging or a pier, hit his head and kill himself and then be in the water."

"Really," said Travers, with the most courteous display of ignorance. "But it would have to be a remarkably vital blow to kill a man stone dead before the body in the course of the next second or so hit the water."

"I grant you, sir, but it's happened." Then he wagged a mysterious finger. "But you haven't heard half yet. All we've said so far is that we know he was dead before his body entered the water—and that there aren't any marks of a struggle on him. But what about this, sir? *After he was dead, he was shaved.*"

"Good Lord!"

"Yes, sir; the post-mortem proved that beyond all doubt. And to show what they *can* prove nowadays, they say he had a thick beard and it was taken off after death *by a dry shave.*"

"Good Lord!" said Travers again.

"Mind you, that makes it easier," Pettingford said. "We might find out who he was when we comb the doss-houses for missing men with a beard. But on the other hand, sir, we can't be certain of murder. Manslaughter?—yes. Two of them might have had a row and this one been hit or pushed so that he fell, then the one who did it might have got the wind up and shaved him to hide his identity and then tipped him in the river. By the way, his pockets were cleared out too. He hadn't a copper on him. Not a dirty handkerchief, nor anything."

Travers gave a Whartonian grunt: "Hm! Most complicated, as you say."

"Ah! but wait a minute, sir." Pettingford had deftly arrived at the grand climax. "You haven't heard it all yet, sir. What would you say, sir, if I was to tell you that the coat and trousers he had on were brand, spanking new?"

"New?" Travers's fingers rose to his glasses. "And what about the rest of his clothes?"

"A very worn vest, sir, and a shirt. Cheap quality but fairly clean, the shirt. Boots worn but reasonable. Socks, cheap cotton ones. Braces neatly repaired with string."

"I see," said Travers. "Still more complicated, but again it might make things easier. You might find where the new coat and trousers were bought. You have a rough idea when."

"I know, sir, but what gets me is why he had 'em."

There was an implied question. Travers did his best to answer it off-hand.

"I haven't the faintest idea, unless he was cutting a dash. He might have displayed some money and his new clothes and then been killed for the sake of the money. You said he hadn't a copper on him."

"That's an idea, sir." Then he shook his head. "But if he had money he didn't give himself much of a blow-out on the strength of it. All there was inside him was tea and slab."

Travers winced and the trend of the conversation was changed.

"But you won't be wanting me at the inquest?"

"Oh, no, sir. It'll only be a five minute job."

Travers rose. "Then if I can be of no further use to you, I think I'll move along. Of course if I can be of service in any way, you've only to ring me up."

"Thank you, sir," Pettingford said. "And if you do happen to have any ideas, sir, perhaps you'll be so good as to pass them on now you know the ins and outs. And now if you'll make yourself comfortable here, sir, I'll just see if the surgeon's come and if there's anything fresh turned up. Sorry to keep you, sir, but that's better than having you all the way back here again."

So it was past eleven o'clock when Travers left Dockway Hythe. Two traffic jams held him up badly and Big Ben was striking when at last he drew in at the Embankment.

But during that tedious ride things were happening near Garrod's Heath. At nine o'clock that morning a gang of twenty men had begun opening out that drainage trench, which was then a good ten feet deep. The trouble was, moreover, that the foreman on the job had not been sure to within a score of yards where the open trench had been on that vital Tuesday night.

Norris and Menzies were in charge, and Mott was there too. Menzies, the surgeon, was an old-timer with—as Travers once remarked—as much sense of the sad splendour of death as a greengrocer might have in the presence of a decapitated turnip. So the talk was about anything but what might lie at the excavated bottom, and there was much stamping of feet and cursing the cold, and the splash of the yellow water that came from the hose as the men worked.

Wharton had come by at about ten, and had stayed for a minute or two and no more. Mott had ventured to ask him what he expected to find if there was any luck; whose he thought the head might be, in fact.

"Don't know," said Wharton. "But there's three of you to find out."

"Very useful information," growled old Menzies when the General had gone. "How's he think I should know? And it's not my job."

"Mott's our standby," Norris said. "What with that Wimbeck Street affair and one thing and another I hardly know a soul at this end."

It was just after half-past eleven that a shout came from the trench, and the three were over in a flash.

"Something here, gentlemen!" the foreman was calling, and almost at once up came a soggy mass.

"My God!" said Norris, "it's the clothes."

Menzies called back to one of the men. "You with the hose, there! Turn it this way and wash that mud out."

There was another shout from the foreman at the trench bottom, but it had a strange quality of fear.

"Here is something, sir."

Menzies was on tenterhooks at once.

"What is it, the head? . . . Get out of the way there and let me come. . . . Pass me that pail down. . . . Now then, steady! Lift it with the shovel. . . . Easy now, easy."

He came up and the pail with him. Its contents seemed no more than a something embedded in yellow, soggy clay.

"You with the hose," he said. "Draw it this way. . . . Give it to me and let me do it."

Norris came over and watched.

"No sign of the hand yet. Looks as if it isn't there."

Menzies tipped out the pail's contents and again plied the hose. Features were beginning to appear.

"An oldish man by the look of him," he said, and then a queer thing happened, for he was all at once clutching Mott's arm.

"My God! it can't be. . . . How can it be?"

Mott was licking his lips.

"It is him . . . yet it can't be." He shook his head. "Reckon I'm going mad."

Just as Travers drew in the Rolls outside the Yard, an idea came to him. All that journey from Dockway he had been thinking over the queer affair of the dead down-and-out, and the thing that had intrigued him most was the brand-new clothes. Now, as he drew the car to a halt, he was wondering why he had forgotten to ask Pettingford if the clothes had been a good fit. Maybe they had not belonged to the murdered man after all.

Then again, thought Travers as he crossed the pavement and passed through the door, there is always the question of tailor-mades and reach-me-downs. But hardly tailor-mades, perhaps—

"Oh, Mr. Travers, sir!"

Travers looked round to see Lewis. There was something sheepish about the sergeant's grin.

"Can you spare me a minute, sir? In here, sir."

"Anything up?" Travers said.

"Yes," said Lewis, and gave the same sheepish grin. "A bit too much, sir. Looks to me as if I'm due for the high jump."

"Surely not," said Travers. "But what's happened?"

"You knew we were sitting on Johnson's tail this morning? Well, sir, he's the one that's happened. He's slipped us."

"That's bad," said Travers.

"Don't I know it, sir. But it wasn't anybody's fault. I had three men on him and they reported they'd picked him up—at least, one of them reported. Next I heard was they'd lost him. It seems he took a bus for Oxford Street and he nipped out all of a sudden and was in Windridge's before you could say knife. Which way he came out is what did the trick. Or he might be there now for all we know."

"I don't think I'd worry," Travers said.

"There's nobody here, sir," Lewis went on, "so I reckon you're off to Garrod's Heath; if so, sir, you might break it gently to the—to the Super."

Travers smiled. "I expect I can do that much for you. I thought of calling the station now to find out if I were going or not."

"I'll get them for you, sir."

He buzzed through and waited till the call came. Travers took the receiver.

"Hallo! That Garrod's Heath? . . . Ah! good-morning, Mott. How are you?"

Mott was bursting with some story or other and wasted not a second on unnecessaries.

"You haven't heard the news, sir?"

"What news?"

"Well, I haven't heard what the Super thinks of it, because I came straight back here. What do you think we found, sir, in that trench?"

"Not the head?"

"Yes, sir, the head. And whose head do you think? . . . Mathison's, sir, *Old Mathison's!*"

"But—but . . . Are you there? . . . I say, Mott, are you mad or am I—?"

"That's what I said, sir."

"But it's preposterous! Mathison was alive twenty-four hours ago."

And then all at once Travers was letting the receiver droop. Without knowing it, his hand replaced it. The hand groped for his glasses and he began a slow, instinctive polishing. Then for a moment he was motionless as if the thoughts trembled on a hairbreadth of fate that a breath would shatter.

"Lewis," he said, "could you call your men off?"

"Call them off, sir?"

"Yes. I take it they're reporting to you here. Call them off and stand by here yourself. When they're all in, you report to Garrod's Heath. I'll accept responsibility."

"Johnson's out of it, sir?"

"Yes," said Travers. "There's no point in following him up. It'll do harm rather than good." He smiled. "You needn't breathe a word now about your men having lost him."

"Thank you, sir," said Lewis and looked sheepishly down. Then he suddenly looked up. "Something in the wind is there, sir?"

"Yes," said Travers. "I'm not sure, but I think I know. Before midnight this case ought to be over."

CHAPTER XVII
THE NET IS SPREAD

Then again Travers's lean fingers went to his glasses, and he stood for a long minute in thought, while Lewis watched him anxiously.

"Why should he head straight for a big store, Lewis? It wasn't a sudden idea. He was making for there from the start."

Lewis looked surprised at the question.

"Easiest place in the world, sir, to slip anyone you knew was tailing you. He knew he had to go in by one door, sir, but there were twenty doors to slip out at."

"To slip out at," said Travers reflectively. "I wonder. But there's another way of looking at it. He could enter as one man and slip out as quite another."

Lewis stared, mouth gaping.

"Just as a matter of interest," went on Travers, "why not ring up Windridge's hair-dressing saloon and find out if within the last hour or so they've had a man with a beard come in to have it shaved off."

Lewis was dialling at once. Travers strolled out to the pavement again, sniffed the air and looked apprehensively at the faint mist that lay beyond the river. Lewis's voice was still to be heard when he came in again but in another minute the sergeant was hanging up.

"You're right, sir. They did have a man, and it was him. And by the way, sir, there was something about an overcoat he left behind. A blue overcoat with a Bond Street tab."

Travers flushed slightly. "It'd be Johnson all right," he said. "And he'd got plenty of money on him. No fake glasses, Lewis, and no beard. Your men would never recognise him when he left the barber's chair. Then a different hat; a new overcoat too, maybe, and there you are."

"I see, sir. You guessed it'd be a hopeless game so that's why you told me to call my men in." Then he stared again. "He's going to bolt, sir. That's it; he's going to bolt! He's got wind somehow that we're wise to that little arson affair down at Wapping."

"I wonder."

"Do you reckon I'd better get a description out, sir?"

Travers thought for a moment.

"Do you remember his records when he was convicted for the Porburgh job? What he was like then?"

It was Lewis's turn to think.

"Yes," he said. "I've got him taped, all right. He was clean-shaved. Looked like a naval officer to the life." He nodded. "He'll make for one of the ports."

"All the more reason why you should hold your hand," Travers said. "But there's something I'd like you to tell me before I go. You're a Londoner bred and born. Just step out here and have a look at the weather. It looks to me as if it might come over foggy."

Lewis had a look. Then he shook his head.

"There won't be any fog, sir. It ain't sunny enough, sir, and there's too much of a breeze. That mist means rain, not fog."

Travers gave a curious smile that looked like relief.

"Then there's plenty of time. And now do something else for me. Ring up my flat and ask Palmer to fetch home the car. I'm taking a taxi."

A nod and a smile and he was gone. Lewis gave a shake of the head and turned back. An old sergeant came across from a side room.

"Mr. Travers, wasn't it?" he said.

"Yes," said Lewis. "One of the best, he is too. What I call a toff."

"Wish I had his perishing money," the other told him.

"Money!" Lewis sniffed. "It's his brains you want." He took another quick look in the direction of the disappearing Travers. "Wish to hell I knew what he was off up to."

Travers took a taxi in Whitehall and arranged to be driven to Garrod's Heath. At the fork short of the suburb he had the driver circle round north. A hundred yards short of the cinema he paid the man off and then on foot proceeded warily in the direction of Ropeling's rooms. A reasonably obvious plain clothes man stood on the pavement opposite, eyes on the apparatus in a radio dealer's window. Travers looked round, caught sight of a small boy, and beckoned him over. A sixpence was exhibited and certain instructions rehearsed. Then the boy was running up to the shop window.

"Please you're to go to the police-station quick. Inspector Mott says so."

The man ran his eye over him, nodded an O.K., and shot a quick look at Ropeling's front door. The boy scampered off as instructed, but the man was thinking better of it when it was too late to call him back. Another moment of thought and he was making for the side lane and the rear of the house, doubtless to confer with his colleague. Travers nipped across and was knocking at the front door.

"Is Mr. Ropeling in?" he asked the landlady, and was already stepping inside.

"Yes, sir, but he's still at his lunch."

"That's all right," said Travers, who had timed his call with that hope of a late lunch in mind. "Give him this card, will you, and ask if he'll see me at once on a very important matter."

In a moment he was being shown in but he had a word with the landlady first.

"In a few minutes," he said, "there may be a knock at the door and a tallish man may be asking if Mr. Ropeling's in. You're to say he's out. In fact it would be better if you strained a point and said he went out a few minutes ago."

He closed the door urbanely and turned to the startled curate.

"How are you, Ropeling? Sorry to come in on your meal. But it was really desperately important. Please go on eating and pay no attention to me whatever. Mind if I just draw this blind slightly?"

"But I don't understand—"

"I thought perhaps you wouldn't," Travers said. "But go on with your meal—please."

Ropeling shook his head like a man at an utter loss, then pushed the plate aside.

"I have finished—really. I mean I—"

"Sit down here then," Travers said. "And may I take this one. Quite a friendly visit, you know. A bit uncouth perhaps, and unexpected, but you know the old tag: desperate ills and desperate cures, in fact."

Ropeling was staring with the quick frightened wonder if Ludovic Travers had suddenly gone mad. Now he remembered, he had once read a note in the press. A lack of conventionality and certain eccentricities—

"For you are in a desperate way, you know," Travers was going on. "It may be only a question of minutes before you're under arrest."

A faint flush of understanding came to his face.

"Under arrest?"

"That's what I said. For complicity in robbery, and it may even be—murder."

His eyes goggled.

"Your every movement is being watched by the police. They were aware of the fact that yesterday afternoon you did some telephoning from Westgrove North, and they know why you chose that particular place. If you look out of a back bedroom window you'll see a man keeping the house under observation—or he may be at the lane where he can now watch back and front. You see, I got rid of the man at the front so that you and I could have a secret—er—conference, shall we say. I'm afraid the man may be back as soon as he knows he's been tricked." He broke off to listen to the quick patter of feet. His voice lowered. "That's probably him now."

There were steps on the path and a knock at the door. Voices were heard as a mumble, for the wall was thick. The door closed. Travers was on his feet and beckoning Ropeling over.

"Quick! . . . There he goes—look! . . . He's telling the other man to stay where he is. . . . Now he's off again. To raise the hue-and-cry for you, I expect."

He turned back to the chair again and watched with quizzical eyes while the other sank nervously into his seat.

"Now I wonder if you'd like to tell me about everything. I can't promise it shall be in confidence, but outside the police nobody shall know a thing."

Ropeling drew himself up in the manner of a man who feels in his inmost heart that he was of the stuff of which martyrs are made.

"I'm sorry, but I'm afraid I've nothing to say."

"A pity," said Travers sadly. "But I fear I rather anticipated it. And I wonder if you're waiting for me to tell you the truth about Mathison—and yourself."

Ropeling shook his head. For an indecisive moment he sat licking his lips.

"You regard me as a man of honour, I hope," Travers said. "I trust you'll believe me when I say I'm here in your own interests. If you wish me to, I'll tell you the truth about the man you knew as Mathison."

"It was true then? . . . The tales that are going about?"

"What concerns you and me," Travers said, "is not the things that are true. I'd like to know the things that are *untrue*. The things he told you when he saw you yesterday morning."

Ropeling shook his head.

"I can't do that. I gave my word and I won't break it."

"Oh, dear, dear," said Travers, with a look of humorous despair. "Then perhaps you'll allow me to tell you the truth. I warn you that I shall have to be blunt. I shall have to tell you, for instance, that you were just the dupe and stalking-horse of a crafty knave. He used religion as a cloak, and you and that collar you wear were merely part of his camouflage. Old Mathison, as he was pleased to be, the sidesman at St. Elfrida's and—if you'll pardon me—the friend and constant host of Mr. Ropeling, could never be connected with the Garrod's Heath burglaries."

Ropeling's face had flushed. But though his look was somewhat foolish he still shook his head.

Travers shook his head too.

"Well, perhaps I'd better come direct to the point." He leaned confidentially forward. "Shall I tell you what transpired between you and Mathison yesterday? He came to you in a great hurry. An unfortunate occurrence, he mentioned maybe. Said that owing to a series of misunderstandings or it might have been that he had been badly let down by a friend, he was likely to be drawn into trouble with the police. A temporary and easily explained affair which was nothing more than a misunderstanding, and which he was then that very minute going to clear up in London. Perhaps the police wouldn't come after all. Perhaps already they'd realized the whole thing was a mistake, but—and that's where you came in, my dear Ropeling. You were to phone to a certain address in town—an hotel, I imagine—and from Westgrove North, if you discovered before a certain time that the police *were* interested. The whole thing was clothed with speciousness and a secrecy that would have deceived the elect. You were deceived, but you landed yourself in Queer Street with the police." He shook his head sadly. "Yet somehow I don't blame you."

Ropeling drew himself up. His cheek still held that flush, but it was a flush of annoyance—and with Mathison, as Travers surmised. Dignity had been injured and martyrdoms had become as vain things.

"In a way I still hold I was right."

"Of course you were," Travers told him heartily. "What more sacred than a promise, even to a rogue? But what I have just guessed at was apparently approximately right." He smiled. "So you're released from the promise you made Mathison. I've released you myself."

Ropeling was still shaking his head.

"It seems incredible to me. I can hardly believe it."

Travers tried a little pomposity. The moment, it seemed to him, was awaiting it.

"You've got to believe it. Scotland Yard doesn't lie. It's the servant of the law and the law means impartiality; majestic impartiality." He cleared his throat, feeling that the fine outburst had hardly been one of his best. "But I'll tell you something else. Mathison was on the point of being arrested in town and he gave his name as Ropeling. He was trying to get you involved, so as to keep the police off him till he had time to get clear."

And then Travers judged the time had come for a little legal, moral blackmail. He waved his hand carelessly.

"But all that I hope I shall be able to keep from becoming public. I think I can say that I shall do my utmost to make sure that nothing is known that might do you any harm in the parish."

Ropeling was rubbing his hands nervously together.

"I'm sure I should be very grateful. Mind you, I still hold that I wasn't to blame—altogether." He shook his head. "But other people mightn't see it like that."

"Exactly," said Travers. "That's why I'm determined to keep your name out of things. But Mathison mustn't be allowed to get clear. The law won't stand for that. Your name won't be brought in but you owe a duty to the law." Once more he leaned forward confidentially. "I wonder if you'd like to do something for us? I'm sure you would. And so we'll push this table back, because we haven't much time."

"The table back?"

"Yes," said Travers. "We're going to rehearse a play. A playlet, it might be better to call it, or even a short episode. We've got to make up the words as we go along, and there may be half a dozen different series. You know, like openings in chess, and the corresponding moves. Ready for the table? Right. You take that end and I'll take this."

It was past three o'clock when Ropeling and Travers came boldly out at the front door. Both halted for a minute and surveyed the sky. A few drops of rain were already falling and the clouds lay heavy and dark.

"Better than fog," Travers said. "Fog would have ruined everything. But still I don't like it. We'd better step out."

There was no looking back at the man who both knew was following behind. When they stepped inside the station the first one they saw was Inspector Mott, and he stared at Ropeling as if he were seeing a ghost.

"You know Mr. Ropeling," said Travers amiably. "We've just been having a little talk at his house."

Norris came out then and Lewis with him.

"Mr. Ropeling's going to do us a great service," Travers said. "He's going to assist in the little job of laying somebody by the heels."

"Come along in to my room," Mott said. He was still looking somewhat bewildered.

"Sergeant Lewis reported just now," Norris said. "He said you as good as told him to, sir."

"That's all right," said Travers. "I'll take responsibility. Now where's Superintendent Wharton?"

"He went back with Menzies," Norris said. "I think they were going straight to Sir Barnabas with that head and clothes. Perhaps you didn't know about that, sir."

"I heard about it from here," Travers said, and then Mott cut in. His first hysterics were things of the almost forgotten past.

"I reckon you knew I was joking, sir, about that head being old Mathison's. Anyone'd know it couldn't have been. I knew you wouldn't take me seriously."

Travers caught the inquiring glance in Ropeling's eyes.

"Of course I didn't," he said to Mott. "We all know the age of miracles is over. You didn't dig up part of Mathison. He's still loose. How long he'll be so is a different matter."

Mott suddenly stared.

"Now I've got you, sir. You and Mr. Ropeling here have got some scheme or other to get him in a trap."

"You never can tell," said Travers enigmatically. "But about Superintendent Wharton, Norris. It's most frightfully awkward. I've got to take a responsibility and I'd rather not. Just over a half-hour and it'll be getting dark. I wonder if it'd be any use trying the Yard. Would you mind?"

"I'll get them for you, sir," Mott said, and hurried out.

Travers looked worried.

"I'm afraid it's too late already," he told Norris. "He hasn't time to get here before it's dark, even if he is at the Yard. Better let me have the key of The Rockery, I think, so that Mr. Ropeling can be pushing on ahead."

He went out with Ropeling to the main door. When he came back Mott was reporting.

"He isn't there, sir. Anything you want to send? We're still holding the line."

"Just a minute," said Travers. "Let me think. There may be the very earthquake of a row after all this."

His fingers went to his glasses and then at once fell again.

"We've got to gamble. Take this down and make sure they get it correctly:

Superintendent Wharton. Remain at Yard till further message, however late. Desperately important. While waiting get from Pettingford of Dockway story of Limerick Crown. Travers."

There was silence in the room till Mott came back.

"We've got to work quickly," Travers said. "We've got to be in Mathison's house—funny I never can think of him as Luke—

before it's even dusk. Get some food of any sort, Mott, and from anywhere, and make it enough for five. A loaf or two and some cheese will do, and a thermos or two of tea'd go down well. Get them to the back door of The Rockery yourself, and at once. You, Norris, and Lewis, come separately. Slip in the back way and the door'll open and let you in. Just a moment, Mott. If you can rake up a gun from anywhere, I'd rather like to have it. Then I'll be moving on." Then all at once he was shaking his head. "Almost forgot the most vital thing of all. If by any chance Superintendent Wharton doesn't get that message at the Yard but comes here instead, leave word he's to stay here. Tell him it's life and death."

Mott arrived last and was through the door as soon as Travers had it open. The wet was running from his hat.

"Settled in for a bad night, sir."

"I know," said Travers. "That may make things awkward. Let's go in the living-room to the others. We haven't got more than a quarter of an hour before it's pitch dark out there. The trees don't help much either."

Ropeling had a fire going, and with the easy chair drawn up and a book at his elbow, he looked as if he had owned the house for years.

"You stay here," Travers told him, "and we four will go upstairs to the front bedroom which will give Lewis and his sharp eyes the chance to look out of the window. Are those curtains all right?"

Ropeling said they were drawn as directed, with just a slit to show through towards the road.

"Right," said Travers. "Then we won't turn on the light till we get down again, which should be in five minutes. The back door's locked, by the way."

The four trooped quietly upstairs in the inside dark.

"You squint out by that corner," Travers told Lewis, "and we'll stand back here. The idea of all these preparations is this. To-night, when it's pitch dark, our visitor may come. It may be by the front door or it may be by the underground passage."

There was the passage to explain and how it worked, though Travers was of the opinion that it would not be used that night.

"But we've got to make sure," he said. "Still, by whatever way he comes in, he'll make for the living-room because he'll have seen the light from outside."

"He wouldn't walk right in a trap like that, surely, sir," broke in Mott.

"Mr. Travers knows," Norris told him quietly. "He'll do the ordering and we'll do the rest."

"We're all in it together," Travers said. "Anything outside there, Lewis?"

"Not a thing, sir. One or two people going past—that's all."

"Then to get on," said Travers. "When our man steps into the living-room he'll find Ropeling. Practically every question he may ask has the answer all prepared ready, and in the course of the brief talk our friend will certainly give himself away. Then a moment will come when he'll have to be collared, and until that moment there mustn't be a whisper. If Superintendent Wharton should come here and be seen, and alarm him, for instance, that might be disastrous. Everything understood? Then we'll move off down again. Wait though. I've got an idea. Lewis, you'll remain here. Norris, slip off downstairs and turn on the living-room light and turn it off again at once. Just a flash."

It went on and in the second of visibility Lewis saw the streak of light across the dark, sodden lawn.

"That's your signal," Travers said. "When that streak of light disappears—and I shall operate it from behind the curtains—you sneak downstairs to the front door, carrying your shoes in your hand. Open it and shut it again as if you've come in. Then slip on your shoes and switch on the hall light and make straight for the living-room, and be ready for things to happen."

He made Lewis repeat till each move was clear.

"Will you have any food here with you?"

"No, thank you, sir. I'm not hungry."

"Then you're lucky," Travers said. "I had my last meal at half-past eight. Besides, we may have to be here till midnight or after—you never know. Nothing may happen and then it'll be all night."

"I'll risk it, sir," Lewis told him.

"Right," said Travers. "Then we'll go and have a look at that underground passage, and then the mine's set."

CHAPTER XVIII
TRAVERS KNOWS

Travers had searched that passage and had again emerged.

"I don't think he'll come this way," he said, "but the partition door's open if he wants to try it. Now we've got to decide where the rest of us are to go."

There was a cupboard under the hall stairs, where the woman had kept her cleaning oddments. Mott went in there and found unexpected room to stretch his legs.

"If our visitor does come," Travers said, "and if he dodges Lewis in some way and bolts upstairs, you nip out of the front door and watch the windows. Any food?"

Mott had brought sandwiches, and he kept one of the flasks of tea.

"Not a sound, whatever happens," Travers said, "even if we all have to be here till next morning."

The thick plush curtains of the living-room were not drawn close to the bay of the window, but ran straight from wall to wall with a consequent recess. There in the corners Norris and Travers were to wait.

"That's our risk," Travers said. "If he gets suspicious and comes over here to have a look, then we must go for him. Let's hope he doesn't. What we want is to hear him talk." He gave a last look out from his corner. "Turn on the light when you're ready, Ropeling. And don't forget we're all here."

"I can look after myself," said Ropeling valiantly.

In a few minutes a ravenous hunger came over Travers and he made a meal. From his corner Norris was invisible, for a heavy mahogany table stood in the window and the streak of light through the curtain slit seemed high above like a star.

Then the house settled down to a strange and utter quietude. It was as if one lived in the country of the blind; or like being in darkness and listening through earphones to a play which never began, though its faint preliminaries were now and then heard. There would be the fall of a chance coal, or a little cough from Ropeling; the rustling of the leaves of his book, and once that almost monstrous noise when he made up the fire. Outside, the night seemed still, and the rain made no more than a faint patter on the misty glass.

The old-fashioned marble clock on the mantelpiece tinkled the half-hour, and then the watchers in the dark could strain their ears to follow Ropeling's steps and sounds. He brought the kettle from the kitchen and made a place for it on the hob. There was an opening of kitchen drawers and the tinkle of china as he prepared his tea. Then at last his meal began, and was over. The tinkle of china came again as the cloth was cleared; the fire was stoked up and the house settled once more to an uncanny quiet, with now and again the rustle of a leaf as Ropeling turned a page, and the old sounds of the fire, or little coughs as a man makes when unaware of them.

The clock tinkled a new half-hour. Travers stirred gently on the hard boards and knew the moment had come for hope. At six o'clock there would be passing the first city men from the railway station, and from then till half-past seven people would be abroad outside whatever the night. So for a half-hour there was now the first of the vital times when the visitor might come. From now on there must be a straining of ears for a sound; at the gate, it might be, or the stealthy lifting of the trapdoor in the room across the hall. But somehow he knew the entry would never be from there, and then a mild panic seized him as he wondered what might have been unthought of—a swarming up the pipes maybe, to a back bedroom....

There was a sudden sound as of two quick deliberate taps on the floor above.

"What's that?" came Norris's whisper.

Travers hissed him to silence. Lewis, it must be, signalling that something had been seen. And then at once there was heard the click of the latch of the gate and feet were on the front path. They neared the door, and as they neared Travers' heart began a sudden racing.

There was a knock at the front door and in the stillness of the house it sounded and seemed to echo like a clap of thunder. Ropeling gave a little nervous cough and his feet were heard on the carpet. Then they sounded in the hall, and there was the opening of a door.

"Is Mr. Mathison in?"

"I'm afraid he isn't," Ropeling said. "That is, not at the moment. Can I give him any message?"

There was silence for a few seconds as if the caller were thinking things over.

"When will he be in? Do you know?"

"Well, that's hard to say. Would you care to come in and wait?"

There was another hesitation but no more words. The door was closed again and feet were heard in the hall. Ropeling began a courteous chattering.

"A dreadful night outside, isn't it? . . . Won't you leave your things out here? They're rather damp, you know. . . . Then we'll go in, shall we? It's quite possible Mr. Mathison may be in at any minute."

"You're all alone here, are you?"

The words were like a challenge. The caller suspected some trap and was standing his ground. But Ropeling had entered the room, still talking cheerfully away.

"As you see. Just making myself comfortable as if the house belonged to me. . . . Mr. Mathison and I play quite a lot of cribbage, you know. I'm a bachelor and he is—as you know. I've got quite in the habit of making the house my own. . . . Do come and sit down, won't you? I'm afraid I can't offer you tea or anything because the woman always goes home of an evening."

There was the shuffling of a chair.

"You don't know where he is, do you?"

"Well, I'm afraid I don't," Ropeling said. "To tell the truth, he's rather mysterious about his movements, if you know what I mean." The tone changed to a mild consternation. "He wasn't expecting you, was he?"

"Oh, no." There seemed some grim irony in the voice. "He wasn't expecting me. Just a little surprise."

"You're not a relation of his?"

There was a silence. Then the answer was thought out.

"What makes you ask that? Do you know any of his relations?"

"As far as I know, he hasn't any," Ropeling said. "At least I've never heard him mention any."

"You haven't heard him talk about his brother?"

"Why, no," said Ropeling. "I didn't know he had a brother . . . . You don't mean to tell me that you—"

"That's all right," the voice cut generously in. "You weren't to know it."

"But what a surprise for him!"

"It'll be a surprise all right." The same grim irony was there.

"Well, I *am* delighted, Mr. Mathison. I suppose I must call you Mathison. But of course. How silly of me."

"Mathison," the voice said, and the word was lingered on the palate. "Yes, you might as well call me Mathison." The tone changed to a kind of slow, cold questioning. "So you keep him company of nights? Sit up for him when he's out?"

"Yes," said Ropeling. "That is—well, yes."

"Pretty quiet down here, isn't it?"

Ropeling tittered.

"You might find it so. I mean, there's always something to do . . . in a way."

"Something to do, is there?"

"There was all the excitement of the burglaries," Ropeling was suddenly saying, as if desperately anxious to announce a cue. "We actually had a burglar try to get in here. On the Tuesday evening it was. The night before they discovered the body in the bonfire."

"I haven't heard about that. Been abroad and just got home."

Ropeling plunged into an account.

"Who did it?"

"The police don't know," Ropeling said. "They haven't found out."

"Not the police here? Haven't they found anything?"

"As far as I know, not a thing—I mean, about who did it. It frightened your—your brother pretty badly, Mr. Mathison. That was why he decided to sell this house and leave the district."

There was a grunt, then the sound of an uneasy shuffling in a chair.

"You were reading, weren't you? Don't mind me. You get on with your book."

"I wouldn't dream of it," Ropeling said. "I was just passing the time."

The room held for a moment a disturbing silence.

"I don't think I'll wait after all. What's your name, by the by?"

"Ropeling. . . . I'm at the church where your brother is sidesman."

"Then I'll be going, Mr. Ropeling. I expect I shall meet him somewhere outside. Don't worry if he doesn't turn up till late. He mayn't even turn up at all."

"But surely—"

"I might take him back to town with me—*What was that?*"

At the first mention of his going, the long arm of Travers had reached up to the gap in the curtains. Now there was a sound at the front door as of somebody entering.

"Stay where you are—you! . . . Don't stir, d'you hear? . . . I'll speak to Mathison myself."

The voice had changed to a cold, deadly menace. As the curtain went cautiously aside Travers saw Ropeling backing nervously and there was a something that had gone through the door.

"Get him, Lewis!"

Travers's voice was shrilling. Norris had made a leap for the door and in the passage-way there was all at once a thudding and a scuffling. Then there was a snarling like that of some netted, struggling beast and a yell from Lewis and all Travers saw was the mad fighting of a mass of men, with whirling arms and legs that appeared in the faint light from the living-room door. There was that frightening snarl again, and then up went the hall light and Ropeling peered out. Travers made for a pair of legs and Lewis was yelling again.

"He's got my arm! He's got my arm!"

Norris's fist thudded. Ropeling seized a whirling leg and held on. Mott was growling blasphemously between his teeth and his fist was thudding too. Then in some queer way there was a sudden quiet. Men sorted themselves out and one was motionless on the floor.

"Lash up his legs," Norris said. "Don't matter what with. Use your handkerchief. . . . Get him over on his belly and find something to lash his legs to the handcuffs." He bent down for a moment. "He'll come round all right—blast him! He's only knocked out."

They trussed him up. Lewis looked savagely down.

"Had my arm in his teeth, sir. Like a mad animal, he was."

"Johnson, isn't it?" said Norris. "I thought I spotted his voice. And look what he had in his pocket, sir. Got it out of Frisch's old metal yard, I should reckon."

It looked like the sawn-off upright of an iron bed; shaped like a small knobkerrie and heavy as lead.

"Yes," said Travers. "That's what he did the murders with."

"You mean he—"

"Get him away," said Travers. "He frightens me. Get him away before he comes round."

"He frightened me, I don't mind saying," said Ropeling with a little titter. "His eyes were just like a snake's. It was like talking to somebody dead. Somebody who didn't answer. Somebody who knew you were telling him lies."

Travers smiled. His hand fell on the curate's shoulder.

"You're a hero, Ropeling. You've fought with beasts at Ephesus. We can't thank you too much for what you've done."

Ropeling smiled gingerly, then shook his head.

"Those lies I had to tell him—"

"Not lies," said Travers. "Merely adjustments of truth. Now let's get our hats and we can keep each other company as far as the station. Inside an hour we shall have to explain all this to Superintendent Wharton."

But however bellicose Wharton's first tones may have sounded over the phone from the Yard, and whatever his final rumblings when he had heard Travers's last words and was about to hang up, there was a fine and heartening joviality about his voice as the waiting Travers heard it from inside the-police-station at Garrod's Heath.

"Here we are then. . . . Mr. Travers here? . . . All right, all right. I'll find my own way in."

He came in, snapping his eyes at the sudden light.

"Well, you got him then?" he said to Travers. "I guessed something was in the wind when they gave me that message of yours. Where's everybody?"

Mott and Norris had gone with Johnson, Travers said.

"Much trouble, was he?" Wharton asked.

"Fought like a wild animal at the house, he did," Lewis said. "He came at me, sir, before I'd properly got my boots on, and I hadn't time to switch the light on either."

"Did he say anything?"

"Not a thing, sir. When he came round he just glared. Enough to give you the creeps."

"He'll get clear with Broadmoor," Wharton said, and took off his heavy coat. "Your man brought me in your car, Mr. Travers, but I take it you're in no great hurry." He stirred the fire and gave a knowing nod. "Didn't I keep insisting all along that Johnson was the key? Didn't I insist on having him tailed when it might have meant trouble?"

"You did," said Travers. "And if you saw Pettingford and heard all about the Limerick Crown, you know as much as we do."

Wharton shot him a look.

"I wouldn't go so far as that. I'd like to hear your point of view. How you worked it all out."

"It worked itself out," Travers said.

"You're too modest," Wharton told him, and cast a genial eye in the direction of Lewis. "You tell us all about it. Some of us never went to a Police Collect. It'd be a bit of a treat for us to listen to a demonstration—if that's what they call it. You tell me everything you didn't have time for over the phone."

"Well, if you insist," Travers said. "But I'm making no claims for subtlety. I don't mind trying to follow up how things worked themselves out. It might be interesting too to see where we went wrong."

"That's better," said Wharton, and settled himself comfortably in his chair. "And start off with that old Porburgh job. I still don't quite see how you came to fit things in."

Travers smiled, if somewhat ruefully. "You mean the clue of the Unknown Fourth. That was my Quatre Bras, and might have been a different sort of Waterloo. That's where I went absolutely astray."

"Astray? Why, you were always harping on that clue!"

Travers shook his head. "You listen to me, George. I went astray over that clue of the Fourth Unknown. And look at the chances I had! No sooner did Watts mention him than he kept nagging away at me. He was presented to me as the vital clue and all I had to do was fit him in—and I couldn't do it. All the time *you* were the one who was right."

"I was right!"

"Yes," said Travers. "You were right. Didn't you insist that the old Porburgh Case contained in itself everything necessary to solve the two new cases? And so it did. I was wrong because I couldn't place X after Watts had virtually mentioned him. I connected X with the bonfire body and with the J. Scott who did the actual killing of Carberry—both assumptions right and yet neither seeming quite to fit. And now I know the simple solution of everything was there under my nose, *and within the framework of the old Porburgh Case, as you insisted.*"

"Just how?" asked Wharton, stirring in his seat.

"Well, take that case and its three principals— Carberry, Luke and Johnson. Add X—the fourth, and let's apply the four to the Wimbeck Street and Garrod's Heath Cases in the light of the knowledge we possessed almost at once. Carberry was eliminated, because he was dead. The bonfire body must have been that of X, because its prints and measurements didn't tally with those of anyone else. Luke was a free man, wandering about Heaven knows where, because he wasn't accounted for, and he wasn't X. That leaves the fourth as Johnson, who must therefore have done the killings; in addition to which he was the only one who physically resembled J. Scott."

"You're right," said Wharton. "It was there and we didn't see it."

Travers heaved a regretful sigh. "Well, it can't be helped, so let's make a start on Luke and his brother—"

"Johnson, sir?" asked Lewis promptly.

"I'm afraid not," Travers told him. "When Johnson told Ropeling he was Mathison's brother, he was casting out feelers for information, and he wanted an excuse for his call. But the brothers Luke, I'd say, were from the Colonies and came over here about two years before the old Porburgh affair.

"What I'm leading up to, or trying to work out, is how they evolved their scheme of inverse double identity. Let me explain. There's nothing more common, as you yourself know, George, than cases where, by means of disguise, a man can give himself a dual identity. But inverse double identity is when two people who have or have not need for disguise, pose as one person. All I want to say about that so far—and remember I sit here as an Aunt Sally to be shied at—is that I am of the opinion that in their Porburgh days the two brothers had not realised the value of the weapon against law and order which they had in their hands. All I say is that when the Porburgh house was burnt down there was no secret passage discovered, or we should have heard of it."

Wharton nodded in agreement there.

"About the brothers," Travers went on. "I propose in what I have to say to call them Luke and Mathison, Mathison being the one who lived here under that name. It was Mathison who was caught red-handed at Carberry's house. His brother burnt the house down that same night and got away with what valuables there were hidden in it. When Mathison came out of jail,

Luke had set up house at Bournemouth. It was then I claim that the inverse double-identity first really dawned on the pair. One must deduce that from the fact that when one became suspect, the other was able to claim a perfect alibi for him." There Travers smiled dryly. "While one brother was doing a job, the other was probably playing cribbage with some gentleman whose testimony was irreproachable.

"But the two were scared and they removed to Garrod's Heath, where Mathison became the public character. Here they worked out the scheme, profiting by previous mistakes. The rockery and passage were made so that there could be exit and entry independent of the house. By adjustment of each other's facial characteristics—and there weren't many, or Mott would never have thought it was Mathison's head that was exhumated—they made two people near enough like one. Shape of beard and manner of doing the hair were important, and Mathison may have adopted a stoop because he was two inches taller than his brother. Those and any other personal peculiarities would be sufficient. Also, though there was a room which the woman was never allowed to enter, I don't think the two brothers necessarily lived together on the premises. Before and after a job—yes. But if Luke got far enough away when a job was done, that satisfied the scheme. It would have been intolerable for a man to have been cooped up all his days in that workroom and where he dare not sleep for fear of his snores being heard by the woman, even though that woman was probably carefully chosen by Mathison as being somewhat deaf. Still, all that can be worked out and maybe Mathison will tell us when we lay hands on him—if ever. So I pass over the two jobs here, and how the two called a halt so as to feel their way, and how Luke went to America and ultimately came back. What we now want to arrive at are the events of the last fortnight, which means going back to Johnson."

"Yes," said Wharton, and stirred expectantly in his chair. Lewis's eyes never moved from Travers's face.

"Johnson," said Travers slowly. "Johnson and his obsession. Johnson fretting out his heart and nerves in jail. He may have laid the death of his wife to Mathison and Carberry, but what he was like when he came out, we know from what he subsequently did. What to call his mind I hardly know. Watts said he was brilliantly clever and absurdly ingenious by turns. I'd add that he was warped and twisted; cunning as a weasel and cruel as—as—"

"As hell," said Lewis.

"Yes," said Travers. "And he was raving mad with one obsession and in the matter of that obsession incredibly sane. He knew the old story that if a man stands all his life in Piccadilly Circus, sooner or later the man he's looking for will pass by under his nose. That's why he became a match-seller—beggar, if you like. He changed his own personality and he dedicated his life to finding Mathison—whom he knew as Luke—and Carberry. Carberry no doubt he hunted for in the reference books, but the change of name threw him off the scent. And I'd say he found Carberry first. One day Carberry walked past a match-seller's pitch. The match-seller followed.

"Now what happened when Johnson had Carberry marked safely down? Well, he must have worked his brains to find a way to kill him without risking his own neck. And not only that. Johnson wanted to keep an eye on Carberry because he might lead him to the man he knew as Luke. So he worked out the scheme for an assistant. Johnson was saving his money because one day he might badly need it. He frequented doss-houses and he was always patient. Then he found the man he wanted.

"Some quiet, decent, unfortunate soul he must have been, and of an age and a height with himself. Johnson asked him if he would like to go shares— approaching him warily of course. The poor devil jumped at it. Johnson had him grow a beard and trim it torpedo-shape. Then when the two wore precisely similar clothes—red muffler and curious hat, for instance—and dark glasses, who was to know? One doesn't make a familiar of a beggar. If one does he can always assume a deafness. You see him and you never even say to yourself, 'Yes, that's my beggar.' No, you accept him as a matter of course, and you accept his voice in its mumbled thanks. All therefore that Johnson had to do to assume his own double identity, was to tell his man to keep that motionless statuesque attitude and to coach him to know faces and report fully the occurrences on the days when he took his turn."

"You're not worrying about chronological sequence," Wharton said apologetically. "What I mean is that Johnson mayn't have fixed up with his double till he first saw Luke."

"That's right," Travers said. "I'm making hypothetical times and orders of happenings because they fit in. We know when Johnson hired that shack off Frisch, for instance, and we must assume he always had in mind how he could get rid of his assistant if there was sheer necessity. Close his mouth for ever, I mean. We know also that in course of time Johnson recognised Mathison one day in Piccadilly and followed him to Garrod's Heath. After that there were two murders to be planned." He gave a slow shake of the head. "Can't you see Johnson standing there all day? Static, I called him. Standing there and knowing the luck he had had in finding the two he wanted, and still not knowing how the one thing could be done. Watching the faces of his regulars and mumbling his thank-yous, and thinking and thinking. Then Yawlings came along and sent a chill through his heart.

"Johnson thought the police were wise to who he was, and if murder was done, then the first suspect would be himself. But the police didn't bother him and perhaps he felt a kind of security after a time. Then the scheme came—a mad, jumbled scheme, like himself, and some of it made up on the spur of the moment. Which brings us to the weekend prior to the murders."

There Travers polished his glasses and took a breather.

"Johnson was haunting the neighbourhood of The Rockery, using the fog as cover, and Mathison saw him there and reported to the police because he thought him a police spy. Mathison had long forgotten Johnson and his threats or else he thought himself secure. And so to the Tuesday night.

"Luke left the house after tea and while Mathison and Ropeling played cribbage, Johnson was on Luke's heels. He picked up Luke after the job and killed him where we found the blood. Then he had him across the road in a flash, and went through ail his pockets. The burglary proceeds you can bet he took, and

I'll wager if you ring up Norris you'll find they are in that belt he was so anxious about at the hospital. Then I'd say he got Luke's clothes off and hacked off the head and hands with his knife. Then he thought it might be better if he hacked off feet as well. Just as the missing head threw us off the scent as to why the hands were missing, so the missing feet would have thrown us still farther off the same scent. Then he was disturbed perhaps and he wrapped the parts of the body in some of the sacking and draw farther into the gorse. Then he saw the bonfire, or maybe he had been making for it from the first. He must have known all the neighbourhood of the Common fairly well. He knew enough about the horse-trough, for instance, to mention it in the fake letter that was slipped in Carberry's pocket.

"He left with the head, clothes and both hands in more sacking and found his way to The Rockery again. He didn't know of the underground passage, but he knew the house was empty, so he thought of ransacking it and maybe disposing of head, clothes and one hand there. But Ropeling disturbed him as he was breaking in, and he bolted. Remember that he didn't see Mathison. He saw only Ropeling.

"Then he tramped on towards town in the fog and either remembered the cutting if he came that way by bus, or else blundered on it, and there he hid the head and clothes. The hands were in his pocket and then he made his way to town for an arranged meeting at Wapping with his assistant. He would hear the news; what regulars had been along, what happened and so on, and he also put the assistant on the job for the following afternoon and evening.

"What happened then, you know. He killed Carberry and used the hand. By a childish sort of intricacy he tried to involve Carberry in the bonfire killing or lay a complicated false trail by slipping the note into his pocket. Then he joined his assistant at the Wapping rendezvous, where I would say they had some hot tea and slab—thick bread and butter, isn't it?—while Johnson gathered each item of news, particularly the things that happened round about six o'clock. When Johnson was dead sure of enough facts to establish the alibi he struck the poor devil on the head and the blow killed him. Johnson dressed him in the clothes bought for the occasion, and burned or sank the navy-blue suit. He also went through his pockets and took the poor devil's share of the takings, but he didn't think of searching his boots where the old chap had hidden a coin that looked as if it might be valuable. Then Johnson shaved him and he shaved him dry. That's what first made me think. Johnson didn't shave, so he bought a razor ready for the job. But he forgot the brush. Only a bearded man would have had no brush."

"You're right, sir," broke in Lewis. Wharton gave him a glare.

"If so, it was a lucky right," said Travers. "However, Johnson had a perfect alibi, thanks in part to myself. All that remains is what happened when you, George, had that brilliant idea of confronting Mathison and Johnson. No wonder Johnson flopped down in a fit. *He saw in flesh and blood the man he had killed*. And no wonder when he came round he babbled about Luke."

Once more Travers gave a slow shake of the head. His fingers went to his glasses and fell again.

"One little point can be cleared up now. Mathison certainly never recognised Johnson when he walked by him on that inspection test. We know that for this chief reason. To-day Johnson undisguised himself. He discarded his glasses and his beard. Part of that was paradoxically as a new disguise, so that Lewis's men should never know him. But I believe the main reason was a far grimmer one. He came here to recall himself to the man he knew as Luke. Before he killed Luke he was going to give a dreadful zest to the killing. '*Look at me,*' he would say. '*Now do you know whom I am?*'" And there Travers gave another shake of the head. "That's all. Except that to-night after the rest in hospital had given him time to think things out, Johnson came back to complete the job that had been half done. He came to kill the right man."

Wharton gave a sideways nod of approbation. "To finish the job and kill the right man. You're right. Seeing Mathison the other day gave that brain of his the last tilt."

There was silence for a moment or two and then Travers got to his feet.

"To-morrow suit you, George, for clearing things up? If so I'll be pushing on. I feel unaccountably tired."

Wharton was all concern at once.

"My dear fellow, do. We're staying on for a bit. Any time to-morrow that suits yourself. And what we'd have done without you . . ."

His voice was lost and its profusion of thanks. Lewis listened for a last time and then whipped quickly round to a something of which he alone in the room had been aware—a narrow slit in the room beyond. He was grinning as he pushed the door open.

"Hallo, you! Had a good earful?"

The station-sergeant grinned too.

"And what if I have?"

"Oh, nothing," said Lewis graciously. "Lucky for you, though, the Old General didn't know you were having a listen-in."

"Rare smart one, that Mr. Travers," the station-sergeant said. "Lousy with money, too, so they tell me; and no more swank than you or me."

"Keep your eyes open too, don't you?" Lewis told him ironically.

But the other was giving a shake of the head.

"Wonder what Johnson did with that second hand. He didn't tell us about that."

"What's it matter?" said Lewis. "Some people are never satisfied. Is there anything else you'd like to know?"

"No," he said slowly, "I don't know as there is."

"I thought perhaps there might be," Lewis said. "You might like to know who killed Cock Robin?"

He cocked a quick ear and knew the returning steps for Wharton's. As he closed the door he fired his last sarcastic shot.

"Because if you'd like to have an earful of that, I'll get you the answer from Mr. Travers. I'll lay you a fiver he knows."

THE END

Lightning Source UK Ltd.
Milton Keynes UK
UKHW020219071222
413495UK00010B/815